NO FILTER

NO SHAME SERIES BOOK 1

NORA PHOENIX

Love,
Nora

No Filter (No Shame Series Book 1) by Nora Phoenix

Copyright ©2017 Nora Phoenix

Cover design: Sloan Johnson (Sloan J Designs)

Proofreading: Courtney Bassett

www.noraphoenix.com

PUBLISHER'S NOTE

This novel depicts mature situations and themes that are not suitable for underage readers. Reader discretion is advised. Please note there's a trigger warning for mentions of sexual abuse.

1

Indy Baldwin was dying for a frappe, but he was shit out of luck. The sign stated the machine was broken. He'd have to settle for ice cream, then. He debated in front of the freezer section for all of two seconds before deciding on a half pint of Rocky Road.

It cost more than he could afford to spend, but fuck it, he craved a pick-me-up. An egg sandwich alone wasn't going to satisfy him. Besides, the ice cream here was wicked good and, as far as Indy was concerned, the whole point of shopping at Stewart's, the New York chain of convenience stores. People said the coffee here wasn't too shabby either, but Indy wouldn't know since he hated the stuff. You could smell it walking in, on account of the pots that always brewed. Handwritten, colorful signs advertised pumpkin spice coffee, even though fall was still three weeks away.

He picked out a few groceries, stacking them on his left arm. His broken right arm still hurt too damn much to carry any weight, even in the cast. He performed a perfunctory check on his appearance as had become his habit when he'd started dressing as a woman. No one had ever seen through his disguise, and he wanted to keep it that way.

Indy trudged to the back of the store to grab some healthy snack bars. It was impossible to cook when he lived in his car, and these snuck some fiber and protein into his meager diet. He'd lost too much weight as it was lately. Another reason to indulge in a little ice cream.

The egg sandwich balanced precariously on top of the single serve yogurt, so Indy kept an eye on it to make sure it didn't fall off. Where was a shopping basket when you need one? Or a fucking carriage? A cart, he corrected himself. They called it a cart in these parts. Another sign he was wicked tired—he fell back on the dialect he was trying so hard to get rid of.

He should have shopped at a supermarket. Or Target. It would have been cheaper and more anonymous. But after his 5k run, his body had ached, and he'd felt weak and dizzy from hunger. Changing in his car into his female disguise— he couldn't run dressed as a girl, since workout clothes revealed too much—had cost more time than he'd planned. He needed a quick bite before parking his car for the night. Two days prior, he'd discovered the perfect spot: a parking lot near a nature preserve. Quiet, little chance of people seeing him, yet relatively safe.

A lean guy—the only other customer in the store— towered over the snacks section, studying the various offerings. Damn, he was tall—at least six foot two, Indy estimated. A dark blue cap the same color as his T-shirt hid most of his face, and his hands were stuffed in the pockets of a pair of tight dungies—jeans. *Use the right word, moron. Stop with the fucking Boston slang already,* he chided himself.

The man's jeans outlined his long, toned legs and one hell of a perfect ass. Too bad he was not a member of the snap-decisions club Indy belonged to. Why did he have to be in the exact spot that Indy needed to be? After a few seconds, Indy decided he'd been patient enough.

"Excuse me," he started, pitching his voice a tad higher. Hours of practicing ensured he had his female voice down pat.

The guy jumped as if Indy had shocked him with a Taser and backed up, hands flying out of his pockets in front of his face. Wow, talk about a fight-or-flight response. He must've completely surprised him.

"I'm sorry, honey," Indy drawled, laying the accent on thick. He'd left Atlanta the day after he'd broken his arm, but the Southern charm and accompanying drawl suited his purposes for now. "Bless your heart, I didn't mean to startle you. I wanted to grab a few bars, if that's okay?"

Wide-open blue eyes stared at him from under a Patriots cap that matched the tight-fitting shirt he was sporting. At least he supports the right team, Indy thought wryly.

For a few seconds, neither of them moved, and then the guy lowered his hands in clenched fists and stepped aside. If Patriot Guy wasn't so scared out of his mind, he'd be damn cute. Well, even spooked he was a looker, the butterflies-inducing result of angel mixed with a hint of bad boy. Bright blue eyes in a chiseled, smooth face, dark eyebrows, sharp nose, and luscious lips, framed by damn sexy stubble.

"Thank you, honey," Indy said, raising an eyebrow when the guy didn't react. *Okay, then.* Either this guy was a total weirdo, or he didn't like people. Or both. Either way, not his fucking problem. He had a bigger issue, which was how to pick up the snack bars with his right arm in a cast.

He should've been more careful during that last jiujitsu training. Cockiness, that's what had happened. Reckless overconfidence. He'd been so excited to get some training hours in that he'd refused to tap out his opponent in time. The snap of his bone breaking had sent a gasp through his partner and the professor. Stupid, plain fucking stupid. Anyways, only two more weeks till the cast would come off.

After fumbling to get the three bars he wanted—Patriot Guy still staring at him like a damn statue—Indy gave up that approach. He put his groceries on the floor, took the bars he wanted and stuffed them clearly visible in the front pocket of his girly, tan capris. He let the ends stick out so nobody would think he was trying to steal them. Getting arrested for shoplifting was about the worst thing that could happen to him. He needed to stay as far away from the boys in blue as possible, which was why he forced himself to stick to all speed limits, and used his fucking blinkers like a grandma. Getting pulled over—or even seen—by a cop could very well get him killed, so he wasn't taking any chances.

Loading his groceries on his left arm again, he turned toward Patriot guy to thank him. Southern girls were polite like that, after all, and he had an image to uphold.

His gaze was aimed at the floor now, fists clenched and body tense as a runner ready to start a race. What was the deal with this guy? Seriously.

In the background, the doorbell jingled. Right, his exit cue. *Bye, bye, weird guy.*

"Gimme the fucking cash!" a young male voice yelled.

Fucking hell.

A quick look over his shoulder to the front of the store revealed a scene that made Indy's stomach churn. The cashier stood frozen to the spot, his eyes wide in terror under his uniform visor, as he faced a guy dressed in black with a ski mask over his face. The robber wielded a Magnum .45 in his shaky right hand.

Indy lowered himself to the floor in an instant, letting the groceries slide out of his grasp. What a fucking mess. That kid behind the register had better cooperate. Ralph, his name was Ralph—Indy had spotted his name tag out of habit when he walked in. All he had to do was hand over the cash in the register, and nobody would get hurt. Hopefully.

Patriot Guy. Indy had forgotten about him. He turned his head. The guy was still standing there, nailed to the floor. What the hell was he doing? Why wasn't he on the floor? Disn't this chowdahead have a survival instinct?

"Get the fuck down," Indy whispered urgently.

"Gimme the fucking money!" the robber shouted again.

In the background, a commercial for Stewart's ice cream was playing. "Kids in sports uniforms get an ice cream cone for only fifty cents!" Fuck, no. The only thing missing from this nightmare scenario was a couple of kids walking in.

"I'm trying!" Panic reigned in the cashier's voice.

"I can't be here." Patriot Guy's voice came out a hoarse whisper. "I can't do this."

He was deadly pale, body trembling, wide-open eyes darting back and forth. Little pearls of sweat glistened on his forehead, and he forced breath puffs out of his clenched jaw.

What. The. Fucking. Hell.

"Get down, you fuckwad!" Indy whispered again. "You're gonna get shot!"

The guy didn't seem to hear Indy and took another step, whimpering like a puppy being kicked. He moved like a robot, completely rigid, as if he was sleepwalking and not really present. Another step and the robber would spot this idiot, might feel threatened and shoot him. Fuck, Indy couldn't let him do this.

Indy jumped up and clamped the guy's arm tightly. A

shooting pain tore through his broken right arm and hand, but he ignored it as he hooked his own leg behind weird guy's right leg and let himself fall backward on the floor. The move was deeply ingrained, practiced thousands of time in jiujitsu, but this time he couldn't do a break fall—a maneuver aptly named because you broke your fall by slapping your underarms and hands on the floor. He had to hold on to the guy, and he couldn't slap the floor with that useless broken arm.

Fuck, this was gonna hurt.

Indy moved with the falling motion as much as he could, but his head smashed into the floor, then snapped back again as weird guy's weight slammed into him.

Holy shitting fuckity fuck!

Pain exploded through Indy's body, but he managed to hang on to the guy and brace his fall. Indy's arms pinned the much taller man against his body. He pressed his head tightly against his own neck and for good measure, he hooked both his legs around him. He had no idea why this fuckwad wanted to walk into a shooter's path, but he damn well wasn't going to let him.

Indy was on his back on the cold, dirty linoleum floor; a hard, male body pressed against his. His muscles stiffened as his heart went into overdrive. A wave of nausea barreled through him, making him swallow furiously. His skin broke out in a fine sweat, and he jerked in a raspy breath. He hadn't been this close to a man since...

Fuck, no. Don't go there.

Focus. You have to fucking focus.

Now was not the time to panic. He had far more pressing problems to worry about. Damn, that fall hurt. His head throbbed like a motherfucker, and little specks danced in his vision. Indy blinked a few times, the colorful spots persisting.

"No, no, no, no..." Patriot Guy groaned, pushing against Indy's arms. His cap must have come off as they fell, and he thrashed his head around in a futile attempt to break free. Indy moved his left arm slightly, increasing the pressure on his head to keep it down. Despite outmatching Indy in height and weight, the guy stood no chance against Indy's experience.

Indy's body shook with the effort. He was too close. Any second now Patriot Guy would realize he was being held down by a man, not a woman, and then what? Indy's disguise would be blown to hell, and he'd be in hip-deep shit.

What the hell was wrong with this guy? Why wouldn't he stop fighting? He was in full panic mode, way worse than Indy's state of mind, but why?

Indy's eyes fell on a bulleted silver chain around the man's neck. He made the connection instantly.

Dog tags.

Veteran.

PTSD.

This guy was experiencing one hell of a panic reaction triggered by the robbery. Well, shit.

What could he do to help him snap out of it?

"You're okay," he whispered.

He'd seen this on Grey's Anatomy when Owen had flashbacks. How did they bring him back? Senses, he had to engage the guy's senses to make him aware of where he was. Grounding, they'd called it. That all sounded nice in theory, but how comforting was the reality of being in a store that was getting robbed? Shit, it had to be better than whatever this guy was remembering, right?

"My name is Indy, and I've got you. You're safe."

He put as much warmth in his soft voice as he could manage under the circumstances. Fuck, his system was still on full alert with a body tightly pressed against him. Nobody had even touched him in a year and a half, and now this.

It's too much. He's too close.

Focus, dammit.

"As long as we stay on the floor and he gets his money, we'll be fine. You're okay, honey. I've got you."

The man kept struggling in blind panic. Fuck, it sucked to hold him against his will, but what else could Indy do? It beat the hell out of him getting killed.

He needed more senses. Smell was a powerful one. What could he make him smell? He'd taken a shower after his run—he'd snuck into a YMCA—with this floral-scented body wash, and he still smelled pretty rosy. Maybe that would work?

"Smell my hair. Do you smell the lavender in my shampoo?"

Indy lifted his head up and turned his curls close to the guy's nose. He'd grown his hair to shoulder length since deciding to disguise himself as a girl, and it was longer than it had ever been.

"Maybe you can even smell my shower gel and body lotion. It's Dove. I don't know if it's true what they say that it contains real cream, but whatever. It smells great, and it makes my skin wicked soft."

Indy was babbling, his accent slipping and his voice getting too low, but he was trying, for fuck's sake.

Still nothing. Auditory, smell. What else? Visual. It was risky because anyone looking too closely could see past the makeup and women's clothes and recognize the man underneath. What other option did he have?

"Lift your head and look at me. Look at me."

When the guy didn't respond, Indy let go of him with one hand, tightening his injured arm around the man in a secure grip, which fired another blaze of pain through his body. He cupped the man's sweaty, pale cheek and raised his head slightly. The unfocused, panicked gaze in his eyes told Indy he wasn't able to see anything right now.

Shit.

What could he do to bring him back? Taste and touch, those were the only two left. But they were on the floor of a store during a fucking robbery, what the hell could he make the man touch and taste?

You.

Without thinking too much about it—because thinking would make what he was about to do fucking impossible—Indy loosened his grip and dragged the guy higher, to bring his head to the same level as his own. He was still unyielding in Indy's arms.

Indy hooked his legs around the man's thighs again and yanked his head down, crashing their mouths together.

Oh, God.

Shit, did he even know how to do this anymore? He hadn't kissed anyone in…two years.

Technically, two years, three months, and fifteen days.

Not that he was counting.

Not that those kisses were ever any good, or worth remembering in the first place.

Not that Duncan wanted much kissing anyways.

Too romantic. Too time-consuming. Duncan's main objective had been to get off and who needed kissing for that? Mouths were good to stick your cock in—or so Duncan had stated repeatedly.

Fucking stop it! Focus on the present.

Patriot Guy wasn't kissing him back. No wonder, Indy was assaulting his mouth with the finesse of a ten-ton steamroller.

Indy softened his lips and explored the guy's mouth, coaxing him to open up and respond. Come on, kiss me back, he willed him. When the guy remained frozen, Indy's tongue peeped out to lick the plump, soft lips. Oh, fuck, they tasted sweet and salty at the same time. The man's stubble sanded Indy's own clean-shaven chin, sending delicious tremors through Indy's body.

Wait...Was he...? It couldn't be. He couldn't like this, could he?

A bubble of panic rose up again in his belly, but he shoved it down. He was okay, no one was forcing him to do anything. His hands wound around the guy's head, caressing his wavy, dark hair that was a tad too long. Indy's fingers trailed his smooth skin, his tight jaw with the pleasantly rough stubble.

Please, kiss me back. Work with me here.

Suddenly, the man's whole body relaxed as if the air was let out of a balloon. He stopped struggling and in surrender, sank into Indy. Indy froze for a moment, bile rising in his throat, then willed his body to relax. *You can toss him off any time you want. You're holding on to him, not the other way around.*

The man opened his mouth and let Indy in, thrusting his tongue into Indy's mouth. He tasted of chocolate, addictive and rich, and Indy's skin tingled as pleasure radiated from his mouth throughout his entire body.

The guy placed his forearms on the floor and put his

hands behind Indy's head, lifting it up to press them closer together. It relieved some of the man's weight off Indy's upper body, which was good, because his ribs hurt like hell. It also increased the pressure on their lower bodies, which ground together. God, he wanted to grind against him, grate his hard cock until... Wait. He was hard. He was hard as a fucking pole. Oh, God, this was bad on so many levels.

Their slick tongues coaxed and explored, danced with each other, kept chasing one another in a sexy game of cat and mouse. The soft sucking sounds made Indy's insides swirl in response. Fucking hell, was this how good kissing was when there were no groping hands, no expectations, no force?

No, he didn't want to think of Duncan now. This glorious kiss, this enticing, seductive battle of their tongues—this was what he wanted to focus on. Hot damn, this guy could kiss.

Giving in to his needs, he gyrated his hips into the guy's crotch, and he connected with a solid erection. It sent a shock wave through his body. A burning heat he hadn't felt in a long time—had he ever experienced this before?— pooled in his stomach. He was so fucking horny. His hole twitched, signaling it, too, was ready for some action.

What the hell was happening?

Reality hit and yanked his mind out of the gutter. Fuck, he was royally fucked. There was no way the guy wouldn't notice Indy wasn't a girl. And when he did, things would go south faster than you could say Indiana Jones.

2

—————

"What the hell?"

Someone was talking to them. Indy knew that voice, but who was it?

The cashier, Ralph.

Patriot Guy's mouth froze on Indy's and his body stilled. Indy pulled back. *Please, please, don't rat me out.*

"You're okay now, honey," Indy said, turning the drawl back on just in time. Thinking was damn hard when his brain was transformed into mush. "We're okay."

"I'm getting robbed, and you're making out on the floor?" Ralph's voice dripped with indignation.

Indy lowered his head to the floor, his core muscles screaming after the extended workout they'd gotten. Patriot Guy's eyes flickered in mild panic, then focused on him, narrowing.

"How are you doing?" Indy asked, raising his voice to his pretend-girl pitch and cupping weird guy's cheek, his eyes pleading with the man to help him maintain his disguise.

"Shouldn't you be asking me?" Ralph asked.

"Well, sugar, I didn't hear a shot, and considering the

fact that you're walking and talking, I assume you survived," Indy answered, his eyes still focused on the bright blue eyes inches away.

"I'm okay," Patriot Guy said, his voice hoarse.

"That's mighty good to hear," Indy said. "You were about to do something stupid, honey, so I stopped you."

Patriot Guy blinked. "I was?"

"You don't remember?"

"Sorry. I kinda blacked out, I think."

"Bless your heart. You're fine, now. Do you think you could get off me now?"

Weird guy blinked again, clearly not entirely out of his episode. At least he hadn't blown Indy's cover. Yet.

"Yeah, sorry," the guy said again, lifting himself off Indy.

Indy unwound his legs, quickly pulled his blouse down so it covered his groin, and let his arms drop dead to the floor. Holy shit, everything hurt. His head pounded like a fucking jackhammer, and ice-cold stabs pierced his arm like when he'd broken it. He closed his eyes for a second.

So. Much. Pain.

"Are you okay?"

Indy opened his eyes. Patriot Guy lowered himself next to him, studying Indy with furrowed brows, his mouth tight. He'd asked a question, hadn't he? Shit, his brain was slow. Yeah, he'd asked if Indy was okay. He could lie, of course, pretend he was fine. Another wave of pain clobbered his head. No, this was stupid. He'd taken a hard blow to his head. He needed to be checked out. A possible head injury was not something to ignore if you were by yourself. Fuck, he'd seen more than one scenario of delayed consequences in Grey's. He could have a fucking brain bleed! But how could he get checked out without revealing his gender? Or his identity?

"My head had a rather unfortunate close encounter with the floor, and my broken arm hurts something awful." He clenched his teeth and breathed through the pain, pushing himself up sideways into a sitting position. "Oh, shit!" Indy bit his lip at the unladylike exclamation he'd let slip.

"What happened?" Ralph asked, concern ringing in his voice for the first time.

"I fell," Indy said when he was confident he could talk again with the right voice and accent. Holy fuck, his upper body ached like a sonofabitch, too.

"You fell." The disbelief in Ralph's voice was obvious.

"Yes, honey, I fell."

"With him on top of you?"

"Why yes, I sure did."

"And that seemed like a good time to make out?"

"Do you have a problem with that?" Indy was about to run out of patience with this kid.

Ralph shook his head. "You're nuts, both of you. Thanks for nothing. I was in mortal danger, you know? You could've tried to help me."

Indy smirked. "Mortal danger? Feeling a tad dramatic, are we?"

As Ralph sputtered, Indy's eyes traveled to Patriot Guy, who was making a call on his cell. "This is Joshua Gordon. I need an ambulance at the Stewart's on Route 146...yes, same place that got robbed...female, about eighteen, possible concussion and a broken arm, in stable condition, awake and alert. Please transport to Albany General per patient request."

Indy raised his eyebrows when he hung up. "Per patient request?"

Patriot Guy shrugged. "My friend works in the ER there. Problem?"

"No problem, honey. Merely curious. Delighted to make your acquaintance, Joshua. I'm Indy. I'd shake your hand, but moving seems to be a mighty bad idea right now."

A smile tugged at the corner of his mouth. "Call me Josh."

He knows. His smile said he knew, yet he'd described Indy as a female. Why? Maybe it was his way of thanking him? Whatever the reason, Indy was grateful as all get-out. Fuck, Josh was so cute, his eyes as blue as calm water. And he was gay. No doubt about it, Indy's gaydar was going off like crazy.

"You guys didn't even know each other?" Ralph's voice whined at a frequency that tested Indy's patience. "Sheesh. I've heard stress brings out weird stuff in people, but making out with a complete stranger during a robbery? If you're that easy, why don't we—"

Ralph stopped talking when Josh raised a single finger and shot Ralph a look that would have made weaker guys wet their pants. "Shut the fuck up. Right now. Or the shitty day you thought you were having is about to get way worse. You do not want to get on my bad side, trust me."

Oh my, Josh had a backbone. Hot damn, that authoritative don't-fuck-with-me tone was seriously hot. Even through the pain, Indy's body buzzed in response, his cock still halfway hard. It had to be because of the kiss. After all, he hadn't even been close to another human being in over two years, so no wonder the kiss had affected him. Simple biology. It didn't mean anything. Neither did the fact that they'd both become hard. They'd made out, of course they would get boners. Everyone would, right? Especially since they were both gay.

In the distance, sirens announced the arrival of the cops.

"I'd better talk to them," Ralph said, shooting Josh a careful look. "Make sure they have a solid description of the robber."

"You do that, Ralph," Indy dismissed him, his voice cold with disdain. The little shithead had called him easy. He might as well have called him a slut. Ironic, considering he'd only fucked one man his entire life—or rather, had gotten fucked by one sorry excuse for a man—and look where that had gotten him. And no, he wasn't counting Eric, because that sonofabitch didn't even deserve to be mentioned.

"You may want to get another sandwich," Josh remarked.

Indy glanced at the groceries he had dropped onto the floor. The sandwich container had burst open, spilling its contents on the coffee-stained linoleum. The ice cream was half melted by now, looking forlorn on the floor next to the snack bars.

"Well, fuck," Indy said and carefully leaned back against the shelves. Ralph wasn't anywhere near, so there was no need to keep up appearances.

Josh shifted till he sat across from Indy on the floor, his back against the other side of the aisle. "Thank you," he said after a spell, studying Indy from between his lashes.

"You're welcome."

"I have...issues. I don't do well with stressful situations." He spoke low and precise.

"I gathered as much." Indy kept his voice level. This could not be easy for Josh to say.

"How did you manage to tackle me?"

"I have a brown belt in Brazilian jiujitsu."

"Impressive."

Indy smiled. "Even more impressive than my kissing skills?" He had to keep this flirty and easy. As he had discovered in the last two years, it was the best way to keep people from seeing the real him—the person who had to stay hidden to survive.

Josh's gaze shot to the floor. Was that a blush staining his cheeks? Fucking hell, he was adorable. But why was he blushing? Indy had expected anger, embarrassment at being kissed by a strange guy, especially one that was dressed like a woman, but not this. It couldn't be the kiss itself. Josh was so damn cute he'd have men lining up to kiss him.

"What, no comment?" he teased Josh. "And you were such a prolific speaker so far."

Josh's lips curved shyly, making two dimples appear. Indy sighed softly. God, Josh had the sweetest smile. It surprised him, the effect this complete stranger had on him when he hadn't felt anything even remotely similar in years, if ever. The combination of boyish cuteness and that shy, self-conscious attitude totally got to him.

And the guy was one hell of a kisser. Fuck, that kiss had made Indy block the pain in his head and arm and everything else—no small feat under the circumstances. More surprisingly, it had taken away his initial panic. That was the biggest fucking miracle of all since even the smallest touch scared him shitless these days. He was skittish as a rabbit around people.

Maybe Josh had this effect on him because he'd been the first to touch Indy in a long time. Could it be that he'd been unconsciously starving for touch, even though it scared the fuck out of him? God, his head throbbed, trying to make sense out of it. It didn't matter anyways. Josh and he would go their separate ways, never to see each other again.

"The police want to talk to you," Ralph shouted from the front.

Indy froze, his mind suddenly on high alert. Of course there would be cops involved. It was a robbery. All he had to do was act normal and it would be fine. He was not a suspect, so there was no reason to check his background, right? Oh, fuck, what if Josh let slip Indy wasn't a woman? He did a quick check on his appearance, straightened the now crumpled and stained blouse he was wearing, righted his filling-stuffed push-up bra, and fixed the thin scarf around his neck that covered his Adam's apple.

Play it cool. And for fuck's sake, keep your accent strong and your voice high.

Indy raised his eyes to find Josh studying him with a curious look. He wanted to ask him, beg him not to say anything, but wouldn't that trigger more curiosity?

Josh hesitated for a second, but then he got up. "I'll ask them to come to you," he said.

Maybe he'd gotten the message without Indy saying anything. Damn, he hoped so. He watched Josh walk away gracefully, his long legs eating up the ground with ease. Indy sighed, pinching his eyes closed when a shooting pain burst through his head.

Please, God, let this cop be shitbrained and nearsighted.

"Miss, I'm Officer O'Connor. Are you okay to answer some questions?"

Indy's stomach soured.

He'd pronounced his name O'Connah. What were the odds of running into a fellow Bostonian in upstate New York?

Fuck.

You should have never traveled back so close to home.

O'Connor, Irish name. If he has ties to the Fitzpatricks, you're dead.

At least he called me miss. Play it cool. Nothing is lost. Yet.

Indy opened his eyes. A police officer lowered himself to the floor in front of him. The guy was built like a defensive end with a broad chest, strong arms, and thick legs that almost burst out of his uniform. Masculine face, dark buzz cut, strong jaw, sharp and assessing dark blue eyes. This cop was anything but shitbrained and nearsighted. Figured. God hadn't answered one of Indy's prayers in, like, forever.

"Sure, Officer," Indy said, drawing out his vowels.

"Can I start with your name and a phone number where you can be reached?"

"Indiana Baldwin, Indy." The phone number rolled off his lips easily enough, the drawl thick and his voice soft and feminine. He could do this.

O'Connor scribbled down the name and number in a tiny notebook. "Can you describe the robber, Miss Baldwin?"

"Call me Indy, Officer. He was a bit taller than the cashier, slender build."

"Any idea of his race?"

"I'm sorry, Officer, I couldn't see, what with that cliché ski mask on his face."

"Did you get a look at the gun?"

"Magnum .45. I'm from the South where we hold the second amendment in high regard," he explained when O'Connor looked surprised that a Southern lady could identify the weapon so easily.

The cop nodded in appraisal. "How did he come across to you? Any idea of age?"

"Young. His hands were shaky, for sure. He didn't look like he had a whole lot of experience doing this. But you should be able to get that off the security footage as well."

The officer sighed. "Unfortunately, it looks like the camera directed at the register wasn't working. We only have him entering and exiting the parking lot on foot."

"Well, color me stupid. Don't tell me that asshole is going to get away with this."

Josh grinned, an irresistible smile that caused Indy's heart to skip a beat.

"What are you laughing at?" he asked good-naturedly.

"You. You've got quite the mouth on you for a Southern Belle," Josh answered, his grin stretching even wider.

Indy merely lifted a brow at the double meaning of Josh's words, and it didn't take long before Josh realized what he'd said. "That's not what I meant. Fuck," he stammered.

Indy laughed. "Why, thank you kindly, sir. I told you my kissing skills were impressive."

Indy focused back on Officer O'Connor who stared at Josh with a strange expression. "Sorry, Officer, inside joke," Indy said. For whatever reason, Josh had decided not to rat him out. Thank fuck.

O'Connor almost imperceptibly shook his head, then refocused on Indy. He was gripping his notebook so hard his knuckles turned white. What the fuck was his problem?

"How did you get hurt?" he asked Indy.

Indy's eyes flashed to Josh, and he gave a slight nod, still blushing fiercely from the unintended innuendo. "I had to take this kind gentleman down, as the robbery triggered a PTSD episode with him. He was panicking and would have gotten himself in harm's way, had I not taken him to the floor."

The incredulous look O'Connor gave Indy was almost insulting. Fuck him for underestimating women. And short, scrawny guys in this case, though the cop didn't know that.

"You took him down," O'Connor said.

"I sure did, Officer. Would you care for a demonstration?" Indy's tone was steel, covered in sugary sweet syrup.

"Naw, that won't be necessary. I was merely surprised that you could tackle him."

"She has a brown belt in Brazilian jiujitsu," Josh said with audible pride that made Indy smile, even if he wouldn't have divulged quite that much information to the cop himself.

"You a vet?" O'Connor asked, his eyes trailing to the dog tags under Josh's shirt.

"Yes, sir, Army."

"I was a Marine."

A look of understanding passed between the men that made Indy's skin prickle. Both had seen more than they had ever wanted to. What was O'Connor's story? There was more to the cop than was obvious at first glance.

"How did you know what to do? How did you snap him out of it?" O'Connor asked.

There was no way this was an official question. O'Connor wanted to know this on a personal level, but why would he be interested? Maybe he had friends who suffered from PTSD? Wasn't a stretch, considering he was a former Marine.

"I remembered from a TV series that you have to ground someone experiencing a PTSD episode, evoke multiple senses to make them aware of their surroundings. I talked to Josh, told him to smell my hair as I had just washed it, and tried to get him to focus on me. When that didn't work, well, I saw no other option but to kiss him."

"You what?"

"I kissed him. Taste and touch are such powerful senses and kissing evokes both. And my, my, it surely is a sweet distraction, isn't it?" Indy said with a wink to Josh.

"She's got impressive kissing skills," Josh confirmed, his ears fiery red. "And it worked. I've had worse ways of coming out of a panic attack."

O'Connor studied Josh for a second, and something

Indy couldn't identify flashed over his face. The cop almost seemed surprised by Josh's remark. O'Connor smiled, one of those polite gestures that didn't reach his eyes. "I can imagine," he said stiffly.

"The ambulance is here," Ralph shouted.

O'Connor raised himself to his feet and extended a hand to Josh. Josh froze for a second, then slowly accepted it and let himself be pulled up. He kept his eyes aimed straight at the ground, avoiding the cop's look. O'Connor seemed to wait for Josh to acknowledge him, but let go of his hand when Josh stayed mute.

O'Connor frowned, then extended his hand to Indy. There was no way Indy was going to let the cop touch his hands, since all the hand treatments in the world couldn't make them feminine enough. Besides, he felt like he'd been hit by a truck. Standing up was about the last thing he was interested in right now.

"Sorry, Officer, I appreciate the offer, but I think it's wise if I stay seated for now. I'm not feeling well."

"We'll let the paramedics take care of you in that case. Thanks for your info, Indy. You've been helpful."

"You're more than welcome..." Indy let his voice trail off, hoping O'Connor would supply him with his first name so he could check him out, find out if he was connected. The Fitzpatricks still had cops on their payroll, even if the family was nowhere near as powerful as it used to be.

"Connor."

"Your name is Connor O'Connor?"

"Nah, everybody calls me Connor."

"That begs the question as to your real name," Indy said, acting playfully.

"I don't think it's any of your concern," O'Connor replied, his jaw setting.

Indy bit back a laugh. Like the cop was any match for Indy's stubbornness. He was a fucking pit bull once he wanted something.

"Oh, I'm almost certain it's something weird, like one of them new age names. Winter maybe, or Current. Or a made-up name. Or it's something embarrassing, like—"

"Ignatius, all right? My official name is Ignatius."

No sir, he wasn't happy with him. But at least Indy had his full name. That made things a hell of a lot easier. "I am so sorry to hear that, as that name must've gotten the living daylights beaten out of you in school. No wonder you went with Connor. It suits you."

A look of pure shock was followed by an amused smile in the cop's eyes. "You don't have much of a filter, do you?"

Indy smiled, satisfied he'd managed to keep up his front. "No, sir, not according to my momma, I don't. Good luck on the rest of your shift, Officer. Stay safe."

O'Connor nodded, then took a step back as he turned to Josh. His expression changed to neutral as he extended his hand. "Hang in there, Josh."

Josh was a good inch taller than O'Connor, but the cop still dwarfed him because of his size. Josh took his hand but kept his gaze glued to the floor. O'Connor seemed to wait for Josh to look up, but gave up after a few seconds. With one last look at Josh—who was still avoiding the cop's eyes like the plague—O'Connor left. Josh didn't raise his head until the cop walked away, apparently still a bit sluggish, because he kept staring at O'Connor until he walked out of sight.

Indy blinked a few times. Was his vision getting more blurry? One thing was certain, the first thing he was gonna ask for in the ER was the mother of all painkillers. The incessant pounding in his head was killing him, and his ribs hurt like a motherfucker with every shallow breath he drew in.

"Tell those paramedics to get a rush on," Indy said. God, his voice sounded weird. Distant. "I'm not feeling well."

He sagged back farther against the shelves, unable to hold himself up. A stabbing pain tore through his head, then everything went black.

Screaming sirens dragged Indy out of the deep, cold black. He fought to open his eyes.

Too dizzy. Too much pain. Too tired.

Did they drug him?

God, he was so fucking helpless unconscious.

The black sucked him right back under.

Sudden silence shocked him awake. Doors opened. Rattling sounds. His body jolted even though he was restrained in some way. *What the hell?*

Still too far gone to stay awake.

Damn it.

More darkness.

A steady rhythm of bleeps. The wicked pounding in his head was so blinding he didn't even consider opening his eyes. His left arm was tied to something, preventing him from moving it, while his right arm had a sort of band around his biceps. His left index finger was compressed in cold, plastic pressure.

Where the hell was he?

His heartbeat accelerated, and adrenaline rushed

though his veins. What the fuck had happened? Why was he tied down? Had they found him?

No, no, no...what would they do to him this time?

They wouldn't let him survive, not after what he'd done. His mouth filled with acid, and his back flared, remembering. Horrific pain, the smell of burning flesh. Their laughs as he was dying.

"She's waking up," a female voice announced. "Her pulse is spiking."

"Indy?" a warm, male voice spoke. "Indy, are you awake? Don't panic, you're okay."

He opened his eyes out of reflex, but blinding lights stabbed his head so fiercely his stomach rolled. He dry heaved, pinching his eyes shut again. A warm, strong hand touched his left arm. He recoiled on instinct, his heart rate speeding up even further.

What will they do to me? God, help me.

"Don't fucking touch me!" His voice was raw, hoarse.

The hand disappeared immediately as Indy instinctively brought both his arms up in a defensive position. His right arm came up, though he could still feel the weight of the cast and that weird band around his biceps, but his left arm was restricted in some way. He jerked it again.

He was tied down. Fuck. He had to get out of here.

Fight, he told himself, forcing his will to push through his muddy brain. *Fight your way out of this. You've done it before.*

God, everything hurt. His head, his chest, his arms, his whole body. What the fuck had happened to him?

"Untie me..." he demanded.

He clawed at whatever was restraining his arm, unsuccessfully trying to rip it off. The panic was rising in his throat, his stomach, his lungs. He couldn't breathe, his heart hammering in his chest.

"Get this fucking thing off of me. Let me go!"

He screamed, fought, yanked at cords he couldn't see.

"Everybody out," the male voice ordered in a tone that demanded immediate obedience. "Get Josh in here."

Footsteps as people left the room. A door opened and closed. Quiet footsteps came closer. Indy let out a groan of frustration when he couldn't get whatever was restraining his arm off. Why did everything hurt so fucking much?

"Josh, talk to her. Maybe she'll remember your voice."

"Indy, you're okay. You're in the ER. Remember the robbery? You took care of me, but you hit your head, and you blacked out."

Indy stopped fighting when the sweet, timid voice hit him. It sounded awfully familiar. He knew this voice, this guy.

A wave of memories hit. Shopping at Stewart's. Patriot Guy. The robbery. Josh. He'd called an ambulance, said his friend worked in the ER. That's where he was, the ER.

He sniffed, his nose tickling with the familiar cocktail of antibacterial hand sanitizer, the strong detergent used on the bed linens, and the cleaning disinfectant. For fuck's sake, he'd spent enough time in a hospital to recognize it.

"Indy, my name is Noah Flint. I'm a friend of Josh, and I work here as a physician assistant."

It was the male voice, the authoritative one. Indy flinched, his entire body still on high alert. The adrenaline pulsated through his system, like he'd thrown back three energy drinks.

"I'm going to take the blood pressure cuff off of your right arm, since it bothers you, okay? You also have an IV in your left wrist and there's a heart rate monitor on your index finger. Are you okay with those, or do you want me to take them off?"

"Off."

"Okay. To do that, I need to touch you. Is that okay?"

Indy grunted his consent. Warm hands gently removed whatever was around his arm, barely touching him. The pressure on his index finger disappeared. The room quieted as the bleeps stopped their insane racket, and his own ragged breathing was all that was left. He forced himself to relax, to slow his heart rate down. He was okay and nobody was attacking him.

"Indy, I'd prefer if the IV could stay in, since you may need meds later. I can unhook it from the pole for now so you can move your arm more. Would that help?"

"Okay."

He didn't trust himself to say more than that, knowing he didn't have it in him to play his role right now. Shit, how badly had he fucked up? He'd dropped his accent. They knew he was a guy even though they kept referring to him as a she. Would they ask questions?

"Josh, can you hit the lights? Indy, I'm dimming the lights for you, okay? Josh told me you hit your head hard, and it seems like the bright lights are bothering you. Let your eyes adjust and then you can open them if you want. We'll wait till you're ready."

The man's calm voice steadied Indy. It drew him in like a beacon, a lighthouse promising a safe harbor.

He released a quiet exhale when the bright lights went out. They'd irritated his head even with his eyes closed.

"Better?"

"Yah."

They waited patiently until he was ready to open his eyes. Indy slowly blinked. His head still pounded like a jackhammer, but the relative darkness in the room helped. It was still light enough to see the two guys standing elbow to elbow at the foot of his bed. Josh was looking at him with concern, but it was the guy next to him that made Indy blink again.

He was younger than Indy had expected, with a serious, hard face. His dark blue scrubs seemed to be a tad tight for his powerful chest and arms, and he stood a few inches shorter than Josh. He had short, blond hair and looked like he hadn't seen the sharp end of a razor in a couple of days.

"Hi," Indy said gamely, drawing out the sound.

"You okay now?" Noah asked, not sporting the impatience or irritation Indy had expected. If anything, he looked curious, which was not good, because it would trigger questions Indy had no intention of answering.

"Yeah, I'm good."

"Do you remember what happened?"

"Had to take Patriot Guy down and smashed my head into the floor. And I may have cracked my arm. Again."

"Patriot Guy?" Josh asked.

Indy sighed. "I had to call you something, since I didn't know your name."

"I've had worse nicknames," Josh said with a soft smile on his lips.

"Can you tell me where it hurts?" Noah asked.

Indy closed his eyes, mentally scanning his body as he'd done countless times after Duncan had done a number on him. "My head. Feels like a concussion. And my right arm may have sustained some more damage. You may want to run an X-ray." His accent was back. Thank fuck. Though it was probably too little, too late. He opened his eyes again, wincing as even that small move triggered a fierce pulse of pain behind his eyes.

"Are you telling me how to do my job?" Noah asked, amusement lacing his voice.

He had a nice voice. Warm and reassuring. Wait, he'd already thought that before, hadn't he? And the man had asked him a question. Fuck, thinking was hard when your brain had been replaced by cotton balls.

"Just a suggestion. I've been here before, so I know the drill," he explained.

Light and easy, that was his way out. Noah had seen him panic, so he'd know that Indy had some kind of trauma in his past. Hopefully he could prevent the PA from running any more scans because they would definitely raise questions.

"Are you okay with me examining you? We can take as much time as you need. You can call me Noah, by the way."

Indy studied the physician assistant who observed him back with quiet patience, standing so close to Josh their bodies were touching. He had an interesting build, Indy mused, with an incredible upper body but relatively lean legs. Indy's eyes fell on a silver chain around his neck. The same bulleted chain that Josh was wearing. Dog tags. That must be how they know each other. Army buddies.

He made a decision. "Okay."

Noah nodded. "Can I ask a nurse to help?"

"Yah. Yes," he corrected. Deep South, not Boston.

"Josh, you need to step out now. Can you ask Jessie to come back? Indy, is there anyone we can call for you?"

"Josh can stay," Indy said. He'd subtly ignored Noah's question. Hopefully, the guy would get the hint and drop it.

"No, he can't. No relatives or friends in the exam rooms. Josh knows. He can wait in the waiting room."

"You're bossy," Indy complained. The quicker he slipped back into the slightly flirty Southern Belle persona, the faster everyone would forget he'd been acting all weird.

"It takes one to know one," was Noah's fast reply.

Josh chuckled, elbowing Noah in an affectionate gesture. He shot Indy a reassuring glance. "Trust me, Noah knows his shit. You'll be fine."

"He'd better know his shit, 'cause I wanna get the fuck outta here. I fucking hate hospitals."

Oops. Not exactly Southern Belle language.

Josh laughed out loud as he made his way to the door. "Told you she had a mouth on her."

"You're talking about my kissing skills, right?" Indy asked, his voice light and teasing.

"You kissed her?" Noah's voice was dripping with incredulity, but there was a hint of something else as well. Indignation? Jealousy? Interesting. Almost as interesting as the fact that both men kept referring to him as a female when they damn well knew Indy was a guy.

"Technically, she kissed me," Josh replied. He was too far away to see him in the dim lights, but Indy had no doubt he was blushing again. Too fucking cute.

"Why the fuck would she—Never mind. We'll get to that later," Noah responded, turning back to Indy.

Josh left and a few seconds later, a young female nurse stepped in, wearing scrubs with purple flowers. Purple flowers, for fuck's sake. There really was such a thing as being too girly.

"Jessie, can you start with checking her vitals again and then run a full blood trauma panel? I'll do a head exam first."

The nurse nodded and grabbed the blood pressure cuff, reaching for Indy's arm. Indy flinched, a soft grunt escaping his lips.

Noah swore. "Back off," he ordered. "I'll do it myself. Wait outside until I call you in."

"I'm sorry," Jessie started, wringing her hands.

Indy was sure the poor girl was about to start crying. No wonder when your boss was that hot and he looked at you like you were a fly he was about to swat.

"Out." Noah gestured at the door, and Jessie hurried out.

"That poor kid is bawling her eyes out right now, you know that, right?"

With uneven steps—for some reason he was favoring his right leg—Noah made his way to the right side of the bed. "She was unprofessional."

Indy studied his serious expression. "She's young and she wasn't thinking."

"She should know better and if not, she has no business working in an ER."

"Maybe you make her nervous. You're pretty good looking, honey." It was one of the things Indy liked about pretending to be a woman: you could get away with saying shit like that without getting your head bashed in by someone taking offense. Guys tended to not respond so favorably when it was another guy commenting on their looks.

Noah chuckled, which was not the reaction Indy had been expecting. "Trust me, she's not nervous because of my looks. She knows she doesn't stand a chance."

"Not your type?"

He shook his head, still laughing. "Not even close."

He wondered what Noah's type was. Older? Indy guessed the PA to be in his late twenties, so maybe the guy liked women a little closer to his own age? Jessie couldn't have been more than twenty, maybe twenty-two, max. Pretty close to Indy's own age.

"Can I put the cuff back on?"

Indy nodded. He winced as pain stabbed behind his eyes. Noah wrapped the cuff around Indy's arm and pressed a button. The sleeve filled up with air, compressing his arm. It slowly released, beeping when it had found his blood pressure.

"Your blood pressure is returning to normal. Extend your index finger for me so I can get a pulse." He clamped the pulse meter on Indy's finger, and it, too, started beeping.

"Any important medical history I need to know? Major surgeries? Allergies? Previous trauma? Medications?"

Yeah, like he was gonna share his shitlist of medical stuff. Not happening. "No allergies. No meds. I've had surgeries, but none that are relevant to this." He'd conveniently skipped the question about previous traumas. Maybe Noah wouldn't pick up on it.

"Describe your fall for me. How were you hit?"

"I tackled Josh in a full frontal tackle, so I had his weight on me when I hit the floor backward. My head slammed into the floor, and my right arm took a hit, probably when Josh's weight crashed into me."

"Can you follow the light with your eyes? Don't move your head."

Noah tracked a path with a small flashlight, and Indy obediently followed it despite the pain it caused in his head. Sheesh, light really was the enemy right now. The PA next shone the flashlight in each eye, undoubtedly checking his pupil reflexes. Also not good for his headache. Sticking the light in his breast pocket, Noah reached out with both hands to Indy's head, and waited for him to nod his consent. He gently probed the back of Indy's head, prodding in different places.

"Nauseous?" he asked.

"No. Just a blinding headache."

"We'll get you some painkillers when we've got all your results. We need to make sure we've got the full extent of your injuries first. I want to listen to your breathing."

Fuck. He'd see his back. He'd ask questions, become suspicious.

"Do you need me to wait for a minute?"

Indy swallowed. "Can you listen to my breathing without looking?"

Noah didn't even hesitate. "Sure."

Noah popped his stethoscope in his ears and closed his eyes. "Put it above your right nipple…"

Indy slipped the cold metal under his bra and filling. Damn, what a nuisance for girls to have to wear that shit every day. It bugged the crap out of him every single time he had to put a bra on.

"Take a deep breath for me. Now your left…breathe in… and out…okay. You can't reach your back, so I'll put it on, but I promise I won't look, okay?"

Indy knew what was coming, but when Noah's fingers touched his back he still tensed. Would he stop when he reached the ragged skin? There was no missing the scars, not where he'd have to put the stethoscope.

Noah's movements were steady and continuous as he put the cold circle on Indy's back, listened, then moved it to the other side, and listened again. If the man felt the scars, he didn't show it in any way. Noah kept his eyes closed until he'd taken a careful step back and Indy had time to lower his blouse.

"Thank you," Indy said softly.

"No problem. Your breath sounds are good. Do you have any pain other than in your head and your arm?"

Indy hesitated.

"Look, Indy, I understand this is intrusive, but I want to make sure you're okay. Taking Josh's weight means you took a hard hit on your body, and I'm concerned about injuries to your upper body."

"My back hurts," he admitted, his stomach sinking. Noah was right. He could've been injured there. It hurt like a bitch. For all he knew, he was sporting a few broken ribs. Sure felt like it.

"Will you allow me to examine it?"

Indy bit his lip. Noah had listened to his breaths without looking. He must've felt something on Indy's back, because the scars ran all the way up. Yet he hadn't said anything. He knew Indy was a man, yet again he hadn't said anything, had respected his privacy. Indy had little choice, but that wasn't what made him decide.

"I trust you," Indy said. He expected Noah to start examining him immediately, but he didn't. Instead, Noah lowered himself on the bed, again putting all his weight on his left leg.

"Thank you for your trust. It means a lot to me."

His closeness didn't bother Indy at all. Noah's eyes were focused on him but not in a creepy or uncomfortable way. He was reading him, trying to gauge what he needed.

"What happened with Josh at Stewart's?" Noah asked.

"I startled him even before the robber came in and he reacted strongly, almost like I'd shocked him. I think he never came out of that. Then that guy started waving his gun and he panicked. He wanted to walk out, but he woulda gotten himself shot."

"So you tackled him."

"Yeah. I spotted his dog tags and figured he must be having some kind of panic attack. I tried to calm him down, tried grounding him, but he kept fighting me. That's why I kissed him."

"You saved his life. You realize that, don't you?"

Indy's breath stuck in his chest. "I couldn't let him get shot," he whispered under Noah's intense gaze. His eyes were kind, even if his face was still stern.

"You saved him by doing something that must've gone against all your instincts. Josh, he means the world to me, and you saved him. I'm in your debt. I need to make sure you're okay, but I want to do it in a way that respects you and your privacy, and without causing you stress. Let's forget about hospital policies or forms or medical charts and all that bullshit. I'll bend and break the rules if I have to. Tell me what I need to do."

Indy studied the kind man sitting so close to him, his insides strangely warm after Noah's passionate words. Could it be that for once in his life Lady Luck was on his side? About fucking time. "If you run scans, you'll discover old injuries. I don't want to talk about those, and you can't report them."

"I understand."

"My back..." Indy broke eye contact and stared at his hands. "My back is scarred. Don't ask me why."

"Okay."

"And please put my gender down as female."

"How about I don't ask too many questions, and you tell me what you think I should know. I trust you to share what's important for me to treat you. Does that work?"

The tightness in his chest became a little less. "Thank you."

Noah dipped his head. "I know your head must hurt like a motherfucker, but I'll need to turn the lights on to see anything. Is that okay?"

So much for the professional language the PA had used so far. Seemed Indy wasn't the only one pretending to be someone else. "Yeah."

Indy turned himself on his stomach with difficulty, pain shooting through him at every little move. He hid his head under the pillow. The lights went on, and Noah walked back to the bed and sat down again. Wasn't that a tad personal for a doctor? Or a PA, in his case. They usually stood, or bent over in weird angles, but Indy couldn't remember one ever sitting down on his bed. Especially not this close to him. Not that it bothered him, because it didn't, and maybe that was the craziest thing of all.

"Is it okay if I lift your shirt now?"

"Keep talking to me. I need to hear your voice," Indy whispered. As long as Indy could hear Noah, he knew it was him, not someone else. Not Duncan. Or worse, Eric.

Noah didn't miss a beat. "You a football fan?" he asked, gently lifting Indy's blouse.

"Yup, one more week till the regular season starts. Can't wait."

Indy was waiting for Noah to freeze or gasp but he simply kept talking. "Being from Georgia, you're probably a Falcons fan, right? Can't believe a girl who is savvy enough to snap a guy out of a panic attack by kissing him would support a team who threw away a twenty-five point lead in a Super Bowl."

His fingers probed Indy's back, undoubtedly checking his ribs. Indy gasped when Noah hit a tender spot. "What's your team? You a Pats fan, like Josh?"

"Hell, yeah. Since the day I discovered football. Brady, Gronk, Amendola, they're my guys."

If only he knew. Indy should hit back with the expected insult from a supposed Falcons fan—something along the

Pats are cheaters line—but he couldn't. He wouldn't dare jinx the team that had his true loyalty.

"Can you turn on your back for me?"

Indy kept the pillow on his face as it shielded him from the lights that hurt even with his eyes pressed tight. Noah's warm hands gently touched the front of his rib cage, slipping under the bra without hesitation or comment, systematically checking for damage. Then his hands withdrew and he pulled Indy's blouse down, covering him with the blanket.

"Keep the pillow on your face while I draw some blood, okay?"

Indy stretched his arm so Noah had access. He drew the blood quickly. Thank fuck he'd always been an easy stick because boy, he'd been poked and prodded enough these last few years to last a lifetime. If he never, ever saw a damn hospital from the inside again, he wouldn't mind.

"Ok, done. Let me hand these off to the lab, okay?"

Thank fuck that was over.

Noah got up from the bed, walked to the door with a heavy step, and the lights went off. Noah stepped out for a second, saying something Indy couldn't quite pick up, then came back inside.

Indy let go of the pillow, and Noah sat down on the bed again, letting out a soft groan. He had to be sporting one hell of an injury, because he didn't seem like the type to whine over a little pain.

"Indy, you have a large bruise forming on your back, right below your left shoulder blade. Trauma protocol says I consult with my attending, who will no doubt order X-rays of your back. As a PA I can't order scans, nor sign off on them, so my attending physician would have to see them, and he might start asking questions when he spots your other injuries. I'm relatively sure your ribs are bruised and not broken, but you may have a hairline fracture. In both cases, a tight binding and rest to heal properly are the prescribed treatment plan. The choice is yours: do you trust my medical judgment, or do you want me to run scans and maybe field questions you don't want to answer?"

The choice was easy. "I trust you. I thought both soldiers and medical people were the obedient, rule-following type, though. How did a rebel like you end up here?"

For the first time, Noah touched Indy without asking him, taking his hand and pressing it lightly. "Thank you for your trust."

Indy never even tensed up. Instead, his body tingled at the sensation of Noah's strong, masculine hand around his own, much smaller hand. "You didn't answer my question."

Noah let out a sigh. "I never wanted to be a soldier, nor a physician assistant," he said, letting go of Indy's hand. "But that's something I don't like to talk about. Listen, I do want to ask my supervisor to sign off on an X-ray of your arm if that's okay, plus a head scan to rule out brain trauma. Anything I should know beforehand?"

A head scan? They'd charge at least a thousand bucks for that, if not more. Those things were wicked expensive. "My arm has been broken before, but it won't look suspicious. My head...is it necessary?"

Noah ran his hand through his short hair. "Normally, I'd do it to check for possible brain trauma, especially since you passed out. We could skip it, but then you'd need someone to wake you every two hours to see if you are alert and responsive, tonight and tomorrow night. Sometimes head injuries have delayed effects. Is there someone who can stay with you?"

Indy's stomach sank. Fuck. "No."

"Staying for observation isn't an option either, of course," Noah said. He rubbed his stubble and was silent for a few seconds. "You can stay with me."

"What?" Indy stammered. He was joking, right? He couldn't possibly be serious.

"Me and Josh, we live close to that Stewart's. My shift ended already—I only stayed for you—so we could take you home as soon as your scans are done. I could check on you tonight."

They were roommates, Noah and Josh? *Huh.* Indy couldn't make out Noah's eyes in the darkened room, but there was something in the guy's expression he couldn't determine. "You do that for all your patients?"

"Of course not. But like I said: I owe you. Big time."

What was it between these two guys? There was an emotion in Noah's voice when he talked about Josh, even when he mentioned his name, that was charged with more than Indy could put his finger on. Respect. Brotherhood. A deep affection. It was that sentiment that made him decide.

"Okay."

"What do you mean, okay?"

"Okay as in: okay, I'll stay with you guys."

Noah stepped closer, raised his eyebrows. "Like that? You don't even know us, and no offense, but you're not the trusting type."

Indy slowly pushed himself up a bit. Noah was studying him, reading him again. "You guys are both army veterans. Josh has PTSD, and you feel responsible for him at least enough to say you owe me for keeping him safe during the robbery. You're a PA, and you stayed after your shift to take care of me, even though I'm a seriously fucked-up nutcase. You recognized my hang-ups and managed to work around them, even getting me to trust you. And you didn't react in any way when you saw my back. None of that screams psychopathic murderer to me, you feel me? Also, I'm pretty sure Josh mentioned that brown belt, right? Even with a concussion and bruised ribs, I could kick your ass if you attempted something I didn't want."

Amusement danced in Noah's eyes where respect had been moments before. He understood. "True. I'll put in the order for the X-rays of your arm and check on your labs. I'll send Jessie in to take you up. Try to be nice to her."

"Be nice yourself. It's not me she was scared of. You about reduced her to tears with your barking."

Noah grinned. "But the barking is so effective."

Noah's face transformed from stern and aloof into boyish and vulnerable with that grin. Damn, what a difference.

"After we get your results, assuming they don't reveal anything new, I'll get your discharge papers started and write you a script for meds. We can pick those up when we take you home. If you want, we can drive by your place to pick up some things."

His place. Shit, he hadn't had a place he could call his in over two years. Longer, actually, since the house Duncan had bought him had never been Indy's either. Indy's car came closest, but anyone seeing that from the inside would know he'd been sleeping in it. No, he'd make do.

"That won't be necessary. If I can borrow a T-shirt or something, I'll be fine." His answer left no room for doubt.

Noah narrowed his eyes for a second, obviously curious, but he backed off. "Is it okay if I send Josh in later? He can tell you where we live and arrange the practical details with you."

"Sure."

Noah gave him a reassuring smile and turned around to walk out.

As soon as Noah had left, doubts attacked Indy. He was nuts. Certifiably out of his fucking mind. How could he have agreed to spend the night at the residence of not one, but two guys he didn't know? Shit, that bump on his head must have seriously fucked up his self-preservation skills, because otherwise there was no way he would have made such a rash decision.

But what the hell was the alternative? Staying in the hospital overnight where every examination could trigger alarm bells? The scars were pretty conspicuous, after all, not to mention the whole not-being-a-woman thing. Spending another night in his cramped car, with these sore ribs? Even if he found a cheap motel—burning more cash he couldn't afford to spend—he'd still run the risk of bleeding out in his brain because he'd refused the head scan. He hadn't survived by making rash decisions on important dilemmas like this. No, he'd consistently weighed the pros and cons and had done whatever had made the most sense. And as counterintuitive as it seemed, trusting Noah and Josh right now was his best option.

Jessie hesitantly stepped inside. "I'm here to take your cast off and then take you to radiology, Ms. Baldwin," she said.

"Thank you," Indy said, sending her a friendly smile.

Poor kid, screwing up in front of your hot boss. No matter what Noah had said about her not being his type, there was no way he was not Jessie's type. Shit, he has to be pretty much everybody's type, male or female. Seriously. He certainly is yours...

Noah and Josh were both so fucking sexy, yet completely different. Josh was sweet, adorable, and cute, whereas Noah

—despite his gentle, calming voice and manners—was raw, masculine, and breathtaking. The two of them made a pretty deadly combination.

Asking Indy's permission for every single step, Jessie carefully removed the cast and gently cleaned his arm. Indy's guess was that the girl had gotten some extra instructions aka barked orders from Noah to make sure she wouldn't screw up again. When the cast was off and Indy's arm was clean and resting on a pillow, Jessie unlocked the bed and wheeled him out of the room.

A concussion wasn't Indy's biggest worry. With proper rest that would be cleared in a week, two at most. But his arm and those ribs...they had better be bruised and not broken, otherwise he'd be royally fucked. How was he supposed to take care of himself, protect himself when he was that vulnerable? Plus, living in a car with injuries like that? Pshaw, he'd be so fucked.

Even if he was screwed physically, he still didn't regret saving Josh. He couldn't have let him walk out in blind panic with the high risk of getting shot. With a nervous kid like that handling a .45 bad things could happen, even by accident. Saving Josh had been the right thing to do, no matter what it would cost him. It was a small consolation, but it did make him feel better.

The exams were fast and relatively painless. Luckily, scanning an arm took no undressing and precious little touching. A few minutes later, Indy was back in the ER, waiting for Noah to return with the results of his scans.

Why did his heart rate speed up at the mere thought of this man? It was weird to start noticing guys again. First Josh, whose kisses had totally turned him on, and now Noah who caused his heart to gallop with a simple smile. Maybe his body was ready for sex again, even if his mind wasn't and probably would never be.

The door opened, and Noah stepped in.

"What's the verdict?"

"Your arm is bruised, not broken, and the previous fracture is healing. We'll put on a new cast, give you some pain meds, and then we can go home."

Home. Now, there was a word he hadn't used in a long, long time.

4

I ndy leaned back in the front seat of the car as Josh navigated the sturdy-looking Subaru through the sparse traffic. Out of habit, Indy checked the cars behind them in the side mirror. Nobody seemed to be following them. It was easy to track with so little traffic.

Noah was in the backseat behind Josh, still wearing his scrubs. He sat turned to the right with his right leg stretched out on the seat, rubbing his thigh every now and then. Probably that leg injury Indy had spotted before bothering him. That also had to be why Josh was driving, because Noah didn't seem like the type to not be in the driver's seat.

God, he was tired. Exhausted, more like it. Even after Noah had cleared him to be released, he still had to finish the administrative stuff. He'd paid his hospital bill himself, which had set him back way too much, but he'd had no choice. The hospital administrator hadn't looked suspicious of his story of not having health insurance yet after moving, not when he had an old Georgia address and driver's license to go with the accent. His license even listed him as female. *Thank you, Houdini.*

Noah had to be suspicious after seeing the scars and knowing about the previous injuries. Plus, you know, the whole fake woman thing. Fuck, Noah and Josh had seen him freak out. Yet they hadn't asked any questions. It was a trust that felt unfamiliar, yet good. He had to keep his distance from them, though. He couldn't afford to make friends. He'd get well and get on his way.

The tight bandage Noah had wrapped around Indy's ribs had brought relief. Noah had done it himself instead of asking a nurse and had made small talk the entire time, and it had made it anything but awkward. The heavy-duty painkillers Noah had prescribed had improved Indy's mood even more. He'd received the first dose in the hospital, and they'd just picked up the rest at a pharmacy—which had cost Indy another fucking fortune. It made a huge difference to his headache as he could at least open his eyes without getting stabbed in the head. Still, every bump and dip in the road made him wince. And the meds made it damn hard to concentrate, to think clearly.

"We're here," Josh announced, as he banged a left into a driveway, and hit a button attached to the visor.

Indy wasn't sure what he had expected, but it wasn't the suburban single-family home they pulled into. Holy crap, this was a nice house, illuminated by several outside lamps and garden lights. This was where Josh and Noah lived? He'd expected an apartment. What's the story with these two? It didn't matter. He wasn't here to stay.

"I'll take Indy in," Josh said. He switched the car off inside the garage and pressed the button again. The garage door closed behind them with a buzz. Josh's eyes found Noah's in the rearview mirror. "You go get changed," Josh said.

Indy frowned. Why would Noah want to change so

urgently? Surely scrubs weren't that uncomfortable. From the corner of his eye, he caught Noah climbing out of the car, a pained wince flashing over his face. Josh waited till Noah had disappeared through a white door before he exited the car. He walked around and opened Indy's door.

"Do you need help?"

"Can you unbuckle me? Twisting my back hurts like a mother..."

Josh bent over him, clicking the button to release the seatbelt. As Josh pulled back with the belt, his hand brushed against Indy's crotch. A small shock blazed through Indy. What the fuck was going on? It was like a switch had been flipped, and suddenly his body responded to every little touch. Damn inconvenient, not to say fucking embarrassing.

"Sorry," Josh mumbled. He straightened and stepped back.

Indy extended his hand, and Josh took it without hesitation, sending another sparkle through Indy's body. Josh had a strong grip, more powerful than Indy had expected. Leaning on Josh's hand, Indy turned his body to swing his legs out. He let out a groan as his ribs protested. Josh grabbed Indy's other hand and waited till he pulled himself up.

"Can you walk?"

"Yeah, I'm good," Indy said and let go of his hands.

Josh stayed one step behind Indy as he made his way through the tidy garage to the door. When he got there, Josh reached out around him and opened it. It led into a brightly lit hallway with a small mudroom to the left, a door presumably leading to the back yard in front, and a bathroom and steps to the kitchen to the right.

"Go on in," Josh said.

Indy made his way into the kitchen, which was decked

out like an amateur cook's dream with a double oven, a large five-burner stove, several appliances he didn't even recognize, and more glossy white cabinets than he could count. The gray marbled counter ended in a breakfast area with a couple of black leather bar stools. Little red flowerpots containing various green plants perched on the small windowsill. The faint smell of lemon hung in the air.

The parlor was homey with light gray walls and carpet, a warm burgundy red couch and two big reading chairs in the same color. A huge TV was mounted to the wall, with a nizza sound system and an Xbox. It was all so fucking clean and tidy, so lovely normal, Indy thought.

"The guest bedroom is upstairs," Josh said. Indy slowly climbed the stairs, every step radiating pain to his ribs and head.

"Second door to the right," Josh offered when they reached the upstairs hallway.

The first door was closed, but light was spilling under the door. That had to be Noah's bedroom where he was getting changed for whatever reason. Josh once again reached in front of Indy to open the door and flicked on the light. The guest bedroom was sparsely decorated, but had a comfy-looking queen bed, a dresser, and a small closet. It beat the hell out of the places Indy had stayed at lately, and it sure as fuck was a whole lot better than his car.

"Your bathroom is across the hall. There are towels in the cupboard under the sink as well as some toiletries."

A muffled groan sounded from the room next door. Josh's face tightened. "Can you get yourself comfortable? I'll be back in a minute to check on you and see if you need anything."

Indy nodded carefully. What was going on?

Josh closed the bedroom door, and another door

opened. Low voices drifted through the wall, but they were too soft to make out.

Indy lowered himself onto the bed. Fuck, it was good to be lying down again. The painkillers helped, but his body still felt like he'd gotten run over by a car. He inhaled deeply. The bed linens smelled wicked fresh, like those expensive dryer sheets.

The voices next door continued with some kind of discussion. Were they arguing about him? Did they not want him here? Had Noah spoken out of turn? If they didn't want him, he'd leave. He wasn't staying where he wasn't welcome, injured or not. Where would he go? His heart rate sped up and he clenched his fists. He pressed his eyes shut, not wanting to even think about leaving again.

"For fuck's sake, Noah, are you insane?" Josh exploded next door.

Indy's eyes flew open. *What the fuck?*

Noah said something back—Indy recognized his voice —but it was still too soft to hear.

"Oh, fuck you, you arrogant shit!" Josh shouted.

A door slammed and someone—Josh, Indy assumed by the even and rhythmic steps—stomped down the steps. Shit, he was seriously pissed off. What was happening?

Seconds later, a low, hard thump reverberated through the floor. Oh, God, what was that? Indy scrambled up from the bed and made it to the door, cursing through his teeth at the pain in his head and ribs at the sudden movements.

"Noah!" Josh cried out from downstairs.

Indy yanked the door open. Josh came flying up the stairs, his face twisted in worry. He blew into Noah's room.

"Are you okay?" Josh shouted the question that was on Indy's lips. Indy stood in his doorframe, hesitant to intrude.

"I'm fine. I needed you back here and didn't feel like

shouting, so I kicked a chair over." Noah's voice had a touch of amusement, as if he was satisfied his little trick had worked.

"Oh, I want to..." Josh cut himself off, but the frustration in his voice was unmistakable. Something told Indy they'd been through similar confrontations.

"Trust me, I know exactly what you want to do to me."

"You drive me crazy sometimes, you know that?" Frustration and affection laced Josh's voice. Thank fuck the dispute had been resolved, whatever it had been about.

"Will you trust me when I say this is the right thing to do?" There was that tone in Noah's voice again, the one that made you want to follow him to the ends of the earth and back.

"Always." Josh's voice sounded muffled.

Indy stepped into the hallway. Noah appeared seconds later, balancing his weight on two crutches. He was wearing a Patriots T-shirt that sat tight across his wide chest and biceps and simple white boxer shorts—and his right lower leg was missing. What remained was a red, irritated stump that ended above the knee. Angry scares covered both of his legs.

Indy swallowed, then let his gaze move up again. Noah's eyes were kind, vulnerable. He was showing Indy his scars because he'd seen Indy's. Who was this man? Why the fuck would he do this for a complete stranger?

Nothing could have made Indy feel more accepted than this. Nothing. God, he knew how Noah felt. Completely exposed, stripped bare, even if he'd made the deliberate choice to show this. All Noah wanted was for Indy to look at him the same, to know that his wounds didn't change how Indy saw him. It's what I want more than anything else.

How could he express that to Noah? He could make a

joke about it, or show it didn't make a lick of difference. Dammit, he was too fucking fried to come up with anything funny, and he was so over his fear of touching Noah. Indy's face broke out in a smile as he stepped up to Noah, grabbed his neck and pulled him down to kiss him square on the mouth.

"You're still sexy as hell," he said, letting him go.

Noah's eyes widened and behind him, Josh stood frozen, his jaw dropping. Then Noah smiled, a big, lazy smile that lit up his entire face. Sweet fuck, Indy had never seen a smile like that. It was like lighting a thousand-watt bulb in a dark room and holy mother of all, it was fucking deadly. Indy's whole body reacted to that smile, was drawn to it, drowning in it.

"I take it kissing is your solution for everything?" Noah asked.

Indy forced himself to descend from the light of Noah's smile. "What, you're complaining?"

His stomach turned sour. Fuck, what had he done? He hadn't been thinking. When would he ever learn to activate that fucking filter? He kissed a man. On the mouth. A man who knew he wasn't a woman.

Noah's smile faded into something way more serious, but equally powerful. "No. No complaints," he murmured.

Indy let out a breath he'd been holding. Noah lifted a hand to brush a curl from Indy's forehead, and the tender gesture caught Indy's breath again. He slowly released air as Noah drew back.

Why did this guy affect him so much? Shit, it was equally exhilarating and scary as fuck. It seemed his body was ready to feel again after being dormant and self-reliant for so long. He'd encountered many guys in the last two years, especially since he'd started dressing as a woman.

None of them had affected him. His body hadn't been ready yet to awaken, apparently. No fucking wonder. But today, he'd been ready. Fuck, he'd been more aroused in one day than in the entire two years before, maybe more aroused than ever.

It was a relief, in a way, to discover that part of his life wasn't over. But dammit, it was fucking complicated, too. How could he react this strongly to two guys? That was weird, not normal. No shit, when was he ever normal?

Maybe it was because intuitively, he had trusted both guys. And trust right now was the biggest turn on he could think of, ranking way above a hot body. Sure, both Josh and Noah were hot, but that wasn't what attracted Indy. It was their inherent trust. Noah had trusted him with something few people got to see, and Indy had wanted to honor that. That had to be it. He wanted to reciprocate that trust, include Josh as well.

"Did you tell Josh?" he asked Noah.

Noah understood what Indy was referring to. "No. Doctor-patient confidentiality."

To his credit, Josh didn't ask what they were talking about but merely studied Indy. Josh knew about demons, alright. The guy had PTSD. He wouldn't judge or ask what Indy wasn't ready to reveal. For the second time that night, he made the leap to trust. He slowly turned around and lifted his blouse. Even with the bandage around his ribs, the scars had to be visible.

Like Noah, Josh never gasped. When Indy wanted to drop his blouse again, a flutter of a touch caressed his back. Josh's hand, or maybe just his fingers for it was so feather light, followed the jagged path of the biggest scar. Indy's back tingled where Josh brushed him, sending shivers to his core.

It was seconds at most before Josh dropped his hand. "Thank you," he said softly.

Indy pulled down his blouse, then turned around to face them.

"You're safe here, Indy." Noah's voice was warm, strong, and his eyes beamed.

"I know."

Josh's gaze traveled from Noah to Indy and back, and there was something indecipherable in his eyes. "Let's get some sleep," he said, his posture stiff and his voice pinched.

Indy stepped back. He was still standing awfully close to them both. "Yeah. I'm wiped."

Noah's face shut down. "I have the evening shift again tomorrow, so you can sleep in. I'll wake you every three hours."

"Thank you."

Noah cleared his throat. "Can you give Indy one of your shirts to sleep in? He'll drown in mine," he asked with a sideways look to Josh. It was the first time Noah had referred to Indy as he, but it was okay. They knew he was pretending, even if they hadn't asked why.

Noah's eyes fixated on Indy, who squirmed under his scrutiny. Why was he looking at him like that?

Josh went into the room next door. Noah's room. Their room. Noah and Josh were sleeping in the same room.

Noah was gay.

Shit, shit, shit.

He was pathetic. The biggest fool ever. In one night, he had kissed not one, but two hot guys...and they were together. How the fuck had he missed this? He'd known Josh was gay, but even with that, the thought had never crossed his mind that Noah was gay too. Dammit, Noah had told him they lived together, and Indy still hadn't connected the dots. He was an idiot and a pathetic one at that.

Indy raised his chin, willing himself to meet Noah's eyes. God, Noah and Josh had to be laughing their asses off. Or feeling sorry for the pathetic fucker who'd completely missed they were together. Fuck, he wasn't sure which one would be worse.

But when he met Noah's green eyes, they weren't mocking him, or laughing. Instead, he let his hands fall to his sides with a pained expression. Indy didn't wait for him to say anything, but made his way into his room, closing the door with a definitive click.

Kill. Me. Now.

NOAH GROANED. A sharp pain stabbed his leg. The leg that no longer existed. The leg that was buried somewhere in Afghanistan, courtesy of a well-placed IED he'd hit while trying to get to a wounded soldier. It had to be one of the most frustrating pains ever: to ache in something you no longer had. Phantom pain was, contrary to its name, very real.

His stump throbbed, too. It had been bothering him more than usual lately, caused by the adjustment on his prosthetic leg. The more his scars and stump healed, the better they could fit his prosthesis, but it took getting used to. He'd worked longer than his regular shift because of Indy coming in, and the extra two hours of standing and walking were killing him now. Plus, ever since the amputation in the field over a year ago, the stump had troubled him. It had never healed completely, had become a constant discomfort.

He glanced at the clock. Another half hour before he had to check on Indy for the first time. He was looking forward to seeing him again, talking to him, even if it was under these circumstances.

Fuck, he'd been frantic when Josh had called him from the ambulance to tell him he'd witnessed a robbery and was bringing in someone who'd helped him through an episode. Shit like that could set Josh off, cause him to have a major panic attack. His best friend was fragile, and violence especially was a big trigger. The fact that Indy had saved Josh's life had made Noah like him before he'd even met him. But when Indy had told him he'd kissed Josh to snap him out of the episode, Noah had been...He didn't even have words. Shocked, maybe?

Something about the mental picture of Josh and Indy kissing had triggered him. Had he been angry? He considered it. Not really, no. Not jealous either. More like upset that he hadn't been there, hadn't been a part of it. It didn't make sense at all.

Well, neither did this weird connection with Indy. What the hell was that? It wasn't purely physical attraction, not with him being dressed like a woman, including makeup and all. Not that Noah hadn't recognized the beauty underneath. Those full lips, the almond-shaped eyes, the little gap between his front teeth, and his cute button nose. Oh yeah, he'd noticed, alright.

It was way more than that, though. Maybe it was the mystery surrounding Indy. The boy was underweight, malnourished even. Noah had registered the ribs sticking out, the too-thin arms and legs, but also the frail nails that hinted at a lack of calcium, the paleness of Indy's skin. He'd seen the same in homeless people he'd treated, or neglected kids who'd been physically abused. But Indy had been clean, had not shown any sign of drug use.

The conundrum of his gender made the puzzle even more complex. Josh had whispered a quick plea when they'd brought Indy in: "Protect her gender." What the hell was going on in Indy's life that he felt the need to hide his gender and identity? It could be that he was transgender, gender neutral, or simply enjoyed cross-dressing, but combined with everything else Noah had witnessed, it felt like more.

The old injuries Indy had hinted at, those horrific scars on his back—he had survived one hell of a trauma. Noah didn't judge how people survived. How could he when he hadn't learned to face his own trauma in a healthy way? If Indy didn't want to talk about it, if he chose to hide behind a mask and even a different gender, Noah would accept that. He was damn curious—how could he not be?—but wouldn't ask questions.

Indy's scars hadn't made him less appealing to Noah; on the contrary. They shared that, didn't they? For once, Noah didn't feel the need to cover himself up, to keep that part of him hidden. No one had seen his stump, except Josh and his own doctors and therapists.

And when Indy had stepped up to him, had kissed him... God, it had been like he'd been zapped. All his nerves had been on fire, his body tingling with want. He'd grown hard from a simple kiss. Sexy as fuck, Indy had called him. Noah wanted to do so much more than kiss him...

Luckily, his shirt had been long enough to cover his erection. And even more luckily, Josh had been standing behind him and had never caught Noah's reaction to that kiss. Hopefully. He'd hate to hurt Josh as well. How could one kiss from a guy he'd met only hours before have that effect on him? Even now, thinking about him, his cock stirred.

But oh, that look when Indy had deduced he and Josh were more than friends, that they weren't merely sharing a house, but a bed as well. The embarrassment had been easy to see, but also the pride and determination to cover it up. Fuck, he'd hated hurting Indy like that, especially after the incredibly risky move of kissing another guy. Indy hadn't known Noah was gay, and even if it had been an impulse, as Noah suspected it was, probably fueled by the painkillers that had lowered his inhibitions, it was still a ballsy move.

Wait. He'd labeled himself gay. Was he? He'd considered himself more of a gay-for-you variety since he'd only been involved with Josh. He'd never so much as looked at another man, not even before his accident. Well, Josh, maybe, but that was because they'd been so damn close, and Josh had been openly gay. Of course he'd wondered. More than once if he was honest. But now his attraction to Indy disproved that theory. Hmm, maybe he was bisexual? Did it really matter?

The naked, lean body sleeping in his arms was the living, breathing proof it did matter. He'd have to navigate carefully here, because Josh was fragile. His needs had to come first. Not that Noah resented that. Fuck, no. He could never resent Josh. He loved him way too deeply for that. At the same time, Indy had stirred something in him worth exploring, something he hadn't felt since the loss, as he called it.

The loss of his leg.

The loss of his identity.

The loss of a sense of calling.

He wasn't the same Noah he had been before, and he doubted he would ever be. Of course, it was also the loss for

Josh. Noah might have left a leg in that field hospital, but Josh had left a part of himself in the sand pit that he had not yet learned to live without.

He shifted, trying to find a position where his leg would stop hurting. Josh stirred in his sleep, snuggled closer to Noah and put his head on Noah's arm. They always slept cuddled up against each other since it was the only way Josh could sleep without having nightmares. Noah had gotten so used to it that he himself now had trouble falling asleep without Josh next to him. Tonight, despite a twelve-hour shift and being dead tired, sleep eluded him. His leg hurt too much, and the erection he'd been sporting on and off since Indy kissed him didn't help either.

Another shooting pain tormented his leg, and he bit his lip to keep the wail in that threatened to erupt from his lips. His body tensed, and Josh shifted in his arms, rubbing his bare ass against Noah's equally naked cock. It responded with fervor, and Noah let out a soft gasp.

"Your leg bothering you?" Josh whispered with a sleepy voice.

Noah ordered his cock to back off, but it wasn't hearing him. "Yeah. Sorry to wake you."

Josh wriggled with his ass, no doubt noticing the hard rod poking his cheeks. "'S okay. You need release?"

Noah's jaw tensed. The never-ending battle between what he needed and what he wanted. Another reason he could never resent Josh. They took care of each other. Always.

"Yeah," he admitted with a raw voice.

Josh turned to face Noah. "It's okay, Noah. I got you."

Noah's cock jumped as Josh's hand wrapped around it, pulling slowly at first, then with a firmer grip. Noah closed his eyes as his cock responded to Josh's ministrations. The steady rhythm made him grow rock hard. Josh pulled back the skin, brushed the thick head with his thumb. Noah's spine tingled.

Oh fuck, he needed this. He wanted this. He groaned as Josh's hand formed a tight pressure around his shaft. Noah arched his back, moving with Josh's hand to create even more friction. Josh's thumb found the head again, this time juicing his whole cock with precum.

"Hand, blow, or fuck?"

That simple question had been asked by Josh dozens of times before, but it never failed to hit Noah deep in his core. The fact that Josh even wanted to do this after what he'd been through, it was a fucking miracle. The mere thought of burying himself in Josh's ass had his cock throbbing. He needed something to make him feel anything else but the pain in his leg...and the confusion Indy had brought.

"Let me fuck you. Please, Josh." His voice trembled.

"You know you don't need to ask me twice."

Josh shoved the covers up and climbed up, straddled him, their cocks brushing against each other. Noah reached out and grabbed his friend's shaft, eliciting a soft moan from Josh's lips.

He smiled as his best friend's cock jumped under his loving care and grew rigid.

"Oh!" Josh groaned and flexed his hips as Noah firmly stroked his member. He was nowhere near as hard as Noah, but Noah could remedy that in seconds. Josh was always fast to respond to Noah's touch. Noah added his other hand, grabbing the base of Josh's shaft with one hand and stroking him with the other.

"Shit..." Josh sighed, closing his eyes and leaning back to give Noah full access.

Josh's ass pressed down on Noah's cock, and Noah had to

force himself to keep focused on his friend. Fuck, he wanted to be inside him, but Josh's pleasure came first.

If his leg hadn't hurt so much, Noah would have flipped his lover over and given him a solid blow job. The good news was that Josh loved being fucked, so he was about to become really, really happy. Noah would fill him up and make him come.

When Josh's juices started to flow, Noah released his cock. Josh let out a contented sigh while grinding his ass against Noah's cock, making him tremble. Josh lowered himself to his forearms, brushing a soft kiss on Noah's lips.

"Ready to fuck?" Josh whispered, touching Noah's lips again with another butterfly kiss. God, he was so sweet.

"Always," Noah groaned, lifting his hips to grind his crotch against Josh's ass.

"You sure about that?" Josh teased, maneuvering Noah's cock against his entrance.

What had he ever done to deserve a man as tender and sweet as Josh? Noah reached up with his right hand and pulled Josh's head down, crushing his mouth against his. Josh stilled in surprise—no wonder, as kissing wasn't usually part of the program and when it was, it was initiated by Josh—before he surrendered and kissed him back with fervor.

The intricate dance of their hot, slick tongues released flutters in Noah's belly. Damn, the guy could kiss. Josh deserved so much more than what Noah was able to give him.

Noah pulled his mouth back and rocked his hips forward again, pushing his shaft against Josh's hole. He gave Josh the look that had earned him the nickname The General. "Does that answer your question?"

Most men trembled in their boots when he looked at

them like that, but Josh's eyes lit up. "I love it when you get all authoritative on me."

"I know. Now help me fuck you. Please," he added. He would die before making Josh do anything he didn't want.

Josh stilled. "Stop saying please. You're not asking me for a favor. I want this as much as you."

Noah groaned in frustration. Why couldn't he get it right tonight? "For fuck's sake, Josh, can we please not talk about this right now?"

In an uncharacteristic act of defiance, Josh jerked back the hands that had been caressing Noah's body and pushed himself up on his forearms. His eyes were strangely sad as he met Noah's impatient gaze.

"I'm serious," Josh said. "You always say please, as if I need persuasion to be with you. You know I don't. I love doing this for you as much as for myself."

Did he? Was he getting enough out of this? Maybe, but he was touching on something that dug way deeper than they were ready to handle. Noah had about ten minutes before he needed to check on Indy, he desperately needed to find release, and if nothing else, he had a straining cock that was about to find its own way into Josh's ass. Enough with the talking.

With one move, he flipped Josh off him and turned him on his stomach. He pushed himself up on both arms and, using his good leg, lowered himself on top of Josh.

"Spread your legs," he ordered Josh, the first time he had ordered him to do anything in bed. He bit his tongue to avoid adding the 'please' Josh apparently resented so much.

"Dammit, Josh, spread your legs!" he hissed when Josh didn't respond, rubbing his cock against his friend's ass.

Josh lifted his head off the mattress, looked over his

shoulder and met Noah's eyes with smoldering eyes. "Make me."

A roar thundered through Noah's head. He forgot about his sore leg, he forgot about Indy, and he forgot about not wanting to order Josh around. A desperate need consumed him and filled every fiber of his being.

"Oh, I'll make you," he growled. He rolled off Josh, linking one arm around him to yank them both on their sides in a spooning position. His right hand came around Josh, grabbing his cock in an iron fist. Josh wanted to challenge him? Challenge accepted. He would make him beg before he'd fuck him.

Josh whimpered as Noah's fist pumped up and down. Noah wriggled his left hand between them and found Josh's entrance with his thumb. He played around the tight hole, eliciting soft moans from Josh, as his own cock grew even harder. He pulled back a little and swiped precum off his own cock, lubricating his thumb and index finger. Again, he teased around the entrance while stroking Josh's cock till it quivered in his hands.

"Noah..." Josh whimpered again.

"Noah, what? What do you want me to do?" Noah slid his index finger in Josh's tight hole. "Is that what you want?" He gave the long shaft in his hand a firm stroke. "Or is that what you want?"

"More..." Josh's voice was hoarse and incredibly sexy.

Noah added his middle finger in Josh's ass, moving in and out till the tight hole had made room for a third finger. He found Josh's sensitive spot without effort. Josh bucked against him, writhing in pleasure.

"Is that what you want?" Noah asked again.

When Josh didn't answer but kept gyrating his ass against Noah's fingers, he pulled out and dropped Josh's cock. He brought his mouth against Josh's ear. "Tell me what you want."

"Please."

Noah rubbed his straining cock against his lover's ass cheeks. "Please, what?"

Josh turned on his stomach and spread his legs wide open, giving Noah access to what he had sought all this time. "Please, fuck me... I need you inside me."

Noah reached behind him to grab a bottle of lube from the night table drawer. He squeezed out a glob and coated his throbbing cock. Wordlessly, he nestled himself between his lover's legs and guided his cock into Josh's ass, pushing through the outer ring with ease.

"Yes..." Josh sighed, pushing his ass farther back to pull Noah in deeper.

"Is this what you want?" Noah asked again, forcing himself to pull back.

Why was he was doing this? It was never like this. Sex between them was supposed to be simple, uncomplicated. Simply fucking and nothing else. But tonight was different. He had rarely kissed Josh like that, and he had never, ever made him beg for it. Yet Josh wasn't protesting. If anything, he was more turned on than usual.

"Yes...no... I want more. I want all of you. Fuck me deep...Noah, please," Josh pleaded, pulling his knees up, kneeling in front of Noah, his ass wide open for the taking.

"As you wish." With one strong move, Noah slammed his cock home, all the way to the hilt.

Josh groaned low and deep, ground his ass against Noah. Noah pulled back and set a steady rhythm, gripping Josh's hips and thrusting deep with every move.

Josh's head craned back, and he growled from deep in his chest. "Yes, that's it. Harder, fuck me harder."

His cock buried to his balls in Josh's tight hole, Noah sucked in a shallow breath. Damn, he needed this.

"Oh, so good..." Josh gasped. He fisted the sheets, kneeling even deeper. His whole body shook with the impact of Noah's thrusts. "Don't stop...so deep...so good..."

Noah's ears barely picked up the words over the sound of his own panting breaths. His body thrummed, his cock feasting on the slick heat inside Josh. Forgotten was the pain in his leg, replaced by a singular focus on his dick. God, the pressure...it was incredible. His balls drew close to his body, getting ready to unload.

Josh was almost there as well, his hands restlessly fisting the bed. Noah had never come first when they fucked, and he didn't intend to break that habit.

Josh's whole body tensed, a signal Noah knew well. He lowered himself onto Josh's back and brought his mouth to his lover's ear.

"You have four more thrusts to come..." he said between panting breaths. "One."

He pulled himself out all the way, then slammed home. God, his balls ached, and his thighs shook. So fucking close.

Josh trembled at the impact, his body taut with tension. "Two."

Another massive shove. "Three."

Noah's right hand let go of Josh's hip and circled his lover's straining cock. "And four. Come for me, Joshua."

He buried himself again while jacking Josh's cock once. Josh threw his head back and grunted, blowing his cum all over Noah's hand and the bed. His body shuddered, twitched, his back slick with sweat under Noah's abs.

Noah released the tight grip he had on himself. His balls detonated and his orgasm thundered through him. He pumped into Josh wildly, hot cum blasting up the length of his dick.

"Ugh! Fuuuck!"

With his last bit of strength, he pulled out and slumped on his back, his chest heaving as he sucked in air. Sweat covered his upper body.

"Noah?"

Noah's stomach turned sour at the insecurity in Josh's voice. What had he done? Had he made Josh relive his darkest nightmare?

"Come here," Noah mumbled, blindly reaching for his friend. When his hands found Josh, he pulled him on top of him, their spent cocks finding each other in brotherhood. He wrapped his arms around Josh, putting his lover's head on his shoulder. As always, Josh was careful to avoid his stump, putting most of his weight on his own legs. Cuddling like this after sex wasn't their thing, but hey, nothing was going as usual today, so why stop here?

"Are you okay?" Josh asked.

Despite himself, Noah smiled a little. Even after all this time, it still baffled him that silent, shy Josh turned into a talker after sex. For some reason, Josh was at his most insecure right after his release.

"Yeah. You?"

"Are you kidding me? You went total caveman on me."

Noah froze. Fuck. *You fucked up, Flint.* He swallowed, but the lump in his throat persisted. If he had hurt Josh, if he'd brought back memories for him, had damaged what they had together, he would never forgive himself.

"I'm sorry. Don't know what came over me," he mumbled.

Josh lifted his head up, looking Noah in the eyes. "It wasn't a complaint. That was the best sex we've ever had.

Fuck, Noah, you were a beast." He let his head fall back on Noah's chest, his cheek still damp against Noah's skin.

"Oh," Noah said. What the fuck had just happened? At least he hadn't hurt Josh, on the contrary, it seemed. God, the sex had been off the charts hot.

Just then, his alarm went off. He reached for his phone on the nightstand and silenced it. When he slid back, their still-slick cocks brushed up against each other. Much to his surprise, his cock stirred again. What the hell? They had never fucked twice in one night. Noah usually came twice, but that was because his second orgasm was the one that brought so much relief. Josh would give him a hand job, or he'd jack off again himself.

Josh pushed himself up on his arms and kissed Noah, sliding his groin against Noah's. "Glad to feel you agree with my assessment. I'm game for another round when you're done checking on Indy..." He kissed Noah once more and rolled off him with care.

What was he supposed to say to that? Noah stared at Josh's bare back for a few seconds, unable to find adequate words. The rules were changing at such blinding speed that he couldn't keep up. The kissing, the explosive sex, the tenderness afterward, and now Josh asking for sex all of a sudden. This was becoming so fucking complicated.

His body disagreed with his analysis because the mere thought of another round of that was enough to make him hard again. Maybe he should stop over thinking it all and go with it. Fuck knew he had a tendency to see problems where there were none.

He took a deep breath. *Stop thinking. Just feel.* He leaned over Josh, rubbing his stubbled chin against the soft skin on Josh's arm. With his right hand he found Josh's ass again, which was still dripping. He slipped a finger in.

"You still want more?"

Josh gasped in surprise, then ground his ass against Noah's hand in a circular motion. "Always," he breathed. "Whatever you can give me."

His words stabbed Noah through the heart. He was such a bastard for doing this, for needing Josh and making him need Noah. Fuck, he had to give more, had to even the score, make it up to Josh. But how?

The answer was simple, wasn't it? He could offer something he'd never considered before. Noah closed his eyes. *Feel, don't think.* He brought his mouth against Josh's ear, meanwhile inserting another finger in his ass. There was something deliciously dirty about feeling his own cum in there. Josh's hole sucked his fingers in greedily. Shit, Josh really loved being fucked, didn't he?

"I'll check on Indy. When I get back, I'll suck your gorgeous cock for two minutes...Two minutes of sweet mouth-fucking, and that's it. I suggest you'd better make damn sure you're hard as steel when I get back so you'll be able to blow your load in under two minutes. If you succeed, I'll give you a reward you won't ever forget... Me," he said hoarsely.

A mighty shiver went through Josh as if electricity had shocked him. Had he grasped what Noah was offering?

"I won't disappoint you," Josh said, barely audible.

Noah took another deep breath. Yeah, Josh had gotten the message.

5

N oah had to balance in front of the door to the guest bedroom, leaning on one crutch and dangling the other from his arm so he had a hand free to open the door. Little things like that frustrated him to no end since they were so fucking complicated. At least the pain was almost gone as was usually the case after sex. Release, he euphemistically had called it at first, and they still used that code word. It seemed the physical act of orgasming and the endorphins it released in his body brought relief of his pain at the same time.

"I'm awake," Indy spoke up, his face illuminated by the soft light filtering through the curtains. They didn't have blackout curtains anywhere in the house as Josh couldn't stand the dark.

Indy was lying on his back, his face tilted toward the door. He must've cleaned his face, as all traces of the makeup he'd been wearing were gone. He looked so young, so innocent. Fuck, was the kid even legal? His date of birth had put him at twenty-one, but Noah wondered if it was accurate.

"How are you feeling?" he asked. He bumped the door open with his crutch and came farther into the room.

"Okay."

"How's the pain?"

"It's much better with the painkillers. Not dizzy or sick. My ribs still hurt, but it's doable."

Noah made his way to his bedside. "Can you sit up and move to the middle?" he asked. "I can't do this standing up on my crutches."

Indy slowly sat up and with careful movements scooted over to the middle of the bed. Noah lowered himself on the bed, dropping his crutches on the floor. He'd put on a shirt and some shorts, so he'd have a pocket to carry his light. Plus, he couldn't show up half-naked in Indy's room. He pulled out his light and turned it on.

"Follow the light please."

His eyes were brown now, Noah realized with surprise. Had he been wearing colored contacts? Noah had seen he'd been wearing contacts when he'd been brought in but had assumed they were regular ones. He was going through a lot of trouble to hide his identity.

He checked Indy's tracking, then his pupils. Indy responded well and alert.

"Any dizziness, nausea?"

"Nah."

"Did you sleep?"

"For a spell. I'm sure I woulda slept better if you guys hadn't kept me awake…"

Noah halted in his movements and swallowed. "You heard us."

"It was kinda hard to miss. The walls aren't that thick, and you were right next door."

Noah switched off his light, letting his eyes adjust to the

darkness. "I'm sorry," he said.

Indy crossed his legs, resting his hands on his knees. "Are we talking about the fact that I overheard you guys having sex or the fact that the two of you are together in the first place?"

That was the multimillion-dollar question, wasn't it? What the hell had he been apologizing for? Fuck, he was making a complete mess of things tonight. There was no way he could answer this question without revealing way more of himself than he was ready to.

The funny thing was that he had never wanted to explain himself more than right now. He wanted Indy to understand why he was with Josh, how much they needed each other. But Indy wasn't ready for what Noah had to say. Hell, he was hopped up on painkillers. Hardly the best time for a heart-to-heart. Plus, Noah himself wasn't ready to talk. He hadn't figured it all out, what it meant, what Indy meant, what it said about him and his sexuality. Plus, there was always Josh to consider. Josh, who had to come first, way before what Noah himself wanted.

He sighed, then grabbed his crutches and lifted himself up. "Hang on a sec, I'll be right back." He made his way to the guest bathroom and took a small box and a bottle from the medicine cabinet, stuffing both in his pocket. He limped back where Indy was motionless on the bed.

"Here," Noah said, taking them both out and throwing them on Indy's bed. "Earplugs for tonight and tomorrow night. And after that, you can use the Benadryl. Two tablets will get you drowsy enough to sleep through anything. It doesn't interact with your pain meds. There's a water bottle on your night table. Don't take them the first two nights, though, as I need to be able to assess you for possible brain issues."

Indy lifted his eyebrows. "Were you guys gearing up for another round right now or were you planning on me staying longer than one night?"

Noah turned around, making his way to the door. "Both," he said.

He couldn't look at Indy now, didn't want to see how his words affected him. If he saw Indy's pain, he'd crumble. Still, he had to offer something to help him understand that he wasn't fucking Josh to rub it in.

With his back toward Indy and the door knob in his hand, he said, "Sex helps with the pain."

He didn't wait for an answer, but closed the door behind him. His cock was painfully hard, and he was pretty sure Indy had seen it. It had to be because of the sex with Josh, right? And because he knew he was gonna get more. Give more, he corrected himself. This was about Josh's pleasure, not his own. And his cock had better get that memo, preferably soon.

He made his way into the bedroom to the sound of someone jerking off. Josh had taken his order seriously. He was spread out on the bed, fisting his cock and panting with effort, his head hung back in abandon. Noah stood for a minute, watching him. Fuck, Josh was so sexy when he was pleasuring himself.

Physically, they were completely different. While he himself had a muscular torso and strong arms—a necessary compensation for his weak legs—Josh was lean and toned all over. And his skin was soft, almost feminine, though his beautiful cock proved beyond a doubt he was a man. As his eyes adjusted to the dark, Noah saw Josh's dick juicing with anticipation.

Josh stopped and opened his eyes, slightly raising his

head. "Are you gonna stand there and watch me, or are you gonna make good on your promise?"

Noah dropped his crutches, then whipped off his shirt. "Think you're ready?"

He removed his shorts and boxers with some effort. His cock jumped free with joy, standing erect and ready for action. Too bad it wasn't going to get any, not if everything went according to plan.

Josh sat up, looked at Noah and smiled. "Hell, yeah. I'm not even gonna need two minutes."

Noah turned sideways and let himself fall facedown on the bed, his mouth directly above his lover's crotch. He blew a soft breath, noticing with satisfaction that a mere waft affected Josh.

"And why is that?" he asked, blowing again.

Josh shivered, clenching his teeth. "Because the thought of the reward alone was enough to almost make me come."

"I'm glad to see you are sufficiently motivated, as this is a onetime offer." He slid out his tongue and gave the gorgeous stiff member in front of him a big lap, like he would a lollipop.

"Oh, trust me, I'm motivated."

"Let's start the clock then," Noah said. "Two minutes and counting."

He didn't wait but dropped his mouth down on Josh's cock, taking him in as far as he could. Oh, he knew how to suck cock by now. He'd learned from the best.

Josh let out a loud groan and bucked against his mouth, grabbing his head with both hands. With one hand tight around the base, Noah sucked hard. He pushed the foreskin back with his tongue and lapped at the slit before tonguing it. He went crazy when Josh did that to him, so he figured he'd return the favor.

"Oh, fuck!" Josh groaned, thrusting his hips to get more of his cock in Noah's mouth.

Josh's salty fluids coated Noah's tongue and mouth, and he kept sucking as if his life depended on it. Sucking cock had taken a little getting used to at first, but he loved seeing the pleasure it brought Josh. He'd made a sport out of getting his lover's long cock as far in as he could, succeeding in getting it a little deeper every time. Also something he'd learned from a master cock sucker.

He'd never swallowed. For some reason, he'd always pulled back at the last minute and let Josh come over his hands or wherever. It had felt like a transition he wasn't ready to make, but that had to change. Josh deserved for him to be all in.

Noah relaxed his throat and took him in as far as he could. Josh's constant stream of moans fueled his desire to make this spectacular.

Josh gasped and shivered, sending tremors that vibrated through his cock. His head thrashed on the mattress, and he bucked his hips, seeking more fiction.

Was he really gonna do this? He pushed the thought out of his head. He wanted to do this. He had to do this. He fucking owed it to Josh. Dammit, Josh had gotten hurt because of him, and Noah had to do everything he could to make it right.

Noah came up for air, sucking in some much-needed oxygen, then took Josh in, farther than he'd ever thought possible.

"Noah! Shit...I'm coming!"

Josh's hands shoved Noah back, warning him of the impending release, but Noah dug in, only pulling back slightly to avoid choking.

Josh flexed his back, then made a final thrust in Noah's

mouth. "Oh...yes!" he cried out, shooting his cum down Noah's throat.

Noah's mouth filled with a creamy, slightly salty substance. He swallowed, kept sucking and licking till Josh relaxed.

Wow, that was easier than he'd expected. He smacked his lips at the flavor. It was okay, actually. Pretty neutral and not all that different from the taste of precum.

He'd done it. And fucking hell, so had Josh.

Noah pulled back, dropping Josh's now flaccid cock on his stomach to look at the clock. Josh turned his head at the same time, his forehead clammy. His breaths were slowing down.

"I did it." The sheer triumph in Josh's voice touched Noah deep.

"Technically, I did it, but yes. You made the deadline. Congratulations." He winced as he rolled on his side, maneuvering his stump out of the way.

Josh rolled on his side too, so they were facing each other. He cupped Noah's cheek with one hand, caressing. "Was it...okay for you?"

The question was quintessential Josh. He was always concerned about Noah.

He grabbed the hand stroking his cheek, kissed it softly. "I loved it," he said. "I love seeing you come."

Josh smiled, a sweet and boyish smile.

"Don't you want to know your reward?" Noah teased.

"I'm almost afraid to ask," Josh whispered.

"Why?"

Josh pulled back his hand, wrapped his hands around Noah's neck and snuggled close to him. With his mouth against Noah's neck, he said, "It's okay if you changed your mind."

No. He would not change his mind. He grabbed Josh's head and pulled him back for a hard kiss. "I haven't and I won't. But there's one condition: you have to claim your price. The ball is in your court now. I won't offer again, and I will not fuck you again until you've collected. You get me?" he said with his forehead against Josh's.

Josh nodded gamely. Noah kissed him again. "Now, would you please, please donate a minute of your time to make me come so we can get some sleep? Mouth-fucking your gorgeous dick has left me throbbing, and since I warned you I won't fuck you again until you claim me, I'm left hanging, so to speak." He pushed his solid cock against Josh's stomach for good measure.

Josh laughed softly. "It would be my pleasure," he said. Seconds later, Noah's cock was engulfed in Josh's sweet, sucking mouth. It didn't even take a minute. But when Noah came, it wasn't Josh he was thinking about.

INDY SLEPT most of the day. He'd only taken the earplugs after hearing Josh and Noah finish their second round, and the complete silence had helped him find a deep sleep. Noah had woken him every three hours—how the fuck does he manage that without suffering from severe sleep deprivation?—and had been content with how Indy had responded.

He'd slept and slept and slept and in between, he'd lain in bed, resting. How much of his headache and pain had been caused by that fall and how much by sheer exhaustion? He hadn't been sleeping well the week before—and that was the fucking understatement of the year. His diet had been equally crappy, since he was running out of money, and cooking was impossible in his car.

Josh had brought mouth-watering food. First a fluffy omelet with spinach and some kind of salty cheese, then homemade chicken soup, and for dinner a turkey sandwich. Indy had been ravenous, and every single bite had been scrumptious.

Indy assumed Josh was the cook. His face had displayed an adorable I-really-hope-you-like-it look every time he'd brought Indy something. He was like a puppy, eager to please, even after Indy had kissed his boyfriend. Apparently, Josh was the gracious and forgiving type. Thank fuck for that.

When he'd crawled his ass out of bed to pee, Indy had stumbled into Noah in the hallway. He'd looked wicked hot in his dark blue scrubs, not a trace of tiredness on his face. How he could be ready to work a shift after so little sleep, and look damn sexy at that, was beyond comprehension. He was hotter than McDreamy, that one. Same smoldering bedroom eyes, even if his were green, and not Patrick Dempsey's blue.

Indy himself had looked like crap, judging by the quick peek in the bathroom mirror. Pale as shit, dark circles under his eyes, and sunken cheeks. Fuck, he really had lost too much weight. No wonder his last run had been so slow and gruesome. He'd chalked it up to his broken arm, but clearly his body had been rebelling against the whole concept of running on too little fuel.

He'd needed this time of rest and recuperation. Not only for his body—though he'd asked too much of himself physically—but also for his mind. Not having to worry about where to sleep, what to eat, how to stay safe and unseen, his mind was more relaxed than it had been in a long time. And it was all thanks to Josh and Noah and the uncanny way they'd been able to gain his trust.

Too bad these gorgeous specimens were together because both tempted him to break his dry spell. It was pathetic. As if either of them would ever want him. Look at them, what could he possibly have to offer them? Even if they weren't together, they'd never want him. He exhaled slowly. Of course, they'd never want him. Didn't mean he couldn't dream about it.

Plus, hearing them fuck had made him horny. Like, seriously horny. He'd not been able to hear everything, of course, but Josh had been quite...vocal at the end, so Indy had enjoyed a live audio show of him coming. After that, Noah had let out a moan that suggested it had been his turn, and the whole thing had left Indy rock hard and trembling.

He'd tried to remedy that, but jerking off with your left hand when you were a dominant righty was hellish. And when your ribs throbbed and you had a blinding headache, it was damn near impossible. Finally, he'd put in the earplugs and forced himself to relax and fall asleep. He'd gone without sex or even jerking off for a long, long time, so a few weeks more wouldn't kill him. He'd been more surprised by his reawakened sex drive than anything else, had figured it was a permanent lost cause.

After dining on that mouth-watering turkey sandwich—Josh had put some kind of mayo on it that was the best Indy had ever tasted, creamy with a hint of mustard—he had wondered if he had to leave. Noah hadn't specified how long he could stay, had he? Was he wearing out his welcome by staying another night? Indy had debated it for all of two minutes, then told himself he was fucking crazy for even considering leaving and went right back to sleep.

One more day. Just one more day.

Noah didn't check on him again till after midnight. Indy assumed he'd been working as he was still wearing his scrubs. And his leg.

"How have you been today?" Noah asked, lowering himself onto the bed. Soft light was spilling in from the hallway, illuminating his face. He looked like he was happy to see Indy, even though he was likely in pain again, as he was rubbing his right leg.

"Good. Still tired."

"Josh said you slept most of the day. Rest is crucial for a complete recovery. He also said you ate well, which is a good sign. You could use the calories. Did you take your meds?"

He brought out his little flashlight to check Indy's pupils.

"Yeah. They make me loopy. It's hard to think."

Noah smiled. "They tend to do that. Josh said you were funny and a little loose-lipped. You can switch to over-the-counter painkillers in a day or two."

Loose-lipped. Fuck. Indy swallowed. What had he revealed?

Noah covered his small hand, squeezed it. Indy's heart skipped a beat. Noah was touching him. He waited for his body to react, but the expected fear and panic never showed up. Instead, there was a sense of excitement, his heart rate speeding up and his skin tingling.

"Indy, whatever secrets you have are safe with us."

"Doctor-patient confidentiality?" he asked.

"No. It's called trust, loyalty, and friendship."

Indy studied Noah's kind green eyes. "I have experienced little of that."

Their eyes held. Noah was reading him again, his hand still covering Indy's. He was sitting so close, their legs touching and holding hands, yet Indy didn't feel even the slightest urge to pull away.

"Josh and I have been through hell together, and we're both still finding our way back," Noah said, his expression serious. "All we have is each other. Because we are both emotionally screwed up, we've learned to be honest about what we feel. I know, it's a daring concept for guys to talk about feelings, but we've had to. Josh and I... We've been each other's lifelines. We know that you have baggage, but we're not judging. Shit, we're both carrying way too much around ourselves. And you don't know us very well, not yet, at least. But we have your back. Whatever you are dealing with, whether you want to talk about it or not, you can trust us."

Halfway through Noah's speech Josh had joined them, standing next to Noah, his hand on Noah's shoulder. A unit, that's what these two were, and they were inviting Indy to be a part of it. It was mind-boggling and scary as hell. How would it feel to share the load with them?

You can't. He'll have them killed and you know it.

When the Fitzpatricks found him—and God knew they would at some point—they would have no qualms about collateral damage. Anyone he was close to would be taken down with him, and he would not risk it with Josh and Noah. No, he'd accept their friendship as best as he could, but he'd have to stay at a distance emotionally. He couldn't allow himself to repay their honesty with coming clean himself. One more day, that was it.

"Thank you," he said, reaching for Josh's hand with his empty hand. For a little while, he would revel in being part of a circle, a unit.

For the first time in many years he fell asleep happy. Still horny, but happy.

Indy had spent the second day in bed as well, still wicked zonked. He'd heard Noah and Josh having sex again, which, by the sounds of it, had been satisfactory for both. It had made him hard all over again, but it had also been comforting. He'd thought he would have felt weird hearing them, or even threatened, considering his history. Sex to him had always been about power, punishment even, and in the best case about lust and getting off. But the love between these two guys was clear, and hearing them express it had made him feel safe, included in their unit.

He finally felt better on the third morning. His head had stopped pounding, and his ribs were still sore, but nowhere near as bad as the first day. So he got up and make his way downstairs. He'd freshened up, had shaved the fuzz off his chin, and had pulled his hair back into a messy ponytail.

He reveled in the domestic scene he encountered in the kitchen. Josh, shirtless with tight black boxers on, was preparing what looked like a whole lot of healthy stuffed into an industrial size blender. Indy gulped. Fuck, he was so damn sexy, especially because he didn't know it.

Noah perched on a bar stool at the high end of the kitchen counter, wearing a Pats shirt and white boxers, his prosthetic leg off. He was reading a newspaper, frowning with concentration. They were so casual in Indy's presence, not even bothering to put on clothes. Like it was the most normal thing in the world for the three of them to be in this kitchen.

Indy was overdressed compared to them, wearing Josh's shirt and a pair of too-loose sweat shorts someone had put in his room. He looked like a kid dressed up in his dad's clothes, for fuck's sake. He hadn't even considered putting on his female clothes, though. "Good morning," Indy said.

Josh turned around with a happy smile on his face. "Morning. How do you feel?"

"Still sore, but much better. Dying to get out of bed."

Noah looked up, gave him a quick body-check. "Don't overdo it. Make sure to lie down again after breakfast."

"Yes, doctor," Indy said.

Josh grinned. "He can't turn the medic mode off, it comes with the territory. What can I get you? I've brought you whatever I was having so far, but now that you're up, you can choose for yourself. Are you the healthy type, a cereal person, a full breakfast guy, or one of those don't even talk to me before I have my coffee morning grumps?"

Indy couldn't help but laugh. "Wow. That's the most I've ever heard you say."

Josh shrugged. "I'm shy, especially when I don't know people well. But I don't feel shy with you at all. Plus, I woke up happy today."

"I wonder why," Indy said under his breath.

Noah raised his eyebrows. "Jealous much?"

Josh looked from Indy to Noah and back. "I'm missing something here."

"He can hear us," Noah said.

"What do you mean?"

Indy smiled. Josh was such a fun person to tease. "You're quite vocal when you're...enjoying yourself," he offered.

Color crept up Josh's face. "Oh. Shit. Sorry."

Fucking hell, Josh was so adorable when he did that blushing thing. No wonder Noah loved him. How could you even stay mad at that face? "No worries. Glad somebody was having a good time."

"As I said, jealous much?" Noah's eyes were challenging him to be honest.

Indy said, "Sure, but above all, horny."

Noah's hand, with a mug of what looked like tea, froze halfway to his mouth, while Josh was attacked by a coughing fit.

Why the hell had he admitted the truth? There was something about these two that disarmed all his defenses. For fuck's sake, he'd completely dropped his Southern accent. They hadn't said anything, but there was no way they hadn't noticed he'd switched to a different dialect.

"If you're done choking, I'll have a glass of whatever you're juicing over there, Josh. Thanks," Indy said and lowered himself on a bar stool next to Noah, taking care to keep his ribs as straight as possible. The bending and twisting motions still hurt.

The doorbell rang, and Indy froze. Noah tensed up as well. "Are we expecting anyone?" he asked Josh, who shook his head.

"You'll need to get it." Noah said, pointing at his leg. Josh nodded. "And Josh, don't let anyone in. Indy's not dressed."

Relief flooded Indy. Noah was looking out for him. Josh walked into the hallway and opened the door. Indy recognized the voice.

"It's O'Connor," he whispered to Noah. "The cop from the robbery. What the hell is he doing here?"

Dammit, he hadn't gotten around to researching O'Connor's background. He'd been too busy recovering. But O'Connor had no way of knowing Indy would be here, right? No one knew.

Noah relaxed. "I don't know, but he's getting an eyeful of Josh in his underwear, so there's that."

Indy chuckled. "How long till Josh figures that out?"

"Shit, fuck, hold on!" Josh exclaimed. Indy and Noah burst out in laughter. "I'll be right back," Josh added. The front door closed again with a tolerable loud bang.

"Go upstairs and if he comes in, come down when you're dressed," Noah told Indy. "And you'd better turn your drawl back on."

He'd noticed. Shit. Indy nodded, made his way upstairs as quickly as possible with his injuries. O'Connor's had turned away his face from the door, thank fuck, so he couldn't spot Indy through the glass. Indy encountered a muttering Josh on the stairs.

"You could've said something," Josh complained. "I looked like a fucking moron."

"Sorry," Indy said, inching past Josh and closing the bedroom door behind him. He dressed as quickly as possible. The makeup would have to wait. O'Connor wasn't expecting him here anyway, let alone in full makeup after what he'd been through. He did make sure his pink scarf covered his Adam's apple and took his ponytail out, fluffing his hair up. It would have to do.

When Indy stepped into the kitchen, Josh had let O'Connor in. The cop was dressed in full uniform. Josh was still blushing, now wearing jeans and a black shirt. O'Connor's eyes widened when he spotted Indy walking in, but then he noticed Noah. His gaze flew down to Noah's stump, but he didn't react other than to step up to him and extend his hand. "O'Connor."

"Noah Flint, Josh's boyfriend."

O'Connor's reaction to that news was pure shock. He gave a quick intake of breath, and his eyes went big before he caught himself.

"Oh," he said. "Nice to meet you."

What was he so surprised about? He'd reacted the same way when Indy had told him he had kissed Josh. What was going on there? Surely the sight of two gay men couldn't creep him out, right? It wasn't the 1950s anymore. Sheesh.

"Sorry about my state of undress. We weren't expecting anyone, and I can't get dressed that fast."

Was it Indy's imagination or was Noah deliberately drawing attention to his leg? Noah dropped his hand to his stump, rubbed it. Holy fuck, he was totally playing the crippled card. What the hell?

"No apologies needed. We appreciate your sacrifice," O'Connor said, his tone serious.

"Nice to see you again, Connor," Indy drawled.

O'Connor tore away his gaze from Noah and focused on Indy. "Indy," he said. "Didn't expect to find you here."

"She needed medical supervision after her fall, and as a thank-you for saving my Josh's life, we invited her to stay with us. It seemed like the least we could do."

There was something in his tone that hadn't been there before, something flirty. For some reason, Noah sounded more gay than he ever had before.

"Noah's a physician assistant in the ER of Albany General," Josh added, walking up behind Noah and putting his hand on Noah's shoulder. Noah leaned his head back against Josh's chest, an uncharacteristic gesture of affection and submission for him. Indy wasn't the only one adept at playing a role, it seemed. Noah was claiming Josh loud and clear.

"They've been taking such great care of me," Indy said. "For a couple of Yankees, they sure have Southern hospitality down."

"Speaking of Southern hospitality," O'Connor said, refocusing on Indy, "I was trying to find you. Turns out the phone number you gave me was wrong, and I was hoping Josh would know where to locate you."

Indy forced a smile out. "Oh, my, I'm so sorry about that. What did you want to talk to me about?"

"There's been a silver Chevy parked at the Stewart's for the last few days. It has Georgia plates. That parking lot doesn't allow overnight parking."

Indy met his inquisitive gaze, forced himself to stay silent. He'd learned over the years not to say more than necessary when talking to law enforcement.

"You're not gonna say anything?" O'Connor asked, eyebrows raising.

"I was waiting for you to ask an actual question, Officer."

O'Connor's eyes narrowed. "For someone who says she doesn't have a filter, you're awfully good at evading questions."

"But, sir, you didn't ask a question." Indy pouted his lips, looked at O'Connor from under his eyelashes.

"My point exactly. Is that car yours?"

"Why, yes it is. I'm sorry I haven't been able to pick it up yet."

"She's not medically cleared to drive," Noah said. "Josh will pick it up today and park it here."

"She's staying here?" O'Connor asked, then turned to Indy. "You're staying here?'

Indy ignored the pretzel of happiness and fear in his stomach. "I am. Josh and Noah are wonderful hosts, and I sure enjoy spending time with them. Since I'm between jobs at the moment, I've decided to take them up on their offer of hospitality and explore the region more, once I've recovered."

"As Noah said, it's the least we could do after Indy saved me so heroically," Josh piled it on.

Indy's heart warmed. They were a unit, and he was a part of it. They had his back, just like they'd promised.

O'Connor stared at them for a few seconds. "That's taken care of, then. I'll leave you to your breakfast. Have a speedy recovery, Indy. Noah, nice meeting you."

He looked at Josh, and Indy was sure he was going to say something, but O'Connor merely nodded. As he was walking back to the hallway, Noah called after him. "Out of curiosity, Officer, how did you find Josh?"

O'Connor slowly turned around, facing Josh who had come after him to escort him to the door.

"What do you mean? He gave me his contact info when I took his statement." O'Connor was talking to Noah, but his eyes were on Josh, his face tight.

Noah's smile stayed but his eyes were razor sharp. "His phone number, not his address. You could've called instead of going through the trouble of finding out his address."

What was Noah getting at? Indy looked from Noah, to Josh, and then to O'Connor who looked like he'd been caught with his hand in the cookie jar. What the fuck?

"I could have," O'Connor admitted, his eyes never leaving Josh. Indy's eyes narrowed as it clicked. Fucking hell, he was gay. There was no mistaking the gaze in his eyes when he looked at Josh. Pure want.

"I should have," O'Connor corrected himself, tearing his gaze away and walking out the door without looking back.

"What was that about?" Josh asked when he stepped back into the kitchen.

Noah sighed, an amused smile on his lips. "Dude, you have the worst gaydar in history."

Josh's eyes popped out. "He's gay? You're shitting me."

"Not only is he gay, he was totally checking you out," Indy said.

"He was?" Josh's cheeks stained red again.

"Why do you think he stopped by in the first place when he could've just called you to find out if you had a correct phone number for me? He wanted to see you again," Indy said.

"He's hot," Noah said, adding more fuel to Josh's discomfort.

"He's smoking hot," Indy affirmed. Why wasn't Noah jealous? He seemed more amused than anything else, teasing Josh with Connor's interest. Weird, because he didn't strike Indy as the type willing to share, especially not after he'd claimed Josh so obviously in front of O'Connor.

Muttering under his breath, Josh stuffed the last ingredients in the blender and turned it on.

"I take it I'm staying, then?" Indy asked Noah when silence returned.

"You are," he said to Indy. "For as long as you want to."

"Why?" What did they want from him? Nobody would make an offer like that without wanting something in return.

"Because you need a place to stay."

"Just like that," Indy said, his throat constricted.

"We like you," Josh answered, placing a tall glass with green juice in front of him. "And we protect our own."

It was such a powerful statement coming from Josh, the weaker one in the relationship. It wasn't only Noah who wanted him to stay. It was Josh as well. Like that, they took Indy in and made him feel part of something bigger.

Nobody had ever had his back like that, ever. When he'd become part of the Fitzpatricks, all those big words about being a family and looking out for each other had been fucking bullshit, empty words. When the hit came, no one had stood up for him. But these men, they were completely in tune with each other, and they had made him a part of it. It took his breath away.

"He's crying," Josh said to Noah, a hint of panic in his voice. Indy hadn't even realized tears were streaming down his face. Weird, he hadn't cried in...well, forever.

"These are good tears," Noah said, no trace of doubt in his voice. No judgment either, Indy noted with a warm feeling in his stomach, which only made the tears come even faster.

"Why would you let me in?" Indy asked, fighting the tears back—unsuccessfully. He was a guy, a man. He wasn't supposed to break down like this.

Noah's eyes were kind. "Because I'm a cripple with anger issues, and Josh is a basket case with PTSD. I told you, we're both seriously fucked up. Trust me, you'll fit right in."

Anger issues? What the hell is he talking about? God, he couldn't think anymore. Indy put his head in his hands, surrendering to the tears.

"Do you wanna be held?" Noah asked, his voice a little less secure than it had sounded before. Indy nodded, his hands still hiding his face.

"Come here," Noah said and pulled him off the stool

between his legs, cradling Indy's head against his broad chest. "Something tells me you have plenty to cry about, but you've been holding it all in, so go ahead."

It was as if that permission granted Indy the freedom to open gates that had been closed for such a long time. He stood between Noah's legs, his tiny weight against that solid chest, his head against that broad shoulder, and Noah's strong arms secure and comforting around him.

Then Josh stepped in behind him, wrapping his arms around him from the back and kissing his head. Indy should have freaked out at being held so tight, should have been ashamed and embarrassed about crying and being held by two men, but it was like he was in a safe cocoon where nothing and nobody could hurt him. So he let go and cried until he had no more tears to give. Noah and Josh held him —two solid rocks he could lean on.

"Do you want to stay?" Noah asked when Indy was calm and still again.

"Yah."

He kept his eyes closed, his wet cheek still pressed against Noah's shirt, almost fearing that he'd hear his armor crack. It scared the shit out of him, this weird connection he had with these two guys.

"Is it okay for Josh to pick up your car?"

"Yah."

Another crack. Noah was asking all the right questions, saying all the right things.

"Okay, then."

Indy gently pushed back against their arms, and they immediately released him. He took a small step sideways so they stood in a tight circle and he could look them both in the eyes. "Thank you."

"Noah doesn't want thanks," Josh said. "He hates it when someone thanks him."

Indy tried to lighten the mood. "Well, I'd kiss you again, but since your boyfriend is right here, that'd be wrong."

"Oh, you can kiss him," Josh said matter-of-factly. "We're not together-together."

7

Wth Indy standing only inches away, Noah had prime access to the range of emotions on his face when Josh dropped that little bomb. Surprise, confusion. And one that wasn't so easy to pinpoint.

"I gotta go. I have therapy," Josh said. "I hope you like the smoothie."

Indy stepped back farther, and Noah was left with a strange sense of loss.

"I'm glad you're staying," Josh said, giving Indy an affectionate pat on his back. He was such a toucher who loved cuddling, and he was missing out on so much of that in their relationship.

Picking up on the tension between Noah and Indy, Josh said, "You are staying, right? Noah can explain everything."

He gave Noah a quick kiss on the cheek, then turned to Indy again. "Indy?" Josh said, when Indy stood there.

"Yeah, I'll stay. For now. Can't wait to hear Noah's explanation."

"Good." Josh kissed Indy on the cheek as well, surprising

himself as much as Indy, Noah noted. "See you in a bit. Explain *everything*, Noah!"

The door to the garage clicked shut, and the sound of the garage door opening vibrated in the background. The car started, backed up, and the garage closed again, leaving Indy and Noah facing each other.

"This should be good," Indy said, finding his spot on the bar stool again. He took a sip of his juice, which, judging by the surprised look on his face, tasted way better than the drab color had indicated. "Listen, you don't owe me an explanation, especially not after what you did for me with O'Connor. What you and Josh are or do, it's none of my business."

It had to cost Indy to say this, and Noah appreciated the emotional sacrifice he was making here, even if Indy wasn't aware of it himself. Noah still had no idea what had happened to Indy, or why he was running from someone or something, but he had to have his reasons.

Josh had overheard Indy talking in his sleep, agitated about someone named Duncan. He'd been loose-lipped in his conversations as well, about feeling safe for the first time, about wanting to stay but being afraid to. It all added up to him being genuinely scared for his life, for whatever reason.

Be honest, Flint. You want him to stay. Fuck, you need him to. The thought of him leaving is killing you. And the only way he's gonna stay is if he feels safe.

"That would be true, if it weren't for the fact that you want to stay with us, at least for a while, and you need that explanation to feel safe," he said.

"How the fuck do you do that?" Indy asked with a scowl. "How do you manage to get into my head so easily?"

"It's an annoying habit. Used to drive Josh crazy, too. Still does, sometimes."

"How long have you guys known each other?"

"Since high school. We were fifteen, and I was the new kid. I caught a few guys beating the shit out of him for being gay. Apparently, that was a regular occurrence at that school that everybody knew about and decided to ignore, but I didn't get that memo."

"You kicked their asses. That's wicked pissa, man," Indy concluded, pure satisfaction in his voice. If Noah had any doubt left where he was from originally, that expression sealed the deal. Indy had to be from Boston. Noah filed it away for later. He wasn't going to spook Indy by mentioning anything.

"Sadly, no. It was four against one, since Josh was out of commission by the time I got there, and though I was athletic, I was badly outnumbered and outmatched. So I got my ass handed to me, but at least I didn't go down without a fight. I broke one guy's nose and kicked another in his nuts so hard they were blue for a week, from what I heard. Got suspended for it, which pissed my dad off, of course. He wasn't down with the rainbow, to put it mildly. But since I lost my chance on popularity with that action, Josh and I were thrown together and became friends. We've had each other's backs ever since."

Noah winced as he rubbed his stump. Would it ever stop bothering him so much? He was so done with the constant ache, not in the least because it made him so needy, and he fucking hated that.

"Does it still hurt?"

"It's been hurting like a motherfucker since the last adjustment of my prosthetic leg. It's still healing, so it's not unusual, but it feels good to take it off at home. And the scrubs, they constantly rub against the scars, as do many pants, so I usually walk around in my underwear when I'm home."

"No complaints about that from me," Indy said, then bit his lip in a totally cute way, as if preventing himself from saying more.

"It doesn't bother you?"

"What, your scars and your leg? Or you walking around half naked? Neither."

Noah grinned. "I usually don't let people see it. Not that we have many people stopping by. Josh has a brother, but he lives in DC and hasn't been to visit since we moved here. They're not close."

"No parents?"

Noah's face tightened. How could it still hurt after all these years?

"Josh's parents disowned him as soon as he was of age, because of him being gay. They're conservative Christians and not the good and loving kind. My father broke off contact when we moved in together. Like I said, not a fan of the rainbow."

"But you're not together, Josh said, even though you have sex. So are you bi? Or gay?"

Was he? The lines had become more and more blurred. And it hadn't mattered until Indy had shown up. Why Indy wanted to know if he was gay was understandable, but why had he started caring himself? It's so fucking complicated.

"What Josh and I have, it's not so easy to define. Others draw their own conclusions, also because we're not explaining ourselves."

"Do you want to explain it to me?"

Indy's tone was kind. Curious, but not demanding. He knew like no other that not everything was what it seems and that sometimes you didn't want to explain what was behind the public mask.

"I do," Noah said. "Something tells me you'd understand."

~

*ONE YEAR **and two months before***

The pain was all-consuming. Noah could take the intensity, but the throbbing and burning and aching that never let up wore him down till he was exhausted from fighting it. Lying in a hospital bed with nothing else to do, he was constantly aware of his missing limb, even after three weeks.

His remaining leg and the stump were wrapped in bandages to cover and heal the wounds from the fragments and burns that had ravaged his legs. As an army medic he'd seen his share of horrible injuries, but he couldn't stomach looking at his own. The thought of witnessing his burned and mangled legs formed a sour taste in his mouth. Every time they dressed his wounds, he averted his eyes.

"Noah?"

The timid voice made him swallow back whatever was on his mind and refocus. He had to be the strong one because Josh needed him now more than ever.

"Hey man, how are you?" He opened his arms wide. Josh needed that physical contact. His best friend, impeccably dressed in his combat fatigues, bent over for a solid hug. As always, it lasted a tad longer than was appropriate between straight guys.

Noah didn't give a rat's ass. His previous hospital roommate had already called him a faggot, and he didn't give a shit. Ever since, he'd simply asked the nursing staff in the army hospital to close the curtains between the two beds, and he'd ignored the asshole until the guy had gotten discharged the day before.

"How was the session?"

Josh had come from an appointment with an army psychiatrist to discuss the results of his assessment of Josh's mental health. After Noah's injury, Josh had spent two weeks in a closed ward for 'going off the rails' as one nurse described it to Noah. Noah had been furious with his helplessness to do anything for him, especially since he'd had a pretty good idea of what Josh was suffering from.

Josh pushed out a shivering breath. "They've diagnosed me with a severe case of PTSD," he mumbled, his voice thick with emotion. "I'm getting an honorable discharge."

Noah grabbed his friend's hand and squeezed it. "It's gonna be okay. We'll get you through this."

"How? You have your own recovery to focus on, and I have nobody else. My parents and Aaron haven't even contacted me."

The quiet desperation in Josh's voice had Noah on edge. "You have me," he said firmly. He grabbed Josh's shoulder with his other hand, shaking him softly. "I'm here for you."

"But you're still recovering, and after that, you're going back, right?"

The pain hit him like a stab to the heart, and he swallowed. *Hell, no.* Not ever again. "No, Josh, I won't go back."

Josh's eyes lifted from the floor to meet Noah's. "What do you mean? The army is your dream, your life."

"No, it's not. It never was," Noah said. "It was my dad's dream and his life, not mine. He pushed me into this and I went along. But I've already agreed to an honorable discharge. Graves has promised me he'll help me find a position as a physician assistant in an ER as soon as I'm ready to get back to work. There's a hospital in Albany, New York, that's interested. The trauma surgeon there is a college buddy of Graves, and he's willing to give me a shot. I'm being discharged in a few days and sent to an army rehab center. I've declined their room and board options and have rented an apartment close by. You're moving in with me, and you can help me get better, chauffeur me, cook for me, and in general pamper me. We've always had each other's backs, and that's not gonna change."

Josh broke down, tears streaming down his face. He grabbed Noah's hand and held onto it as if it was the life vest saving him from drowning. Noah's heart filled with compassion. He didn't have a sliver of doubt he was making the right choice. Josh had enlisted because of him, and now he was hurting because of Noah.

If only he'd been there that night. Hell, Josh wouldn't have been there in the first place if not for Noah. Noah didn't care what he had to do, but he would find a way to help Josh heal. He would take care of him, because when he had needed him the most, Josh had been there for him. As a result, Josh was broken in a way that maybe would never fully heal. But dammit, Noah would try. And right now, he knew what Josh needed.

"Hit the lights, would you?" he asked Josh.

"What?" his friend asked, disoriented by the unexpected request.

"Turn off the lights and pull the curtains around my bed. It's the signal to the staff that I'm retiring for the night, and they won't disturb me unless I hit the call button."

Josh obediently got up and did as he was asked. He obviously had no idea why, but he still trusted Noah to do right by him. God, please let him never, ever break that trust.

"Now come here. I'll scoot my upper body over, but

you'll have to lift my legs. One at a time. Be gentle, and it'll be fine."

"What are you doing?" Josh asked with a small voice, while carefully moving Noah's legs to the side of the bed.

Noah clenched his jaw to keep from crying out in pain. He let out a ragged breath.

"Making room for you," he said between his teeth.

"Strip," he said when he'd caught his breath again. "This place is hotter than the sandbox." He gestured to his bare chest and boxers to indicate he wasn't wearing clothes either.

"I don't understand," Josh said, a hint of panic in his voice.

It was hard to find patience when the pain was driving you mad, but Noah dug deep. "Strip down to your boxers, Josh. Trust me."

Josh stared at him for a few seconds, then did as he was told, folding his clothes neatly and laying them down under the bed. Josh's trust in him hit Noah hard, as always, especially considering what the guy had been through. Noah wouldn't have been surprised if Josh had never even looked at him again.

"Come here." Noah lifted his blanket and gestured for Josh to climb on the bed. Confusion painted his best friend's face, then a sweet relief that almost made Noah cry himself. Josh eased onto the bed and Noah held out his arm for his friend to put his head on, then wrapped it around him.

"You're here, and you're safe, and I've got you. Now, get some sleep. You look like hell."

Josh wriggled, clearly scared he'd either hurt Noah or do something wrong. No wonder, he'd been ragged on, bullied, and even beaten up for being gay so many times.

"Put your arm around me. Nobody will see and even if

they do, I don't fucking care. Let me take care of you, Josh, lean on me. I've got your six."

Tentatively, Josh spread his arm across Noah's chest, and to affirm that sweet gesture, Noah pulled it tighter, put his hand on Josh's head. "Are you comfortable?"

"I haven't felt this good in years," Josh said, and the deep emotion in his voice hit Noah deep. This was exactly what Josh needed. Noah wasn't sure if it was because Josh was gay, or if it was his character, or his fucked-up upbringing with parents who'd rejected him, but Josh was a toucher, a cuddler. He'd always reach out to Noah, touch his arm or his shoulder, hug him close. The guy thrived on physical contact until that night that had changed everything.

Ever since, he'd been easily spooked, hesitant, even with Noah. They'd seen so little of each other, with Josh in the locked ward for two weeks and Noah in the hospital. It had taken a huge chunk out of Josh's sense of safety, and Noah wanted nothing more than to restore that, if only between the two of them. And frankly, Noah had missed the hell out of Josh as well, and not just because he'd been worried sick about him.

"Good. Now sleep."

Josh was out like a light, and Noah caught a few hours of sleep before the pain woke him up. He tried to shift, but Josh's weight pinned his upper body down and of course his legs were useless. He couldn't call a nurse, not with Josh being there. Holy shit, Nurse Decker would be shocked if she caught them together. She was a hell of a nurse, but rather prim despite her...inviting figure. Full breasts, curvy ass, a highly kissable mouth. All the male patients had fantasies about her, Noah was sure, and he was no exception. Picturing her in his mind gave him a full-on boner.

Which was unfortunate because, as in many aspects of

his life at the moment, he was helpless there as well. Aside from a complete lack of privacy that prevented him from jerking off, he had the added complication of his injuries, which extended to his thighs. He could reach his cock, but the motion of jerking off hurt his legs—he'd tried. And he feared his jizz would land all over, resulting in some mighty humiliating conversations.

And...that train of thought had made him even more hard. The sensation of a warm, almost naked body draped half over him didn't help either, even if it was Josh. Josh's hot breath against his bare chest only contributed to his arousal. Well, fuck. What was he gonna do now?

"Am I getting too heavy?" Josh's voice was hoarse and sleepy. He stretched his arm, accidentally grazing Noah's hard cock. Both of them froze.

Noah swallowed. When he'd made his plan to let Josh move in, he'd known there would be moments like this. Josh was gay, and their close presence was bound to stir some uncomfortable feelings. They'd had many of those already, even as friends.

When he'd hit rock bottom years ago, he had wanted to be held by Josh, especially when his alcohol levels had lowered his inhibitions. Fuck, those months after losing his mom, when he'd been shit-faced almost every evening, he knew he and Josh had crossed boundaries. Josh had held his head when he'd puked his guts out, had undressed him at times, tucked him in.

And Noah sometimes had weird dreams of Josh sucking his cock, of fucking Josh, even. But those had to be dreams because surely he would remember if it were real. Of course, Josh had never said a word about anything like that happening.

Noah had found himself coping better and better with

Josh's affection, presence, and him being gay. At first, he'd been a bit weirded out by Josh touching him, but now he'd gotten used to it and allowed Josh to hug him longer than others thought was normal. He'd become as touchy-feely as Josh himself, wanting to communicate his affection. Fuck everyone else, he didn't care anymore.

Inviting Josh to sleep next to him tonight, to be held by him, he'd known they were crossing a boundary and entering into new territory. Restoring Josh's sense of trust had been crucial to Noah, but maybe he had done it as much for himself. The distance between them had killed him, too. He trusted Josh to understand, even if he didn't fully comprehend himself what he was offering and why.

Now Josh had inadvertently touched his cock, and Noah could only imagine what had to be going through his mind. Guilt, confusion, lust maybe? Noah guessed, because he was feeling it himself. They had to find a way through this, to help each other. This was Josh: his best friend, the guy who knew everything about him and still loved him, the guy who had endangered himself to be with him. There was no room for discomfort, only brotherhood and friendship.

"Josh, I have a favor to ask you. Would you do something for me?"

"Anything." The answer came without a second of delay, and it told Noah everything he needed to know.

Noah's mind was made up. He took the hand that was wrapped around his neck and put it on his cock, squeezing both. Josh's breath caught, then slowly let out.

"I'm so fucking hard, and I can't do it myself. Please?" Noah's voice was raw.

He removed his hand from Josh's, giving him the option to refuse.

Noah trembled. Had he gone too far? What if Josh was

offended? What if it reminded him of that night? Did he fuck this up?

Instead, Josh gave his cock a gentle squeeze that sent shivers down Noah's spine. "Hand or mouth?" Josh asked.

Noah had not seen that one coming. He had assumed a hand job, but was Josh really offering him a blow job? Could he accept? Wouldn't that be seriously fucked up?

"Noah."

There was something about the way Josh said his name that got to him every single time. There was so much love in there that it humbled him. He closed his eyes, struggling with doing the right thing.

"Noah, I want to do this. I want to replace those memories with something else, something beautiful. You know I love you, and I trust you. Please, let me do this for myself and for you."

Noah nodded, unable to find the words. Josh got up from the bed and grabbed a chair, silently lifting it and putting it next to the bed. He threw a pillow on it, then kneeled on it. Noah didn't need to remind him to not touch his legs. Josh would be careful. With loving hands, he freed Noah's cock from his boxer shorts. It jutted free, completely erect.

"Josh, I haven't jacked off since...since before the accident. I'm on the edge, so be careful, okay?"

Josh sent him a sensual smile that made Noah tingle in anticipation. "I've got you, don't you worry..."

Josh wrapped his hand around the base of Noah's dick, pulling back the foreskin. His cock steeled even harder in Josh's hand. Josh bent over, licked the crown as if tasting it, before closing his soft lips around it to suckle. "Oh, God, yes..."

Noah twitched and moaned as the sucking intensified. It

felt fucking fantastic. Then his cock was sucked into his friend's slick throat, and he couldn't think at all. Josh's head bobbed and squeezed Noah's dick...Oh, damn, he sucked so good.

He took Noah in deeper and deeper until most of his shaft was enclosed in Josh's warm mouth.

"Oh, fuck..." Noah grunted. His balls tightened almost painfully. "I can't... Shit, so good... I can't hold it..."

His entire body tensed and then he let go, the most powerful orgasm he had ever had barreling through him like a shock wave. He lifted his hips and thrust into Josh's mouth, bringing a sweet mix of pain and endless relief. He bucked again, still spurting. All that time, Josh's warm mouth kept sucking, licking, caressing. He took everything Noah gave, and then some.

"Fucking hell," Noah panted. All the tension left his body as he sagged back against the pillows. With effort, he lifted a hand to put it on Josh's head. The short buzz cut tickled his fingers. "Best blow job ever."

Josh lifted his head, causing Noah to drop his hand. Josh caught it and brushed it with a soft kiss while still holding Noah's cock with his other hand. "Thank you for letting me suck you off. At the risk of sounding even more gay than I already am: I love sucking cock, and you taste like heaven," Josh said, his voice dreamy. "I know you're not gay, and I respect that, but I am, so don't ever feel like you are using me. Anytime you need me, ask me. I will never say no, because I love you, and I love doing this for you...and for me."

Josh brought Noah's hand to his own crotch, where Noah encountered a cock that was hard as steel. "You feel me? Blowing you did that to me. Now, if you'll excuse me, I wasn't done yet. That first release was a little...quick and you're still hard, so let's see if we can give you one that lasts a bit longer."

Without waiting for Noah's approval, he dropped his mouth down again on Noah's cock, taking him in as far as he could. Noah's eyes flared, and he inhaled sharply.

"Oh shit... Fuck, Josh, your mouth... Oh, dammit, you're killing me!"

8

Noah's story hit Indy hard. There was such a deep love between these two men, messy and complicated as it might be. He'd never experienced anything remotely similar. What Duncan had felt for him wasn't love. Shit, the guy wasn't even capable of love in the first place. No, Noah and Josh were something else. They'd made deep sacrifices for each other, and there were many layers of guilt and pleasure intertwined.

Something had happened to Josh that Noah felt guilty about, maybe something to do with his PTSD, but Indy wasn't asking. If Noah had wanted him to know, he would've told him. It was complex, intricate, yet beautiful, and also hot as fuck.

They'd moved to the parlor, Indy obediently laying down on the couch per Noah's orders, with Noah sitting in the reading chair across from him. Indy had taken off the scarf and the bra and stuffing he'd been wearing for Connor's unexpected visit. Noah hadn't said anything, had merely looked at him with approval.

Indy discreetly rubbed his cock in an attempt to alleviate

some of his discomfort. Fuck, he'd been horny ever since he'd heard them go at it that first night, and now Noah's story had put his whole body on edge with sheer desire. He swore he could feel his pulse beating through his cock, that's how hard it was. He desperately needed a release, but it looked like he'd have to wait till his ribs stopped hurting so fucking much. The only consolation, though a small one, was that Noah was sporting a boner as well—not that the man did anything to hide it.

Indy shook his head to clear his thoughts. "So to the outside world you're presenting yourself as a gay couple."

"There isn't much of an outside world, but yes. Josh's parents never accepted him for who he was. They're conservative Christians, so him being gay didn't go over well. He has a younger brother, Aaron, but he sided with his parents when Josh came out."

Indy's heart softened. Poor Josh. He deserved better. "And your parents? You mentioned it being your dad's dream for you to be in the army?"

Noah rubbed the back of his neck, his face pained. "My mom passed away a month before I turned eighteen, and my father... Have you ever heard of General Flint?"

Indy gasped. That was his dad? Holy crap. Everyone knew General Flint, the stern asshole who'd made it his sole purpose to reinstate the Don't Ask, Don't Tell policy in the armed forces. Indy knew shit about politics, but he'd followed that one because it blew his mind. "That's your dad?"

"Yeah. You remember him taking a stand before the Senate to defend Don't Ask, Don't Tell? He's a staunch opponent of gays in the military. That's because he despises gay men, thinks of them as weak, effeminate. Can you imagine his reaction when one day, he walked in on

Josh giving me a blow job?" Noah let out a bitter laugh. "He was about to physically attack me, but Josh stepped in."

"Josh stepped in," Indy repeated in disbelief. "Sweet, shy Josh stepped in?"

"Oh, there was nothing sweet or shy about Josh at that particular time. Picture this: I was buck naked and dripping with juices, and Josh was only wearing boxers that did nothing to hide his massive hard-on. He was facing a blazing mad general in uniform, and he never backed down. Josh actually shoved him back to protect me. He can have quite the temper if you push him too far, especially when it comes to people he loves."

Indy was picturing it, and it made for quite the mental image. Dammit, he was about to come in his fucking pants. All this talk about two hot guys having sex was not conducive to losing his erection. If only he was able to touch himself, he would easily come. Twice, at least.

He focused on the conversation. Maybe Noah, the perceptive medical professional, wouldn't notice his permanent hard-on.

"Bad timing on your father's part to come in at that time..."

"I did it on purpose," Noah admitted. "I knew he would be coming by, but Josh didn't, and I asked him to blow me. I wanted my dad to see this, to see us."

"You wanted him to think you were gay," Indy said.

"Yes. I hated that man and everything he stood for. I wanted to break free of him once and for all. This was the quickest way to achieve that."

"Does Josh know?"

"I told him a couple of days later. We have no secrets between us. We can't. It's already complicated enough as it is. We promised each other complete honesty, especially when it comes to sex."

"Are you saying you're not gay?"

It was the question Indy had been dying to ask. Because other than Noah not being gay—which would be weird considering he did obviously enjoy fucking Josh—what the hell could be the reason these two weren't together?

Please, let him be gay. *What difference does it make? He'll never choose you anyways. Not when he has Josh.*

For the first time since Indy had met him, Noah was clearly uncomfortable. He shifted in his chair, cracking his knuckles.

"I don't know," Noah finally spoke. "I thought I wasn't, but I'm not sure anymore. Maybe I'm bi? I mean, I like women as well. I think. I mean, I've had sex with women and enjoyed it, I guess, though it's undeniable sex with Josh is very different. Shit, I don't know. I honestly don't fucking know."

"It's okay," Indy said, feeling how much Noah meant those words. Sex was messed up, or it could be, and it was hard to define yourself when your life was so fucked up.

"You are gay, though, right? I mean, you kissed Josh. And me."

Noah's voice was laced with an uncharacteristic insecurity, one that made Indy feel sorry for the man.

"Oh, definitely. I'm as gay as they come. Proud, rainbow-shitting gay."

Noah let out a chuckle. "How did you know?"

"Jeez, how could I not? I've always been gay. I don't know when you first encountered sex, but where and how I grew up, I was pretty young. Always knew I wanted to be with guys, not girls. I'm the classic queer, you know, too effeminate to even try to pass as straight."

Indy sighed. He'd said too much, perhaps, but he'd wanted to give Noah something in return for sharing so openly about him and Josh.

"But you're not transgender? You don't identify as a woman?"

Fuck, he loved Noah for even asking that. "No. Not at all. But that's all I want to say."

Noah nodded. "Okay," he simply said.

There was a comfortable silence between them. Indy was completely fed up with his cock that wouldn't fucking give up. He'd have to find a way to jack off, no matter how awkward or embarrassing. Hell, Josh and Noah were fucking so loud he could hear them, so it wasn't like they would be weirded out by Indy jerking off.

"I'll ask Josh if he's okay with me helping you, if that's what you want."

Indy frowned. "Help me with what?"

"Help you jack off."

Indy almost choked on his breath. He's fucking kidding, right? "What?"

"Look," Noah said calmly, studying Indy. He made it sound like it was the most natural thing in the world to offer Indy to jack him off. "You already admitted to being horny from hearing us have sex. It's been an emotional morning, and that story I shared about me and Josh turned you on even more. To be fair, I gave you quite the detailed play-by-play. That's as surprising to me as it is to you by the way, since Josh and I are usually tight-lipped about what we do together. For some reason, you made me want to share with you, so I did. But your cheeks are flushed, you've been sporting a hard-on forever, and your whole body is as tight as a drum. I think you're having the same problem I had after my injury: you can't take care of it yourself. If you could, you would've done so already, and you wouldn't still be so turned on this morning. How am I doing so far?"

Indy had heard of guys who could come without being touched. He'd always written those stories off as fables, urban legends. But he'd fucking swear right now that if Noah kept talking like that, he'd spontaneously erupt. Holy fuck, he'd never been this aroused before. Ever. His cock was ready to explode.

He cleared his throat, swallowing thickly. "I'd say your powers of deduction are pretty accurate."

"Indy, you trust us. I know trust is hard for you, but you trust us. You've let us hug you, and you felt safe enough to let go of your disguise. Aside from the fact that you need a release to get rid of the tension in your body, I think it would help you emotionally as well. It may help you heal some of what's inside."

"Ever the medical professional," Indy said, his head swirling with emotions.

"Tell me I'm wrong."

"You're not," he admitted.

Their eyes met across the coffee table, and Noah leaned forward in his chair. "You deserve more than being alone for the rest of your life, Indy. Let me help you gain some freedom back. But the choice is yours. I'll give you the same rule as Josh and I have: you have to ask me. I will not take the initiative; you have to tell me what you want. And I won't do anything until Josh gets home because he needs to be okay with this."

Indy was dizzy with sensations. Why was he even considering this? Shouldn't the thought of a man touching him send him screaming and running in the other direction? It had for the last two years, but he wanted Noah. Fuck, Indy did trust him, and the thought of Noah's hands on him made heat pool in his belly. A relationship was out of the question, obviously, with Indy never staying long in one place and Noah attached at the hip to Josh.

He'll never pick you over Josh. Josh, who is so cute and sweet. Josh, who is not fucked up, like you are. Josh, who hasn't done what you have. You're too dark and twisty, too fucked up.

"Won't Josh have a problem with this?" Indy's voice wavered. "Have you had others since you've been together?"

The beginning of a smile tipped the corners of Noah's mouth. "No. At first, I wasn't in any condition and after that, it never happened. I didn't go looking for it, also because I thought no one would want me looking like this." He pointed to his leg. "But you called me sexy as fuck, so apparently me being a cripple doesn't bother you. As for Josh, let's say he's motivated to grant me this."

Why was everything Noah said so wicked sexy? What was it about him that made Indy lower his defenses, take them down completely? Was Noah just feeling sorry for him? Because desperate as Indy was for a release, he did not need a pity fuck. Or a pity hand job, or whatever. He let his eyes wander to Noah's chest, then lower to his abdomen, and his...holy shit, Noah was still sporting a massive hard-on that threatened to pop out of his boxers.

"As you can see, I have some motivation myself as well," Noah said, following Indy's gaze. With a lazy gesture, he grabbed his cock and gave it a squeeze.

For the first time in forever, heat stained Indy's cheeks. He thought he'd lost all sense of shame, embarrassment, and even arousal, but clearly not. What the hell was happening here?

"Do you like the view?" Noah asked, his voice low, but with more uncertainty than Indy would have expected. Noah was putting himself out there as well. He had said it himself: he didn't expect anyone to want him with his scars —and Indy knew how he felt. Fuck, he'd never thought he'd meet anyone willing to look past his scars and his hang-ups.

"I do. You're beautiful," he said, speaking what was in his heart, ignoring his doubts that Noah was only feeling sorry for him.

Noah visibly swallowed. "Thank you."

"Not just healing for me, is it?"

"No. I didn't realize how much I needed to hear you say that until you did."

Indy bit his lip. "Noah, if we do this...if I agree...it can't come between you and Josh. What you have, it's too beautiful for that."

His eyes burned into Indy's, hot and heavy. "I've wanted you since I met you, but that makes me desire you even more. You won't come between us, Indy, we won't let you. Josh and me, we need each other too much, at least for now."

Indy didn't understand. How could Noah want him? Noah was so sexy, so hot, so confident. For fuck's sake, he was self-assured enough to publicly be gay, even when he wasn't sure it was who he was. What did he see in Indy? He wasn't pretty, he wasn't sexy, and he sure as hell wasn't easy.

"Why do you want me? I'm seriously fucked up and not even close to being handsome or whatever. I'm just a scrawny kid."

Noah flashed his thousand-watt smile at Indy. It lit a fire in Indy's belly that radiated to his arms and legs, to the tip of his toes. It rolled over him like a wave, that smile, reaching deep inside with its light.

"You're fucking beautiful. Your strength, your kick-ass attitude, and your boyish tight body are a total turn on. I love your potty mouth, your fake Southern drawl, and your lack of filter. You must be one hell of a kisser to kiss Josh out of an episode and get him hard—oh yes, he shared that little detail with me. Josh is not an easy guy when it comes to sex, trust me, but you got to him, and I know he would let you fuck him, given the chance. But above all, I want to be with you because despite you being fucked up—your words, not mine—you're so fucking sexy. It's your eyes, they betray everything you're thinking and feeling. You're seeing me, all of me, and you want me."

Sweet fuck, there was enough electricity between them to light a small city. "Keep talking like that, and you won't need to touch me anymore," Indy blurted out.

"Then I'd better stop, 'cause that would be a shame," Noah teased.

"Don't." Indy almost choked on the words. "Nobody has ever wanted me like that, not even before."

Before what? Indy waited for him to ask it, to demand to know what had happened to him, but Noah didn't.

"It scares me," Indy admitted.

"That's okay. You can let yourself open up. It's safe."

Safe. Noah kept using that word, as if he knew how much Indy needed the reassurance. "I know, but I'm still scared as hell. Does Josh know how you feel about me?"

"Not officially. You're the first person I've...responded to since Josh and I started fucking, so this is new territory for us. I haven't told him yet, because I wasn't sure how you felt, but I will. I'm sure he's noticed my reactions to you already. Our sex has intensified since you arrived, so he's reaping the benefits, so to speak."

That created mental pictures in Indy's head that did nothing to quench the desperate need in his body. He had made his decision. Fuck, he really was doing this. He was gonna let Noah touch him. The thought alone sent shivers down his spine.

"Indy, look at me," Noah spoke softly. Indy didn't see the need in resisting anymore and met the man's eyes, surrendering to whatever was happening between them. "I need you to remember three things. First, you can say no right now. I'm asking you if you want this, but it's your choice. Second, you can still say no halfway through. If you change your mind, a simple 'no' or 'stop' is enough. You decide how far you want to go, and I will stop. Even if we ever end up in bed together and I'm inside you, I will pull out if you say stop. I'd rather hurt myself than ever do something against your will. And last but not least: I don't need to hear your story, because you'll tell me when you're ready. But I do need to know if you have any issues with me touching you in a sexual way. If you have any sexual trauma, please tell me, because I'll do my damnedest not to trigger it."

Sexual trauma... Holy fuck, where did he begin? Had sex ever been anything other than a trauma to him? Well, maybe. Duncan had fucked him almost every single day. God, that first time had hurt like a motherfucker, but after that it had gotten somewhat better. Indy had even liked it, sometimes, in the first two years. He'd been way too young, but there had been times when he'd loved being fucked, when Duncan had taken more time.

After that, it had gotten slowly worse. The more Duncan had started using, the rougher the sex had gotten. Indy had learned to cooperate, but even then he'd been tied down, held down with force, fucked too hard. Then Eric had happened. His stomach cramped.

Don't go there. Noah is different. He's nothing like Duncan, like Eric, not even close.

Everything Noah had said and done so far had shown

him to be honorable, a good man. Indy hadn't put much faith in men anymore, not after what he'd been through, but everything inside him told him Noah could be trusted. He wouldn't hurt him. For fuck's sake, he'd outright said so, had told Indy he'd rather hurt himself than Indy.

He'll break your fucking heart, and you know it. He'll never choose you. He'll never love you.

Well, he'd have to risk it. God knew he'd survived worse. He wanted this, wanted him. Wanted to feel what good sex could be like.

"You can't hold my neck down, put any pressure on it, or even pretend to choke me," Indy said. His decision made, he felt calm. "Don't ever tie me up, or physically restrain me in any way. That includes holding my arms or wrists down. If you accidentally do something that makes me defend myself, or if I put you in a hold, tap twice anywhere on my body and I'll let go. It's an ingrained jiujitsu signal I will always respond to."

Noah nodded. "One last question: please tell me you are of age. I've seen your date of birth, but I want to make sure it's accurate."

Indy snorted, his hand flying to his mouth when the sound escaped. Of age, there was a new concept. As if it had ever mattered. Fuck, most of the sex he'd ever had had been before he turned eighteen. Like Duncan had ever given a shit about age. Or consent, for that matter.

"Sorry, you have no idea how unintentionally funny that is. The birthday was fake, but I am twenty, so no worries."

"Okay," Noah said. He looked at Indy with undisguised want, and Indy licked his lips. Noah wanted him, truly wanted him. How the fuck was that possible?

"Okay, then," he repeated slowly. The tension grew thick, the air almost crackling between the two of them.

Noah checked his watch. "We have half an hour before Josh gets back. How about I keep you entertained with the story of how Josh let me fuck him for the first time?"

～

TEN MONTHS **before**

They'd found a rhythm that worked for them both. Noah had daily physical therapy and added his own personal workouts to build his upper body. Josh drove him and waited patiently, reading through stacks of books, till Noah was done. Afterward, Josh would go to his PTSD therapy, while Noah took a swim at the same health care center. It relaxed his body and helped build up muscles in his leg and stump. At home, Josh would cook, do laundry, and keep the house clean, and Noah took care of the financial stuff and anything tech-related.

But the nights made it work. After that second blow job in the hospital, Noah had noticed the pain had lessened. He'd thought it was a fluke, but when Josh gave him another blow job a few days later—which had been equally amazing —he'd experienced the same effect. When the pain got bad, he'd ask Josh to help him find 'release'—and Josh had been true to his word and had never denied him.

On his end, Josh had discovered that sleeping with Noah kept the nightmares at bay. By himself in a bed, the nights were a terror of flashbacks, and he'd wake up screaming and drenched in sweat. But safely snuggled against Noah, he slept peacefully.

The solution had been simple: they'd moved into the master bedroom together and helped each other out. Noah quickly got used to Josh's naked body draped over him, or spooning against him and came to appreciate the closeness it brought. Noah always slept naked since clothes rubbed against his wounds and scars. They had bought the softest sheets and bedding they could find and that worked. And since it didn't seem to bother Noah, Josh had gotten rid of his boxers as well, as he loved the feel of naked skin on skin. They were together, had each other's back.

One night, they were spooning, Josh tucked against Noah's chest. "Why don't you ever come?" The question had been bothering Noah for a while. Josh got hard from giving him a blow job, but he'd never finished. At least, not in Noah's presence.

Josh swallowed. "I wasn't sure if you wanted me to," he replied softly.

"For fuck's sake, Josh, of course it's okay. You're sucking me off all the time, swallowing my cum, or you let me come all over your hands. We are constantly in bed naked together. What makes you think I would not be okay with you coming as well?" To compensate for his angry tone, Noah pulled Josh tight.

"I didn't want to cross any boundaries you'd feel uncomfortable with," Josh said. "I don't want to repulse you."

Noah let go of Josh and grabbed his upper arm to make Josh turn around and face him. He took his friend's face in both hands and looked him straight in the eyes. "You could never repulse me. And you know I'm more than fine with who you are. Seriously, you suck cock better than any girl who's ever tried."

He gave him a quick kiss, something he had never done before of his own volition. Usually, it was Josh sharing affection that way, but whatever. Nothing wrong with kissing, right? He wrapped his arms around Josh again, pulling him tight against his body. At first, the feeling of a naked male had been weird and somehow off, but now he was used to it.

He loved the difference between his own somewhat tough skin and Josh's soft skin. They were so different in every aspect. Even their cocks, now brushing against each other, were different. Josh's cock was velvety soft, but long and slim, where Noah's cock was shorter, thicker and stronger. Nude cocks against each other was also a sensation Noah had come to appreciate. Especially when both their cocks were slick with juices, sliding them against each other was incredibly erotic.

Noah continued, "So if you want something, you need to ask. Do you want me to give you a hand job?" He hesitated for a second. "I'll even blow you, if that's what you want. Can't guarantee I'm any good as I've never done it before, but hey, you could teach me. What do you want?"

"Will you fuck me?"

Noah blinked. The request rocked him to his core. Not what he had expected. Not after Josh's last experience. "You want me to fuck you? Are you sure about this?"

Are you sure you ever want a cock in your ass again after what you went through? He didn't say it, but how did one get over something like Josh experienced?

"I know what you're thinking, Noah, but I can't let that one night rob me from sex for the rest of my life. I loved being fucked. That night, it doesn't change that. It shouldn't. And I want it to be you because I trust you. Please, Noah, do this for me."

How was it possible that as a supposedly straight guy, he was so turned on by the thought of fucking Josh? His cock had jumped up at the first visual Josh's words had put in his head. *Maybe you're not as straight as you think.* "I've never fucked a guy before," he said, his voice raw. "So you'll have to tell me how to do it right, okay?"

A flash of guilt crossed over Josh's face. What did he have to feel guilty for? Surely not for being gay, or wanting to be fucked. Most normal thing in the world as far as Noah was concerned.

"You'll do it?" Josh's voice dripped with disbelief.

Noah grabbed his friend's head, pulled it toward his mouth and kissed him gently. "I'll do anything you ask." He kissed him again, then let go. "So, how do we do this? I'm pretty sure of the anatomy involved, but I can't sit on my knees yet, so what would work?"

"I'll give you a hand job first to make you hard, and if it's okay with you, you can lay on your back, and I can ride you. We can use the massage oil you use for your scars as lube. We don't need condoms since we're both clean."

Noah grinned. "You've given this some thought," he teased.

"It's been on my mind since you allowed me to blow you."

Noah was certain that should weird him out, but it didn't. He was one hundred percent okay with his best friend wanting him to fuck him. How was that for mind blowing?

"Well, let's make that dream come true, then. Except, I'm pretty sure I don't need any help in the getting hard department, because my cock is ready for action."

With a bold move, Josh reached down to grab Noah, giving him a loving stroke. "Can't hurt to give it a little extra attention, right?"

Noah threw his head back and laughed. When Josh was satisfied Noah was hard enough—and he made damn sure Noah was—he grabbed the massage oil. He kissed Noah's cock first, then spread a generous amount of oil over Noah's cock.

Noah swallowed back a moan. God, he loved Josh's hands on his dick, especially with that hungry gleam in his eyes. Josh looked like he wanted to devour him whole, and dammit, it made Noah feel sexy. Wanted.

"It's even more beautiful when it's slick and glistening like this," Josh said with a deep, appreciative sigh.

"You think so?" Noah said without thinking. When had it started to matter if Josh liked his cock? The sheer admiration in Josh's eyes made him quiver inside.

"Hell, yeah. I love your cock, and I love being fucked by you. We'll go slow, as I haven't done this in a while, so I'm tight and you're...well, your cock is really thick, and it fills me to the max."

The dirty talk was turning Noah on even more, especially since Josh was oiling his own ass in preparation. Noah watched, enraptured as Josh slid one finger inside of himself, followed by another as he started stretching and scissoring himself. The soft groans he let out told Noah that Josh was more than looking forward to what was going down. Noah couldn't wait to share this experience with his friend and give him the pleasure he'd been seeking. Oh, fuck, who was he kidding? He couldn't wait to fuck Josh, either. It had to be amazingly hot and tight.

It was funny how Josh was talking about Noah fucking him as if he already knew what it would feel like. A memory of the erotic dreams Noah had sometimes popped up. Noah on top of Josh, ramming his cock in Josh's ass. Him coming so hard inside of Josh he saw fucking stars. He could almost picture what Josh's ass would feel like around his dick, being engulfed in such a tight, slick heat.

Huh. Powerful imagination he had going there. Yup, not

quite so straight. Well, whatever. It wasn't like he cared about that label, or any label.

Josh straddled Noah. Their eyes locked. A tremble tore through Noah. Shit, he really was about to fuck another guy. Not just any guy—Josh.

"Noah...thank you for doing this." The words were barely audible, Josh's voice tight with tension.

Noah grabbed his friend's hand. "Don't ever thank me. There's no room for thanks between the two of us, okay? Just taking care of each other, pleasuring each other."

Josh's face relaxed. He spread his legs, then lowered himself on Noah's cock, seeking the entrance to his ass. With one hand, he spread his own cheeks, with the other hand he held a firm grip on Noah's solid member. Noah's crown brushed the pucker that would give him entry to Josh's ass.

"You guide me in, okay? I don't want to hurt you," he said, letting out a shivering breath.

Josh nodded, teeth clenched in concentration. Noah's cock pushed against the outer ring, then slipped in.

"Oh..." Josh groaned.

Noah closed his eyes and with quivering muscles, waited until Josh relaxed. Josh slowly lowered himself farther and inch by inch, Noah slid in.

He gasped. Shivered.

His cock was engulfed in a hole tighter than anything he'd ever been in, yet it was exactly as he had pictured, as he had dreamed. The warm, slick sensation combined with the incredible pressure on his cock was indescribable. His breath came in puffs as Josh pushed farther and farther down. God, they'd barely started, and Noah's balls were tightening already, sending jolts of pleasure down the entire length of his shaft.

"Fuck, Noah...Oh! So good..." Josh stammered, biting his lip.

The resistance gradually lessened, and Noah's cock sunk in deeper. He blinked a few times to get the droplets of sweat out of his eyes. Even though Josh was doing most of the physical work, Noah was clammy all over from this unbelievable sensation.

"You're so tight," he whispered, watching in awe as Josh lowered himself, throwing his head back in abandon.

Josh moaned. "Holy shit, you have no idea how good this feels. Your cock is so thick, it's...I'm so full of you, and it's incredible."

The last bit of resistance melted away, and Noah was buried all the way. His balls gently rubbed against Josh's ass, tightening further in response to the delicious friction.

"Noah, I'm not gonna last long...I'm already...so close. But I'll make it good for you, I promise. I need to...Fuck, I need to come." Josh started moving, lifting his ass up and thrusting down. After three or four thrusts, he stopped, his entire body shaking with the effort of holding back. "Can you take this? Is it okay with your legs?"

How could he ever refuse anything Josh asked him? Even in the midst of fucking, seconds from blowing his wad, Josh's first concern was for Noah.

"Josh, look at me," he said, his voice thick with emotion. "I'm yours. I can take it. Take what you need."

Josh let out a howl and lifted his ass high up, slamming it down on Noah's cock. Noah's eyes opened wide and a ragged moan flew past his lips. Holy fuck, this felt divine. Again Josh's body lifted and thrust down hard, burying Noah's cock all the way. His nuts pulled flush against his body.

"Oooooh!" Josh shouted and gave one final thrust,

impaling himself all the way, throwing his head back in pure ecstasy as an enormous spurt flew from his cock all over Noah's chest and arms.

Noah had never seen anything sexier and more arousing than Josh losing himself on his cock. Shit, the guy wasn't kidding when he said he loved being fucked.

Josh slowly opened his eyes, blinked, then wiped his brow with a tired gesture.

"Holy fuck, Josh, that was an incredible sight," Noah said. "You came like a geyser."

Josh's eyes traveled to the cum splattered across Noah's chest, and he bit his lip. "I've made a mess," he said, his voice apologetic.

"Don't," Noah warned. "This was amazing."

"Do you want me to finish you with my mouth?"

Noah hated the insecurity in his friend's voice. Josh had been rejected so many times in the past that he always felt like a nuisance. He affirmed him the only way he knew how, by putting Josh's needs and wants first.

"I want my thick cock in your tight ass, because it feels fucking amazing. I want you to ride me hard and deep and use my cock until you come all over me again, and then I'll come."

Josh's eyes flared. Then his mouth curled in a boyish, sexy smile. "With pleasure."

Noah smiled. He'd known the sexy talk would turn Josh on. Shy, sweet Josh had quite the dirty mouth when it came to bed talk. It was an incredible turn on, so it was easy to return the favor.

Josh lifted his hips again and brought them down in a gyrating movement. "I will fuck you so hard," Josh said, thrusting up and down again. "...and so deep..." Noah's balls slapped against Josh's ass from the impact of the shove. "...

and so tight..." Another deep push. "...that you will come harder than you've ever come before."

Noah shuddered as Josh starting riding him for real. The slick heat was incredible, engulfing his cock like a compression sleeve. His hands grabbed Josh's ass, his fingers digging into his cheeks to support the brutal rhythm in which Josh was slamming down. "Fuck, you feel good...Ride me harder, Josh."

Josh let out a growl, increasing the pace even more, almost bringing tears to Noah's eyes. His nuts, which had relaxed a little during Josh's cooling down, resumed their frantic buzzing. His heart was racing, his body drenched in sweat, and his entire nerve center seemed to have moved to his cock. All he could feel was the slick heat and the building pressure. All he wanted was to come hard and long and deep.

He groaned, lifting his hips from the mattress to match Josh's rhythm. His cock was granite, his balls bursting to unload, but he would not blow until Josh had come again. Josh's cock was dripping precum, and Noah grabbed the tight shaft with his right hand, eliciting a deep moan from Josh. Noah pumped him furiously, matching the rhythm from Josh's thrusts.

"Oooohhh," Josh wailed, his eyes crossing. "Oh fuck, Noah...don't stop...don't stop...I'm gonna..."

Noah's whole body tensed as he fought back his release. He couldn't hold on for long anymore.

"Dammit, Joshua, come for me," he ordered and gave Josh's cock a massive squeeze. It erupted in his hands, squirting cum all over, as Josh slammed down on Noah's cock and sent him over the edge.

Noah's vision went red, and a mighty roar thundered in

his ears. His hips thrust up to bury his cock all the way, balls slapping against Josh's ass as he shattered. "Ungh!"

All his strength left him and his hands dropped to his sides, powerless. Josh must have had the same experience, because he flopped down on Noah's chest, panting as if he'd finished a marathon. Noah would have cuddled him, but he simply couldn't lift his hands.

"Josh," he managed to say. "That was the single best fuck I've ever had. Anytime you want me to fuck you, say the word."

9

Indy's boxers were dripping wet with precum, as his cock had been leaking continuously. It was painfully hard, straining against his underwear, fighting to be released. He'd never been this turned on, not to the point where his brain had stopped working and every nerve in his body seemed to be focused on his junk.

Just then, the garage door opened, a distant hum. Noah looked at him, lifting one brow as if to say the ball was in Indy's court.

Was he going to do this? Fuck it, he had already decided to take Noah up on his offer. He merely needed to find the courage to voice his request because as Noah had said: he had to ask for it. And fuck, did he crave the release. His whole body was throbbing and thrumming with red-hot need.

Noah's stories had been so fucking hot. The mental picture of these two guys getting all naked and sexy and sweaty was almost too much. But listening to Noah and Josh's story had done something else, and Indy suspected Noah had done this on purpose: it had made Indy trust them even more. Knowing how wicked special the bond between these two men was, how vulnerable they dared to be with each other, and how they took care of each other assured him he was safe with them.

"Wow, you guys are still talking," Josh commented as he stepped into the parlor. "By the way, Indy, if you want me to pick up your car, you'll need to give me your keys." He stilled as his gaze traveled from Indy to Noah. He undoubtedly detected the tension in the room. "What's going on?"

"Oh, I've been telling Indy stories of how we became fuck buddies," Noah said. "That first time you gave me a blow job and the first time you rode my cock."

Josh's mouth dropped open before he caught himself and closed it. His eyes focused on Indy, narrowed. "That cannot have helped with you being horny already," he said slowly.

All Indy needed to come was someone touching him. Seriously, one touch to his cock and he'd fucking erupt. Stupid ribs. Stupid broken arm. Well, maybe not. Maybe that fucked-up robbery, meeting Josh, and having sore ribs would turn out to be the single best thing that ever happened to him.

Noah and Josh locked eyes, communicating with each other wordlessly. The slow smile spreading across Josh's face told Indy he was on board with the plan. Still, Indy had to ask. Noah would not let anything happen without Indy's explicit consent and didn't that seal the deal for him?

Indy looked from Noah to Josh and back as Josh lowered himself on the armrest of Noah's chair. They were so close, so in tune with each other. He wanted that, opening himself up again sexually with someone he could trust. Maybe with someones he could trust? The idea filled his head. If these guys were that open and okay with their complicated sexual relationship, why not go with the flow? Maybe he could tap into that trust they had going. Fuck knew he could use some of that.

He took a deep breath. It was time to jump. "Which is where you guys come in. Would you care to help a guy out?"

Noah's eyebrows furrowed, but Josh reacted first.

"You mean Noah, not me, right? You said guys, but you mean Noah. It's him you want, not me. I've seen how you look at him, and he wants you, too…I'll shut up now, 'cause I'm babbling. I do that sometimes when I get nervous. But you meant Noah, right?"

"I meant you both."

Josh's head jerked, and he shot Indy an incredulous look. "But…you want him, not me."

A deep sense of calm filled Indy, even though his belly fluttered. "I want you both. I need you both. What you two have, it's beautiful. It's messy and fucked up, but beautiful. I want that. And I don't wanna come between you by choosing one of you. When we kissed, you were hard, Josh. And you gave me the first boner I've had in a long time."

Indy looked down at his hands for a few seconds. This was where it got brutally honest. "I haven't had sex in over two years and for me, sex has rarely been a good experience. The last time I had sex was…fucking horrible. Yes, Noah's stories were hot, and they turned me on. But even more than you guys fucking, the trust between you did it for me. I know that we just met, but I love the trust you have. Maybe you could share that with me and help me regain some self-confidence and faith in people?"

Josh and Noah shared a look stuffed with meaning. How he wanted someone to look at him like that, someday. That much love and trust, it was staggering.

They'll never want you like that. Not when they find out who you are, what you did.

"You can't hold Indy down or restrain him," Noah told Josh. "And we have to be careful with his ribs, so no twisting or turning or any kind of pressure on his torso."

"Okay." Josh nodded seriously, then turned to Indy. "Avoid touching the bottom of the stump. Anywhere else is fine, but the skin of the stump is irritated right now and sensitive."

Indy's eyes burned with tears. These guys were incredible. They did nothing but take care of each other, and now of him. A cripple, a basket case and then him: the paranoid, defensive freak. He did fit right in.

"I don't have much experience, Indy, so you'll have to tell me want you want," Josh said. He was sporting an adorably serious expression, as if he was ready to take notes to pass a test.

"Same here," Noah said. Indy's eyes widened and Josh frowned. "What?" Noah asked defensively. "I enlisted when I was eighteen and thought I was straight, okay? Not a lot of available girls in the army. I only got to fuck girls in the months before I enlisted, but I remember little since I was drunk half the time. Plus, even then, me and Josh were tight, and we hung out together most of the time. Most of my experience is with you, Josh, and you're the only guy I've ever fucked."

"I know for a fact you banged what's-her-name in your dad's office. Lieutenant Dallas," Josh said.

"First, her name was Meghan. You don't call someone lieutenant when you're banging her, as you put it so eloquently. But more importantly, what do you mean 'know for a fact'? It happened only once, and I'm pretty sure I didn't tell you."

A devilish grin spread across Josh's face. "I watched you. We had agreed to grab a movie, remember? I was supposed to meet you at your dad's office, but I got confused on the time and was an hour early. Had quite the front-row seat there to your, erm, activities. She was limber."

Indy hadn't thought it was possible, but Noah blushed. "Shit, I can't believe you watched me, you perv. Probably got off on it too, right?"

Josh laughed. "Hell, yeah. You were pounding away, and I got to watch your gorgeous ass. Exquisite view. Spanked myself to that memory quite a few times."

"Was she any good?" Indy asked, gladly adding fuel to Noah's embarrassment.

"Oh, I'm sure she was. I was eighteen, and she was in her thirties, recently divorced. She came on so strong, and I didn't have the heart to tell her no since she clearly needed an ego boost, so I went along with it. It was nice, and I think she liked it, because she kept screaming my name, but I had no idea what I was doing. And like I said, my experience with guys is nonexistent, except for Josh here."

"Well, that's reassuring," Indy said, his eyes sparkling.

"Luckily, they taught me some stuff in medical training," Noah said dryly.

Indy grinned. "One can only hope."

"So the bottom-line is that none of us know what we're doing, which means we're fucked," Josh said.

Noah's eyes twinkled as he looked at Josh. "Not yet, but that's up to you."

A delightful blush stained Josh's cheeks.

Indy asked, "You guys wanna fill me in here, or is this a private thing?"

Noah gestured to Josh to do the honors. He cleared his throat, fidgeted with his thumbs. "As a reward for certain activities earlier this week, Noah has promised to let me top him for the first time."

"Yup, Josh gets a go at my ass, instead of the other way around." Noah said it so matter-of-factly that Indy almost didn't realize what a big thing this was for them both. Not that he would know, he'd only ever bottomed himself. Like Duncan would ever let me top, fuck no.

"You've never switched?" Indy asked.

"No. I haven't been top ever," Josh said, and Indy noted with interest he wasn't blushing this time.

Noah frowned. "What do you mean, ever? You mean with me, right?"

"No, I mean ever. I've never fucked another guy; I've always been the bottom guy."

Noah's head reeled back. "What the fuck?" he said. "How come you never told me?"

Josh got up from Noah's armrest and kneeled before him on the floor. "Because you would've felt obligated to switch, and it would've been wrong." He kissed Noah's hands, then turned and sat on the floor, his back resting comfortably against the empty spot under Noah's missing leg.

"I've always known I liked boys, ever since I was maybe ten, though I didn't come out until I was fourteen. I was the stereotypical gay kid: sensitive, awkward in social interactions with guys. The kids in school picked up on it easily, especially in high school. My parents stopped talking to me when I came out, and my younger brother chose their side. Fuck, my life was hell before I met Noah. Teasing grew into bullying and then physical violence. I got the shit beaten out of me a few times for acting too gay."

Josh sighed as he looked up at Noah with a deep affection. "Without his friendship, I wouldn't have survived school. But I was still awkward and shy, way too scared to meet other gay guys, let alone date. Finally, I decided I wanted to get this whole virginity thing over with so I liquored up and went to a gay bar. I met this older guy named James who took a liking to me. He was my first, and it was nice. I like bottoming," he said, eying Indy with a quick look. "I love being fucked. It's an incredible feeling, well, with a guy who does it right."

Indy closed his eyes for a second, breathed through the familiar pain that thinking about sex, about Duncan and Eric brought. "I like it, too," he confessed. "When it doesn't fucking hurt because it's too rough."

He opened his eyes again, hoping that he wouldn't find the pity he feared on their faces.

"Yeah," Josh said, a similar expression of pain on his face. "It certainly can hurt like a motherfucker."

Indy didn't ask. Josh's face said it all and so did Noah's hand that came down on Josh's shoulder. What was there to say? Indy didn't need the details; on the contrary. He'd lived them.

Josh let out an audible breath, playing with Noah's hand in a habitual way. It struck Indy again how okay Noah was with Josh's constant gestures of affection. For someone who thought he was straight till a while ago, he seemed to be on board with all of it. The guy had to be bi at least, if not full-out gay.

Josh said, "You know, with two guys having sex, I feel that there's a pecking order. Being top means being in control, being the dominant one in the relationship—at least at that point. I've never been that guy, never felt secure and trusted enough to be anything else than bottom."

Noah had been silently listening, though Indy had seen him react with suppressed anger when Josh mentioned what had been done to him. But now his eyes flared.

"That's bullshit," he said, his voice sharp. "And that's not why we haven't switched positions yet."

Josh ducked a little, then pulled up his legs and lowered his head on his knees.

"Then why?" he asked so softly Indy could barely hear him. "We've been fucking for ten months, and you never even offered."

Indy held his breath. Would Noah get angry? Noah bent forward and simply lifted Josh up under his arms, pulling him on his lap with sheer strength. He clamped two strong hands on Josh's face and kissed him hard on his mouth.

"You're an idiot, if you think that's the reason."

Tears welled up in Josh's eyes, even as he covered Noah's hands with his own in a gesture of sweet affection and surrender.

"Look at me, Josh," Noah commanded. Josh raised his eyes. "I am to blame for that, not you. When we started messing around and then having sex, it scared the shit out of me. Here I was, this self-proclaimed straight guy, and I was getting blown by another guy, literally sleeping with him, fucking him."

"I know it was hard for you. Weird," Josh said, his voice thick with emotion.

"No, it wasn't, and that made it so complicated. I fucking loved it. When you gave me that first blow job, I came harder than I ever had before, including sex with girls. And when you let me fuck you, it unnerved me even more because what should've weirded me out felt so good. Sex with you is incredible, Josh, and that terrifies me since I always thought I was straight. That's why I was so hesitant to cross those last boundaries, why I wouldn't swallow or let you fuck me. Because once I did that, I'd have to embrace that I'm at least bi, probably leaning more toward gay."

Josh's eyes softened. "It's a label, Noah. It doesn't change who and what you are. You give it a name, that's all. And everyone already thinks you're gay anyway because of me, so what's the big deal?"

Noah clenched his jaw. "It would mean he was right."

Indy tilted his head. Who was Noah talking about?

Josh's brows furrowed before his face lit up with recognition. "Oh, babe, he wasn't right at all. God, even if you came out as full-on gay, started wearing fuchsia feather boas and danced in the Pride parade in a pink thong, he still wouldn't be right. He'll never accept you for who you are, not even if you were straight."

His dad. They were talking about Noah's dad, Indy understood. Poor Noah. He and Josh had not been lucky in that department. Indy's mom had done a lot of horrible things—selling him to Duncan took the cake—but she'd never even batted an eye over Indy's sexuality. He'd never even come out. They both simply knew, and it had not been an issue.

"I know," Noah said. "My head knows you're right, but it still hurts. And I'm gonna pass on the feather boa and pink thong, if you don't mind."

Josh grinned. "They'd look good on you."

Noah's face relaxed, a hint of a smile playing on his lips. "Still not donning them."

"We'll see. Now that you're gay, I see a whole range of possibilities."

Noah's eyes found Indy's. Indy sent him a soft smile and got one back in return.

"So why are you willing to bottom now?" Josh circled back to their earlier topic.

"Because of Indy."

"Me?" Indy asked. "What do I have to do with

anything?"

Josh's hands dropped, and he bowed his head. "It's not what you think, Josh," Noah said with a hoarse voice.

"How do you know what I'm thinking?"

Noah lifted Josh's chin with his index finger. "Because you're pulling away right now, in expectation of a mental blow. You think I'm allowing you to fuck me to cover up that I'm attracted to Indy."

"Don't deny it!" Josh's head shot up, an angry blush on his cheeks. "You were hard when he kissed you, and you were angry because he made you hard, and that's why the sex was so different. You've never fucked me that intense."

"You weren't complaining," Noah shot back.

"No, because I'm twisted enough that it completely turns me on when you go all dominant male on me."

"I know," Noah said, with the slightest hint of a smile.

"What do you mean, you know?"

Indy had been tense when Noah and Josh had started arguing. God, would he turn out to be the cause of a break of trust between them? But this was how they worked through issues, apparently. The fact that Josh was still solidly parked on Noah's lap said enough, didn't it?

"When you're on the edge, all I have to do to make you come is order you to."

"Do you have any idea how fucking embarrassing that is? Dammit, Noah, all you have to do is say my full name and I come. Sometimes I hate that you have that effect on me."

"I'm aware, which is why I would never abuse it. Two nights ago was the first time I told you to do something without you obeying me right away. I told you to spread your legs and you didn't."

"Is that why you offered me yourself? Because I had

earned it?"

"No, but it did cross my mind to give you that as a reason when you asked." Noah sighed. "God, you were sexy when you said 'make me.' Total turn on."

Josh smiled a slow, sensual smile. There must've been some nice memories playing through his head. "So why did you offer now?"

"Because I wanted to. Yes, I reacted to Indy, and I still do. I haven't been attracted to anyone since we started our thing, but I am to him. Hell, yes, I want to fuck him, and I'm not denying it. He did make me hard, and I was angry, because it felt like a betrayal to you. But I offered you top for two reasons: the first was to give you pleasure, because after that incredible fuck two days ago I wanted more of that for you. But the second reason was because I wanted to. I want to bottom for you, be fucked by you. I want to know what it feels like and share that with you before I'd even consider sharing it with anyone else."

Indy's body, which had cooled off during the argument, heated up quickly when Noah's words created a picture in his mind that was so wicked dirty and arousing, he had to bite his lip to keep a moan in. Never, ever had a guy turned him on so much with mere words. Then again, never had a guy admitted so honestly that he wanted Indy.

Apparently, it had a similar effect on Josh, because he didn't hesitate, but kissed Noah deeply. And with tongue, by the looks of it.

"Please, Noah, fuck me," Josh moaned, tearing his mouth away. Ignoring Indy, or maybe forgetting Indy was even there, he put his hand on Noah's massive erection. "I need your thick cock to fill me, to fuck me hard. I want you so much."

Without even touching himself, Indy came.

10

Noah caught Indy's deep tremble from the corner of his eyes, and he had a pretty good idea what had happened. But that was not his biggest concern right now. His problem was denying his own raging erection to keep the promise he'd made Josh.

"No. You know what I said. I will not fuck you until you ask me to bottom for you." His cock was cursing him as it was rock hard and dying to get some action. But he would not break his word. He hadn't fucked Josh since he'd made the promise—they'd only given each other blow jobs—and he wasn't going to fuck him now.

Josh looked at him with big eyes, his hand still on Noah's dick. "You can't be serious."

"You know I never break a promise."

Josh squeezed Noah's cock. The press sent a wave of pleasure through his balls and up the length of his erection. "For fuck's sake, Noah, you're as hard as I am. You want this."

Noah clamped down hard on his desires. Knowing Josh was willing, that all he had to do was say yes and he'd find release, it was maddening to deny himself that. Yet he had to. For Josh.

"I do, but that doesn't change a thing. You know what you have to do."

Josh got up from Noah's lap, almost pushing himself off. "This is totally unfair. Every single time you ask for sex, I always say yes. The one time I ask you and you deny me."

Noah's jaw tightened. "That's a low blow, and you know it. I said no because you're asking the wrong question. Ask me, Josh."

Josh whipped around. Indy was watching them in fascination. "He's so hard it's ridiculous," Josh complained to Indy. "He's being a stubborn asshole."

"I have a nice view of his...arousal," Indy said, licking his lips in a way that shot straight to Noah's cock, "And I agree. However, it seems the solution is straightforward. Ask him to let you top him."

"I can't," Josh said. Noah couldn't see his face because Josh's back was turned to him, but the anguish in his voice was palpable.

"Why not?" Indy's voice was warm and understanding.

"You don't understand. I'm not that guy...It's not me. And it's not him. Noah is the alpha, that's how this works. I want to top him, but I can't."

Noah forced himself to stay quiet.

"What do you mean?" Indy asked.

"It's when he goes all alpha on me that I feel safest, most confident. Shit, every time he calls me Joshua I erupt. But he needs it, too. He loves being dominant, taking charge. That night of the robbery, when he was fucking me more intensely than ever before, he came so hard. It was such a deep satisfaction to know I could give him that pleasure."

"You're afraid you can't give him that same pleasure when you top."

Noah gasped softly. How had he missed this? Josh was always so eager to please him, to do whatever brought Noah satisfaction. Noah did get off on fucking Josh, there was no denying it. Being the one on top, slamming his cock into that tight heat—it was an incredible turn on. He'd never realized how it would feel to Josh emotionally, since Josh loved being fucked. Shit, the guy could come by sheer fucking, without ever touching his dick. How had he missed the depth of Josh's insecurity about his ability to bring Noah satisfaction if the roles were reversed?

"Yeah," Josh whispered. "I don't think it would work. He gets off on being in charge, and even if he didn't, I don't have what it takes to be the guy on top. At least, not with him."

Noah opened his mouth. This was bullshit. Indy raised a finger, and Noah shut his mouth again, leaned back to watch. Indy sat up slowly, avoiding putting pressure on his ribs, and extended two hands to Josh. He grabbed Indy's hands, and Indy pulled him down on the floor in front of him. Indy's touch was loving as he lifted a finger under Josh's chin and made Josh look him straight in the eyes.

"Noah told me how you faced his dad when he caught you two," Indy said, his tone kind but firm. "You didn't back down, even though his dad was furious. And I saw you defending me against the cashier when he made those derogatory remarks. I heard you shouting at Noah that first night. Josh, you have as much of a backbone as Noah does, you just don't show it as easily. But it's there. And remember what Noah said? He said it was a big turn on when you defied him in bed. I calculate you're going at this all wrong. You should allow yourself to be the dominant one every now and then with Noah. He needs it, and he wants it. Don't ask him for permission to fuck him. He's given you permission. Take him."

Indy's words shot a jolt of electricity through Noah's body, straight to his cock. The damn thing had been hard the whole time anyway, and it wasn't letting up. Fuck, how could he want them both so much at the same time? Was Josh right? Was he transferring his desire for Indy onto Josh because he couldn't fuck Indy, what with his injuries?

Then why was he craving Josh and not merely the release? It wasn't the idea of fucking that made him so hard. It was the thought of being impaled by Josh's long cock. He wanted Josh to fuck him, wanted to share this with him. And yet he wanted Indy at the same time. Fuck, he was making this so complicated and messy.

Josh rose a little and gently embraced Indy. He whispered something in Indy's ear, but it was too soft for Noah to make out. Josh let go of Indy, and the boy's expressive face lit up with emotions. Joy, excitement, and something that looked a lot like want.

"I'd love that," Indy said, kissing Josh on the mouth. "Are you sure it's okay?"

What were they talking about? It couldn't be, could it?

"I'm fine, and as for Noah... He doesn't have a choice, now does he?"

What was going on here? Much to Noah's astonishment, Josh sat down sideways on the couch, his back leaning against the armrest. He extended a hand to Indy, who kept his upper body straight as he climbed on Josh's lap, facing him.

"Are you comfortable?" Josh asked, gently pulling Indy's ass forward until that gorgeous round butt was snug against his crotch. Noah's breath about stopped. Josh had positioned the two of them in a way that allowed Noah to see every-thing. It was the sweetest torture.

Indy didn't say anything, but raised his mouth to Josh and kissed him. Noah thought it would be a short peck, a quick kiss on the lips, but it wasn't. They sank into each other, and the soft sucking sounds made Noah's balls tingle. If this was how they had kissed during the robbery, no wonder Josh had gotten hard.

Indy lifted a hand, caressed Josh's hair, then pulled his head even closer. Noah fought for control as he watched his lover kiss the guy he wanted with such erotic passion.

Finally, Josh lifted his head. "You really are a great kiss-er," he told Indy in a dreamy voice.

Indy laughed, the happy sound reverberating deep in Noah's balls. "So are you."

Noah wanted him. Them. Both. Fuck, enough with this crap. If Josh didn't get his act together soon, Noah would make him. He was about to explode and couldn't take much more.

"Josh..." he said, his voice menacing.

Josh glanced sideways with a look that made Noah swal-low. Holy fuck, Josh had found his balls, and they were impressive. "Shut the fuck up, Noah. You didn't want to fuck me, so now you get to watch."

Watch? Josh wouldn't...would he? He wouldn't make him watch, for fuck's sake.

"Is it okay if I take your pants off?"

Indy nodded, and Noah clenched his fists. Josh rolled Indy off his lap and back on the couch on his back, supporting him with several pillows until he was raised and comfortable. Josh's hands were steady as he dragged the capris off Indy's slim legs. Indy was wearing red boxers that were stained in the front with wetness, and Noah breathed in deeply.

"You smell different from me or Noah," Josh said almost reverently. He kneeled between Indy's legs on the couch, as if worshiping Indy's body. He trailed a finger up Indy's left leg, stopping at the edge of his boxers, then went down the other leg. Indy didn't even seem to notice Noah, as his eyes never left Josh's face.

Indy spread his legs farther, allowing Noah to see how soaking wet his boxers were. Fuck, the guy must have unloaded months' worth of cum.

"You can touch," Indy whispered. "But maybe you could lose some clothes as well?"

Noah clamped his hands down on the armrests, fighting to stay seated. All he wanted was to jump up and position himself between them.

Josh got up from the couch, whipped his shirt over his shoulders, then dropped his shorts, leaving him in his usual black boxers that fit so snugly around his toned ass. He turned to face Noah for a second, and Josh's bulging erection was hard to miss. Without thinking, Noah grabbed his own cock, squeezing it.

Josh's eyes flared. "Enjoying the show from there?" he said, his voice rough.

Noah wanted to tell him to go fuck himself, but that was exactly what Josh was aiming for. Josh's goal was for him to suffer and fucking hell, he was doing a great job of tormenting him. Time to level the playing field. Noah pulled his shirt over his head, then raised his hips and dragged down his underwear that was stained with his precum. He'd been leaking like crazy since those two had started making out.

Indy inhaled sharply, his eyes on Noah's cock, which

sprang free. Noah leaned back again in his chair and fisted himself a couple of times, dragging his look from Indy to Josh and back. Both guys had their eyes glued to Noah's dick. Josh visibly swallowed.

Noah smiled. "Enjoying the show?" he shot back.

Josh's eyes narrowed, and he straightened himself, tearing his eyes away from Noah. He turned, faced Indy again.

"Want me to take those off for you?" he asked, pointing at Indy's boxers and making Indy smile.

"Yes, please. My top, too."

Josh unbuttoned the blouse Indy was wearing. It was the same one he'd worn during the robbery, and it was still crumpled and stained.

Noah's fist stopped stroking himself as Josh revealed Indy's cock. Like everything else on Indy's body, it was slender and boyish, though he was undeniably hard again. He had little body hair, which Noah had already noticed when he'd examined him in the hospital.

Indy groaned when Josh pulled the boxers down all the way, then kneeled between Indy's legs again. Noah's heart about stopped when Josh looked at Indy one last time and after receiving a trembling nod, dropped little kisses on Indy's legs, all the way from his calves to his upper thighs. He was such a tender lover. Josh held back so much when he was with Noah, not wanting to go too far, be too gay, but now with Indy, he revealed that soft side.

Indy moaned. "You're a tease," he said between clenched teeth.

Josh smiled. "I'm nothing if not thorough." He yanked off his own boxers and lowered himself on Indy, seeking his mouth again.

The sucking noises were killing Noah, and he gripped

his cock hard. What the fuck were these two doing to him? He didn't know whether to be angry at Josh's payback, or impressed. But he would give anything, everything, to be between them right now and fuck either one of them.

Not that Indy was ready for that, not even close. In that sense, Josh's approach was so much better for Indy than Noah's could've ever been. Sweet, non-threatening Josh was exactly what Indy needed, not Noah's bossy MO.

What was happening was about more than payback from Josh. Something was taking place that he couldn't interrupt. Josh and Indy, they didn't need him to be involved right now. They need each other, and they needed him to watch and be okay with it. Noah let out a deep trembling breath and made his peace with being on the sidelines. For now.

INDY'S SENSATIONS were on overload. Josh seemed determined to drive him absolutely fucking crazy with want. He was now rubbing his cock against Indy's, gyrating against his crotch. Meanwhile, his mouth was still devouring Indy's, until he finally pulled back. Josh's eyes were as glazed as Indy suspected his own to be.

"I could kiss you for hours," Indy whispered.

"Same here. Fuck, your mouth is addictive. You're so sweet and tender. I love kissing you," Josh replied, brushing a curl from Indy's face.

Josh slid down, trailing his hands over Indy's smooth chest, and found his nipple that tightened immediately. Josh followed his fingers with his mouth and tongue, kissing and licking Indy's pecs and nipples.

Indy responded with a continuous stream of soft moans and groans.

"You like that, huh?" Josh teased, sucking on Indy's nipple again. It sent lightning bolts to his cock.

"Hell, yeah."

Josh lowered his mouth even farther, following the dusting of blond hairs down to Indy's cock, licking and sucking and kissing every inch of skin he encountered. He slid down the couch, letting his knees lower to the floor.

"Your cock is beautiful," Josh said, lifting Indy's dick and studying it from every side.

"It's too small," Indy said gruffly.

"It's perfect."

"No, it's not. It's too small to bring a guy pleasure."

Josh's head shot up. "Whoever told you that didn't know what the fuck he was talking about. Size isn't important."

Indy bit his lip. He should've kept his big mouth shut. Josh had just been nice to him, and he had to go and ruin it with his pity party.

Josh sat up on his knees, sought Noah's eyes. "Noah, stand up for a sec, would you?" Josh asked.

Noah obeyed without protest, turning slightly. His big, fat cock was rock hard, jutting forward. How was Indy's not a fucking crayon compared to that? That dick was a thing of beauty while his was...disappointing.

"Noah is smaller than me, do you see that? My cock is about two inches longer. But it doesn't matter, since he's not only thicker, but he has that perfect curve. When he fucks me, that curve helps him hit my prostate every single time, and he can make me come without me ever touching myself. Well, that, and I love being fucked. Now look at your cock, do you see you have that same curve?"

Indy nodded, studying the three bare cocks in the room,

his teeth chewing on his bottom lip. Josh had a point about the curve, but surely that couldn't be all you needed to satisfy a guy, right?

"Have you ever topped? Fucked another guy?" Josh asked.

Indy shook his head. As if. It hadn't even been an option, not with Duncan. He did the fucking, and that was it. "No. He said my dick was too small, that I couldn't satisfy him with this...crayon."

A wave of sadness washed over him. He'd ruined it all now. If Josh still wanted him after this, it would be out of pity, right? He lifted his eyes but didn't encounter the pity he'd expected. Instead, Josh's eyes were blazing. He was...mad?

"Fuck that asshole," Josh spit out. "Seriously, fuck him. He didn't know what the fuck he was talking about." Josh's anger dissipated when Indy barely responded. "You don't believe me, do you? Do you honestly believe you can't bring someone pleasure?"

"I don't know. He fucked hundreds of people, guys and girls both, so I figured he knew what he was talking about."

"He didn't," Josh assured him. "He must have been insecure as fuck and a major asshole."

"The latter we can agree on," Indy said. Asshole was too mild a word for Duncan Fitzpatrick.

"Listen, Indy, I know you're not ready for this, but when you are, I'll prove it to you."

"How?"

"I'll let you fuck me, and you can see with your own eyes how much pleasure you can bring me."

Indy's mouth dropped open, and he raised a shaky hand to his forehead. Josh would let Indy top him? What the actual fuck? Josh's face was serious, which meant he wasn't joking. But...why?

"Why?" Indy managed. "Why would you let me do that?"

"Because I love being fucked, I swear. And I like you a lot, and I want to show you how good it can be."

"I don't...I've never..." Indy shook his head, shut his mouth when he couldn't find words.

Josh lowered himself on top of Indy again and kissed him softly. "It's okay. Whenever you're ready."

He dove in deep in Indy's mouth again, licking and sucking and rekindling the fire he'd started before. Indy sighed into his mouth, releasing the tension the discussion about his dick had brought.

Finally, Josh let go of Indy's mouth and started exploring his way down again, dropping kisses on Indy's chin, neck, his pecs, before settling on his right nipple. Indy leaned back with eyes closed, his lips releasing puffs and whimpers.

Josh slid lower, kneeling on the floor again, licking down Indy's stomach until he reached his cock.

"You still okay?" he checked.

Indy nodded. His system was almost short-circuiting with sensations. No one had ever touched him like that, and holy fuck, Josh was worshiping his body, loving every inch of his skin.

Josh's tongue lapped the precum off his cock. Indy bucked off the couch, letting out a loud moan. "Oh, fuck!"

Josh chuckled. "Feel good?" he said with a low voice.

Good? Was he fucking kidding? It was absolutely amazing. Indescribable. And could he please stop talking and get his mouth back on his cock?

Josh must've read his mind, because his eyes twinkled as

he took Indy in his mouth again, until Indy's balls hit his chin.

"Ohhhh...fuuuuuck!"

Indy's hands fisted Josh's hair, desperate for something to hold on to as waves of ecstasy rolled over him. He pinched his eyes shut and let his head fall back.

His cock was engulfed in Josh's wet, hot mouth all the way to his balls. And he was sucking with loud slurping noises that made Indy rise even higher. Indy shuddered, the building pleasure in his system almost too much to bear.

Josh let Indy's cock slide from his mouth until it popped free. Indy opened his eyes, wanting to see what Josh would do next. His dick quivered in Josh's hand, wet and glistening with saliva. Josh took one of Indy's balls in his mouth. Damn, his tongue was...and the pressure...

An inhuman sound fell from his lips. No words. He had no words left, surrendering to the fire in his body that threatened to engulf him whole.

Josh switched his attention to his other nut, sucking and licking until Indy was squirming on the couch. His balls were heavy, aching with the need to unload.

"Oh, please...I need to...Josh, please!"

It made little sense, but maybe Josh had understood because he sucked his cock back in all the way. Gently cradling Indy's balls, Josh went down on him in earnest.

He'd never, ever felt anything like this. He'd always been the one to give blow jobs, but he'd never experienced one himself. Josh's head bobbed up and down as he sucked Indy's cock. That slick, warm, sucking pressure was pure heaven.

"Josh!" It was as much a warning as a shout of gratitude, and Josh never let up.

Indy bucked off the couch, clenching his fists as he

thrust into Josh's mouth in pure bliss. His balls set off with fervor, and he exploded into Josh's throat.

"Fuuuuuuuck!" Indy let out, panting hard. "Thank you, thank you, thank you...That was...oh, my God, that was amazing."

Josh let Indy's cock slide out, licking it clean before he sat up.

"Damn, you taste good." He licked his lips. "And you're very welcome."

Aftershocks were still floating through Indy's body, but he lifted a weak hand to cup Josh's cheek. "Different from Noah?" he blurted out.

Josh grinned. "Yeah. His is saltier, yours is richer. Fuck, you taste good."

His eyes were laughing, and yet tension creeped into Indy's stomach. Would Josh expect him to return the favor? That was how it worked, wasn't it? It was damn selfish to not offer to do something in return, but the thought of having to blow him...Indy swallowed, slivers of fear taking over.

"Do you want me to..." he pointed toward Josh's cock which was rock hard.

"Hell, no. This was for you." He sat up, then leaned over Indy to give him a wet kiss. "When you're ready, you can take me up on my offer to fuck me, but until then I'm more than happy to suck you, anytime. Right now I have something else I need to do, which means you have to move."

A NERVOUS FLUTTER moved in Noah's stomach as Indy got up from the couch, naked and not embarrassed about it, as far as Noah could tell. He'd come so far since the panic attack in the hospital that it was nothing short of amazing.

Josh's eyes made contact with Noah's. Josh grabbed his own cock, which was glistening with precum, and fisted himself a few times. He was damn hard—and so was Noah. The challenge was clear.

"Get over here."

Fucking hell. He was about to get fucked.

"Excuse me?" he said, forcing his voice to be level.

Josh pointed toward the pillows on the couch. "On your back."

Noah found himself getting off the chair and on the couch. His ass was propped up on the pillows, his stump resting comfortably against the soft back side of the couch. The fact that Josh wanted him to be as comfortable as possible made Noah want to surrender more than anything else.

"Guys, should I...?" Indy asked hesitantly.

Noah and Josh answered him at the same time, "Stay."

Indy lowered himself on the chair Noah had vacated.

Josh walked over to the dresser and yanked open the top drawer where they usually had a bottle of lube. He found it, and strode back to Noah, dropped it on the couch.

Their eyes met, and Josh pressed his lips together. Noah shivered. Shit was about to get real.

Josh kneeled on the couch and casually lubed his cock with fluid, efficient moves. Noah watched him, his stomach fluttering.

"Spread your legs."

Noah put his head back against the armrest of the couch. He turned his head to face Indy, who viewed them with heated eyes, a look of complete focus on his face.

When Josh's slick finger touched his entrance, Noah shivered and faced his best friend. He wanted to ask Josh to be gentle, even though he didn't need to. The vulnerability of his position made him weak inside. Fuck, it went against all his instincts, and he had to fight to let go of the control.

Josh's finger pushed against Noah's anal sphincter.

"Bear down on me," Josh said.

God, he knew how this worked, had done it hundreds of times to Josh, so why was it so fucking hard to relax? He overrode his instinctive urge of clamming up and instead pushed back. Josh's finger slipped in. It burned, and it certainly felt strange to have something in his hole. What the fuck was he doing? Could he do this? Would his damaged body even be able to handle this intrusion?

Josh swirled his finger around, and Noah breathed to relax. It didn't hurt. Not compared to, say, getting blown up, or recovering from an amputation. It was more of a discomfort, he told himself. After a bit it felt okay. Not good, but not too bad either.

Josh inserted a second digit, gently pushing and stretching and expanding him. The burning sensation returned in full force.

Was he really gonna do this? All it would take was one word. One 'no' and Josh would stop immediately. But it would also mean that Josh would never try again. Noah wanted this, for Josh. He had to do this, for them both.

"You're so tight, Noah," Josh whispered, and Noah sensed his resolve crumbling.

"Please, fuck me, Josh," he said, pushing his ass back against Josh's fingers. They slipped in way deeper, and Noah involuntarily clenched at the intrusion. Damn, that stung. His breath caught before he pushed out a shaky exhale.

Josh pulled back his fingers.

"Don't stop."

"I need more lube," Josh said. He grabbed the bottle and

squirted some on his fingers. "I won't hurt you, so we'll take our time, okay?"

The fingers returned, this time super-slick with lube. Noah tensed, then relaxed again. He could do this. Fuck, he wanted to do this. How bad could it be if Josh loved it so much? Josh kept stroking him, and the burning subsided.

"Keep going," he urged Josh.

Josh's fingers pulled out, then pushed in again. Noah clenched his teeth at the increased pressure. Josh must have added a third finger, because his hole was being stretched even wider. It smarted like a son of a bitch.

Noah closed his eyes so Josh wouldn't see the tears that forced themselves out of his eyes. There was nothing he could do about his cock, however, which had been hard when they started, but had grown soft as a result of the pain.

"You good?" Josh asked, a tremble in his voice.

"Yeah. I'm ready," Noah said with way more confidence than he felt. But the burning had stopped, and he wanted to get it over with. Fuck, he'd survived being blown to bits, surely he could take a cock up his ass.

The pressure disappeared as Josh pulled out his fingers. Noah kept his eyes closed as heard the lube being opened again and assumed Josh coated his cock once more. His breath froze in his lungs as Josh's cock brushed his entrance. Noah opened his eyes, letting his head drop sideways. Indy's soft eyes were trained on him, his cheeks flushed and his chest heaving with breaths. Indy had pulled up his legs, but his cock was still visible—and it was rock hard. His tongue darted out to lick his lips. Did he have any idea how sexy that was?

"Try to relax, Noah." Josh's voice was tight with tension.

Noah ripped his gaze away from Indy and focused on

Josh, whose jaw was set as his eyes were completely focused on Noah. Noah breathed, then forced his muscles to relax. Josh pushed in against the outer ring and Noah bore down on him, allowing him to slide in a bit farther. Noah's breath stopped, then resumed with effort.

Josh made little thrusts, gently moving in deeper and deeper. Noah closed his eyes, focusing on the sensation of Josh's cock in his ass, even if it was in only an inch or two. It ached a little, but it also gave a titillating, full sensation.

"Are you okay?" Josh asked, stopping.

Noah opened his eyes to find Josh looking at him with concern. "I'm good. Don't stop."

"I don't want to hurt you. You're so fucking tight."

"It's okay. I want this. Keep going."

Josh gave another careful push, adding another inch of his cock inside. Noah closed his eyes again and clenched his fists as pain hit him all over again. How the fuck did Josh do this? How could he take Noah pounding him? And his cock was a hell of a lot thicker than Josh's, so it had to tear Josh apart. He breathed through the sting in his ass. What the hell had he agreed to?

Josh pulled out, which caused a glorious sensation in Noah's ass that spread in tingling waves all the way to his toes. Oh, that had felt incredible. Finally they were getting to the good parts.

"I can't do this," Josh said. Noah opened his eyes. "I'm hurting you, and I can't do it."

Anger and compassion battled inside Noah. He wanted to slap Josh for being so timid, but at the same time kiss him silly for his obvious concern. What could he do to push Josh into committing fully? Tenderness right now would break him, trigger him into complete submission again.

"Man up and fuck me, dammit. Come on, put your

gorgeous cock in my ass and start pounding." He looked Josh straight in the eyes. "Do I look like I will break? If you can take my thick cock, I can take yours."

Authoritative dirty talk: his secret weapon.

Hesitantly, Josh slid in again, and Noah lifted his ass to give it a little extra push. Pain hit, but he forced himself to not show it. Had Josh's cock grown softer or was that his imagination?

"I know how long your cock is, man, I've had it in my mouth. Well, half of it anyway. I know you're not even halfway in, so come on."

Josh's hips pulled back and thrust forward. Another inch in. Noah tried to keep his breaths even. Josh slid out and in again, definitely rock hard now. Could they get this part over with so it would get good? Josh pulling out felt fantastic, but the pushing in was a nightmare.

"Dammit, Joshua, fuck me already!" he groaned. When Josh moved forward for another thrust, Noah lifted his butt off the pillows and moved against him in an opposite push. All of a sudden, Josh's cock sunk in all the way and his balls slapped Noah's ass.

Stars exploded before Noah's eyes as his ass felt like it was tearing, and he cried out. "Fucking hell!"

Even in his pain, he felt Josh move back and grabbed his friend's ass and locked his left knee around his leg, trapping him in place. "You're not going anywhere," he growled.

"Noah, no..." Josh protested, but Noah grabbed his head not too softly and dragged his mouth down for a hard kiss. He plummeted his tongue into Josh's mouth, kissing him as he had never kissed him before. Anything to get his mind off the sensation that his ass had been ripped in two.

The erotic sensation of their slick tongues dueling helped

Noah relax, and the throb in his ass faded, to be replaced by an entirely new sensation. Josh's cock was filling him completely, and he was on the verge of pleasure. He experimentally moved his hips a little, and the ensuing slick friction made him tingle. His cock grew hard, filling him with sweet relief.

He let go of Josh's mouth. "I'm good now."

Josh stared at him as if he was speaking another language. Noah moved his hips again to underscore his point. "You feel good. Now fuck me and make me come."

It was like a switch flipped inside Josh's brain. Or body. Or both. He raised himself up and moved his hips, sliding in and out of Noah in a delicious rhythm. The pain was gone, and instead, there was a wonderful full feeling and a connection to Josh he had never experienced before. Josh rotated his hips, and Noah gasped as a burst of pleasure flooded through his insides.

"Fuck! What was that?"

Josh smiled for the first time since he'd started fucking Noah. "Bingo! That's what's gonna make you come."

He gyrated again, and Noah let out a groan. "Ohhh!"

Josh increased the tempo, and Noah matched his strokes beat for beat, all thoughts of pain gone. Tingles danced on his skin, teasing him with tendrils of pleasure in his belly, his balls, and his dick. Hot damn, this was unlike anything he'd ever felt before.

Then Josh changed his position, and his next thrust hit that magic spot Noah only knew from fucking Josh. He lost the ability to form words and a shivery growl rolled from his lips. Instant ecstasy blazed through his body.

Josh pulled back farther, then slammed home all the way. Noah dropped his arms from Josh's back, no longer able to hold on. The air exploded from his lungs as Josh surged in again. Noah's balls swelled, the pressure almost painful.

"I'll give you four more strokes," Josh said, and Noah laughed at the payback. When Josh rammed into him, his laugh evolved into an embarrassingly long moan. The pleasure inside him surged, radiating everywhere until his skin itched with the need to come.

"Two," Josh said between clenched teeth, burying himself to the hilt again.

"Harder," Noah begged, never thinking he'd be in this position. God, he'd do anything to come, his nuts desperately clinching to unleash.

"Three."

"Dammit, fuck me harder, Joshua."

Josh lost control. Instead of the fourth deep thrust, he erupted into frantic fucking, pounding Noah so hard his whole body moved. Noah's balls detonated with fury, and his cock blew up with an almost painful eruption, spewing all over Josh's torso. Josh didn't even notice, but kept hammering until his entire body tensed, then spasmed as his hot cum filled Noah's ass.

"Ohhhh!" Josh grunted, throwing his head back in complete rapture. A massive shudder tore through his body, and he collapsed on top of Noah.

Noah's arms came around Josh, and he hugged him tight. Their panting breaths mingled, and Josh's heart hammered in his chest, reverberating in Noah's ears.

For the first time after a fuck, Josh was quiet. After a minute, Noah became concerned.

"Are you okay?" he asked the question that was usually on Josh's lips. He kept stroking Josh's back, his head, his lean body, slick with sweat.

"I went total caveman on you," Josh said, his voice barely audible.

Noah smiled, remembering their conversation from two nights before. "Yeah, you did. And I'm not complaining."

"I hurt you."

"For a bit, but it got good after that."

Josh pulled out with a soft sigh that touched Noah deep. The head of Josh's cock plopped out with a delicious dirty sound. Noah's body returned to somewhat resembling normal, which was ridiculous considering he had jizz dripping out of his ass.

Indy.

He'd forgotten about him. He turned his head and found Indy watching the two of them with tears streaming down his face.

"How are you doing over there?" Noah asked, not weirded out at all that Indy had seen all that. If anything, it made him even more proud of what he had done.

"The two of you ... You're amazing. Seriously, I've never seen anything like it."

Josh turned his head as well. "What, you mean the spectacularly clumsy sex we had?"

"What do you mean, clumsy?" Noah said with feigned indignation. "You fucked me good, lover boy."

Josh rose up on his arms to look at Noah. "I did, didn't I? I mean, it took a while for me to get there, but I finished well."

"I'll say. Your cum is still dripping out of my ass."

Josh broke out in giggles and Noah chuckled. Josh swiped a finger down his chest and held it before Noah's face, all sticky and juicy. "You came all over me. Seriously, we're a mess."

"I didn't come," Noah corrected him. "I erupted. Pretty sure I felt it in my pinkie toes."

"Same here. I must have blown my wad halfway up your intestines. Fuck, you are so tight, Noah."

"You're telling me. I took your whole cock in my ass, man. I've gained a whole new level of respect for you after this. I don't know how you swallow my cock in your ass so easily as it's way thicker."

Josh took Noah's hand, laced his fingers through Noah's and kissed it. "I love being fucked by you. Your cock is perfect for me. When you're inside me all the way, I feel so full, it's unbelievable. And that spot I found at the end? You hit that every single time because of the curve of your dick. It's why I come when you fuck me without even touching myself. And by the way, you came first."

Noah smiled at the absurdity of the conversation. Who would have thought a year ago he'd be naked on a couch with his best friend, covered in cum and sweat, with jizz dripping out of his hole, talking about cocks and asses and getting fucked—and all that with another guy watching them. And yet, it felt wonderfully normal and somehow comforted him. While bottoming wasn't an experience he wanted to repeat any time soon—if only because his ass needed some recovery time from that pounding he took— he felt damn good for having shared this experience with Josh.

He turned back to Indy, whose tears hadn't stopped falling.

"He's still crying," Josh remarked. "Should we do something?"

"What, you want to invite him to join our naked and covered with cum cuddle party?"

Indy laughed through his tears, but the tears kept coming.

"Noah, we need to do something," Josh said.

"If you're proposing I pity-fuck him, you're overestimating my sexual prowess, because I'm pretty sure I won't be able to get it up for at least ten hours," Noah remarked.

Josh pinched his butt cheek, hard.

"Ow! What was that for? It's rather sensitive there, in case you forgot."

"Do something, Noah. He's still crying."

"Bring him here, then. I couldn't move if you paid me to. Make sure to ask if he wants to put boxers on or something."

"I can hear you, you know," Indy hiccupped, wiping the tears from his face with a gesture that made Noah's stomach flutter. What was it with this man that hit him so deep?

Josh sat up, straddling Noah. "Why are you crying?" he asked.

Indy let out a shuddering breath. "You were so beautiful together. I've never seen anything like it. Didn't realize sex could be like this."

Noah's heart clenched. He sounded so forlorn, so painfully honest. God, the depths of Indy's pain took his breath away. He deserved so much better. Maybe one day, Noah would show Indy how good sex could be. Until then, he'd be happy Indy had gotten at least a taste after Josh's blow job and through watching them fuck.

"Do you want to cuddle with us?" Josh asked in that sweet way that always made Noah shake his head in amazement. How Josh had managed to stay so kind and tender despite the brutal way he'd been treated all his life, he had no idea. Josh and Indy had that in common, that innate sweetness and tenderness.

"Is it okay? I don't want to infringe on a private moment between you two."

Noah grinned, his heart doing a happy dance. He'd never expected Indy to say yes. "You watched me get fucked for the first time. Pretty sure it doesn't get more private than that. If you want to get sandwiched between two naked guys covered in cum, you're more than welcome."

Indy got up from his chair. Josh stretched himself out at the back side of the couch, opening his arm for Indy to join him on top of Noah. Indy didn't even hesitate—and he didn't put on those boxers, Noah noted—but lowered himself on Noah's chest. Seconds later, Noah was holding two naked guys, his right arm around Josh and his left arm around Indy. It was a good thing their couch was wide and deep. And even better that it had a washable cover.

11

Indy had feared things would get awkward after what Noah had dubbed their covered-in-cum cuddle party, but much to his surprise the opposite was true; it had resulted in an easy familiarity, even more than before.

He'd been there two weeks now, his ribs less painful every day and his whole body recovering well. He had gained weight, gotten rid of the bags under his eyes, and lost the pale, sunken cheeks. His cast was about to come off, too.

At his request, Josh had bought some cheap-ass clothes for him, and for the first time in a year and a half he was dressed like a guy. It felt wicked good, even if he had to get used again to walking and behaving like a guy. Funny how deep his cover as a girl had been.

He hadn't set foot outside the house yet, too afraid to run into anyone who'd met him as a woman. It was ridiculous, since he'd only been in the area for four weeks before the robbery, but he didn't want to take any risks. Staying with Noah and Josh was too good to make dumb mistakes that could ruin it.

They hadn't asked. Two weeks in and they had never asked

Indy about his past, what he was running from, or anything even remotely personal. Oh, they had talked all right, about books—that would be with Josh who read more than Indy thought humanly possible—and movies, about Noah's job, and sports; he'd come out as a Patriots fan, much to the guys' delight. They'd watched their beloved Pats win twice in a row and had celebrated with virgin cocktails, since none of them drank alcohol., Noah had quit after his leg got blown off, too scared he'd become an alcoholic. And Josh, being Josh, had supported him by quitting as well—not that he'd ever been as much of a drinker as Noah, he'd confessed to Indy.

And, of course, Indy had heard them fuck. Every single day. Loudly. He could've used the earplugs, but he hadn't. Sick as it may be, there was something comforting about hearing the guys go at it every day.

They hadn't asked him if he wanted to join in their activities—and he hadn't approached them either. Fuck, that whole experience with Josh blowing him and then watching Josh fuck the shit out of Noah; Indy still hadn't figured out what it meant.

He'd never known it could be like that. The care Josh had taken in prepping Noah, the way Noah had fought against the pain, how they had risen together to climax—completely in sync—it had almost been too intimate to witness.

It had also reawakened him sexually, that much was clear. Every time he'd heard them fuck, he'd jacked off till he came. Even with his sore ribs and his uncoordinated left hand, he'd managed.

He could've asked Noah or Josh to help him. They would've said yes, but Indy didn't trust himself with them. He was already way more attached to them than he should've ever been. How the fuck would he ever walk away from them? He had to, because it was either that, or watch them get hurt the day Duncan found him. But fuck, it would break his heart to lose them. Both of them.

Josh was quickly becoming a close friend who was kind and encouraging. His one goal every day seemed to make Indy happy. Noah too, but since Noah worked, Josh spent a lot of time with Indy at home, and he'd shown he loved taking care of Indy. He had taken it upon himself to teach Indy how to cook, a skill Indy had never had a chance to develop. With sheer endless patience, Josh had shown him to make pasta with homemade tomato sauce—Noah's favorite—as well as a few other dishes. They watched movies together, talked about books, and there was not a better listener on the planet than Josh. Every word out of his mouth was gentle and affirming.

Then there was Noah. Indy was in such deep, deep shit with Noah. God, he loved his strength, his authoritative attitude, his protective demeanor toward himself and Josh; it was all drawing Indy in like a magnet. And that smile, that megawatt smile. Fuck, every time Noah smiled like that, Indy's heart stopped for a second. He was more than halfway infatuated with the man. And that was damn stupid, because aside from the fact that he was in no position to start a serious relationship, there was no way he was coming between Josh and Noah.

As much as both guys had said they were not together-together, Indy wasn't convinced. They seemed closer than ever after Noah had bottomed for Josh, though Indy wasn't sure if he had done it again. He never caught them kissing or doing anything else that would indicate a real relationship aside from the fucking, but there was this almost tangible, unbreakable bond between them. How could he compete with that? With Josh?

He couldn't. Noah would never pick him over Josh. The guy was so much better suited for Noah than Indy was. Sure, Josh had baggage, too, but not the criminal, murderous kind. Not the kind that could get you killed. Aside from that, Josh was closer to Noah's age, much more mature than Indy was, and so fucking cute and kind and perfect.

Even without the whole Duncan mess, Indy had little to offer. He had a high school diploma, and that was it. No degree, no work experience, no job prospects, no nothing. His mother was dead, he had no idea who his father was, and anything he'd inherited from either of them could only be seriously fucked up. And all that was aside from his sexual trauma, the massive scars on his back, and his general sense of being a hopeless fuck-up. No, he wasn't coming between Noah and Josh. They were much better off together.

Dressed in a T-shirt and flannel PJ bottoms, Indy made his way downstairs. Autumn had started, setting the trees in the yard on fire in an explosion of red, orange, and yellow, and bringing cold nights, but downstairs it was comfortably warm. Noah was reading the paper in his usual spot, but Josh was nowhere to be seen.

"Morning," Indy said, always shy at first when it was only him and Noah.

"Hey. How are you feeling?" Noah never failed to ask Indy this, and it wasn't just a polite question.

"Good. Haven't felt my ribs in two days, so I'm officially pain free."

Indy grabbed a bowl from the cabinet.

"Perfect. We'll cut off your cast today. I didn't think you'd want to do an official hospital visit for that, right?"

Indy shook his head, carefully cutting a banana on a cutting board with one hand and putting it in the bowl. He took yogurt from the fridge. "Not if I can avoid it."

"Well, you're lucky you have a highly skilled medical professional at your disposal, who's willing to do a house visit."

Indy grinned as he sprinkled crunchy granola on top of his yogurt. "Don't know about the highly skilled part, but at least he's free."

"That hurt." A smile tugged at the corners of Noah's mouth. "My price just went up."

"Double times nothing is still nothing, you do realize that?" Indy took a bite of his breakfast. He loved these verbal matches with Noah almost as much as not having to worry about what to eat for breakfast every day.

"Who says it was free to begin with? I only offered my skilled services, never said they were free."

"So what's your price?" Indy asked, expecting Noah to launch another joke.

"I want you for the entire day," Noah said.

Indy frowned, quickly chewing to empty his mouth. "What do you mean?"

Noah reached out and circled Indy's good wrist with his right hand, gently pulling until Indy was standing between his legs. "It's my day off, and Josh has some special therapy session, so he's gone all day. I want to spend the entire day with you, and you have to do exactly what I tell you."

Indy's stomach soured instantly. No way. "I can't."

"Which part?" Noah asked calmly.

"I won't let you tell me what to do for an entire day. I can't."

"Why not?"

Indy swallowed back bile as he put his spoon down, his appetite completely gone. Fuck, he shouldn't have to explain this. Noah was observant enough to know why there was no way in hell Indy was relinquishing control of his life. Not even for a day. But how did he clarify without setting Noah off? He didn't want to arouse his anger.

"Do you trust me, Indy?" Noah asked, his eyes drilling deep into Indy's.

Indy bit his lip, cast his eyes down. "It's not about trust."

"Of course it is. If you trust me enough to know that I wouldn't tell you to do anything you wouldn't like, you would have no trouble letting me boss you around for a day."

When he put it like that...Indy did trust Noah. Completely. He hadn't told him anything about his past or what he was running from, but that had more to do with anxiety over how he'd respond and wanting to protect him than with fear of Noah ratting him out. Noah would never do that. The man had already seen so much of him, and he had never crossed Indy's boundaries, not once. But it was too much to ask. He couldn't. How could he tell Noah without hurting him, making him angry, or worse, disappointing him? He wanted Noah to like him. Even if Noah would never love him, not like that, he still wanted Noah to like him.

Noah put his thumb on Indy's mouth, and Indy jumped in surprise. "Stop chewing that beautiful bottom lip," Noah said.

Indy's teeth let go without hesitation, and Noah brushed his thumb over the tender spot. Indy's breath caught. Without thinking, he flicked the tip of his tongue out and licked Noah's thumb. When he lifted his eyes, he found

Noah's gaze focused on him, causing his stomach to swirl. The man was strong, powerful, and fucking gorgeous, dwarfing Indy's slender frame even when sitting.

Noah gently pushed his thumb against Indy's lips, and he opened automatically, letting Noah in. Wasn't that what they had been doing the whole time: Noah gently pushing and Indy opening up without even realizing? Fuck, the man was good.

His tongue found Noah's thumb and licked it, then tasted and sucked. Noah's green eyes darkened and his jaw tightened. Indy sucked harder, pulling the thick digit all the way into his mouth, and Noah let out a soft moan. It exhilarated Indy, this effect he had on Noah. The fact that he could make this big man react with little things like sucking on his fingers; it was a power that made him feel more alive than he had ever felt before. It also confused the shit out of him. Why the hell would Noah want him?

"Indy..." Noah said, dark and low, as much a warning as a plea.

Noah wanted him. Indy couldn't for the life of him understand why, but he couldn't deny it. Not when Noah responded this strongly to such a simple gesture as Indy sucking on his thumb. If Indy wanted to rebuild a life, he had to start with trusting people. And who better to trust than this incredible man, who had shown already in so many ways he was worthy of that trust?

Indy let Noah's thumb plop out of his mouth, kissed it one last time for good measure. "Okay."

"Do you promise to do anything and everything I tell you?"

Indy's teeth went for his bottom lip again, but he realized it in time and held back. He swallowed, nodded.

Noah's face broke in a smile. "Thank you."

"I'm scared," Indy added. Did Noah realize how much this cost him?

"I know. I'll do right by you."

Without warning, Noah put his strong hands under Indy's armpits and lifted him up on his lap, making Indy straddle him.

"Let's start with a nice hug," Noah said, pulling Indy against his broad chest and circling those killer arms around him.

Indy should have been startled, felt threatened because of the unexpected move and the proximity to Noah, but a deep contentment warmed his heart. He was exactly where he wanted to be. So he put his head on Noah's shoulder, wrapped his good arm around the thick neck and leaned in with a deep sigh.

God, Noah smelled so good, an intoxicating mix of his sweat with faint traces of his body wash and his cologne. All male, all Noah, and so damn addictive. Yup, Indy had gotten to the stage where sweat smelled good. Whatever. He breathed in deeply. How safe he felt in this spot, how protected.

"I love how strong and big you are," Indy blurted out. He froze. Fuck, would that be okay to say to Noah? He was flying blind here, had no idea of the rules of this thing with Noah.

"I love your slender body," Noah replied, using those strong hands to grab Indy's ass and scoot it farther forward so their groins were closer together. "Gotta admit it makes me feel like a perv sometimes, because you look so young and innocent, but fuck, you turn me on."

Indy wanted to contradict him, point out that he was anything but innocent and hadn't been for a long time, but he didn't want to break the mood. Noah's words made him all warm inside.

Noah's hand traveled to his head, wrapping a long curl around his finger. "I love your soft curls..." The hand migrated to Indy's cheek. "And your round face with that cute button nose and those chocolate-brown eyes that betray everything you're thinking and feeling." His index finger brushed Indy's lips. "I love your big mouth with those soft, plump lips. Josh told me you can kiss like it's nobody's business. And after you sucked on my thumb, I can't wait to feel your wet tongue and mouth on my cock."

Indy could picture it, his mouth wrapped around Noah's fat cock, licking and sucking him. He didn't mind sucking cock, had liked it before he'd become Duncan's. In the beginning he'd gagged nonstop, even with Duncan's small dick. The guy rammed it in deep, had told Indy he'd better learn how to relax his throat. So he had learned, but the joy of sucking dick had been gone. Plus, personal hygiene hadn't been high on Duncan's list of priorities, and that included condoms. Indy had suffered more than one STD because Duncan had fucked everything with a hole, male and female. He was clean now—and he was damn well going to stay that way.

But Noah would be different. Noah would never hurt him like that, physically or mentally. And after having seen Noah's cock, Indy's mouth watered at the thought of tasting him, pleasuring him. Giving head could be good, with the right man. Josh clearly liked it, had taken such pleasure in sucking Indy off. And damn, it had felt amazing, that warm, wet mouth wrapped around his dick. Fuck, he'd kill to have him do that again. Well, figuratively speaking.

Noah tapped against Indy's teeth, bringing him back to

the present. "I'm completely in love with the little gap between your front teeth."

Indy sighed, melting against Noah as his insides pooled with heat and his cock grew hard. Noah's hand dropped to his neck, then continued to his arm. "I love your body... It's small, yet strong at the same time. I love knowing that you could put me on my back on the floor anytime I crossed a line you didn't want me to."

Indy chuckled. He froze as Noah's hand brushed his back, even though there was cotton fabric between his hand and the scars. "I love knowing how strong you are on the inside. You're a survivor, like me. Total turn on."

Indy let out a breath, shivered ever so slightly. Noah continued his journey of Indy's body, dropping his right hand to Indy's ass and squeezing gently. "Your ass... It's worthy of entire love songs and poetry. Fuck, it's surprisingly round and full considering the rest of your body, and it makes me want to... Well, not sure if you want to know all the details."

A sound rumbled in Indy's chest. He was purring, going all mellow and squishy inside with Noah's words. He cleared his throat. "I do. Want to know the details, I mean."

Noah's chuckle reverberated through his body. "You like knowing what you do to me, huh? All right, don't say I didn't warn you."

Noah's other hand joined in as they slipped under Indy's PJ bottoms and squeezed both cheeks firmly with his strong hands. Indy's cock jumped up in attention and his breath hitched. Noah waited a beat, but Indy pushed out a shaky breath. It was pleasure flooding his system, not fear.

"Your ass, fuck, it makes me want to eat you out—which, by the way, is something I've never done before, just so you know. I want to worship your bottom, then fuck it long and deep until we're both too tired to do anything but sleep. And then I want to wake up and do it all over again." Noah brushed his thumb over Indy's hole, causing him to tremble. "I know you're not ready, and I respect that, but I can't wait for the day that you are. I'll make it good, Indy, I promise."

Noah's right hand moved to the front, wriggling in between their bodies to find Indy's hard cock. He wrapped his rough hand around it, giving it a gentle tug that Indy felt all the way to his toes. "Your cock is gorgeous and perfect. I've gotten quite good at blow jobs, you know. Josh taught me well. I saw how much pleasure he gave you, and I can't wait to do the same for you."

The thought of being fucked again, it made him sick to his stomach, despite Noah's sexy words. His body loved Noah's touch and the images he inspired, but his mind was all but panicking. Bottoming hurt and not in a good way. And Noah was big, way bigger than Duncan. Taking him in had to hurt twice as much. Sure, Josh did it all the time, but he was a good ten inches taller than Indy. Plus, he was used to it. What if he never wanted to bottom again? Would Noah still want him?

"Would you ..." Indy cleared his throat again, his voice hoarse. "W-would you let me fuck you?"

Noah withdrew his hands from Indy's PJ bottoms, leaving his skin tingling. He grabbed Indy's neck and tugged him backward until their faces were inches away, their eyes meeting. Indy fought the urge to look down. What if Noah turned him down? Surely him topping Noah was ridiculous.

"Would I let you...Fuck, yeah. If you asked me, I would drop my boxers and spread my legs for you right now. Just say the word."

Indy swallowed at the truth in Noah's eyes. "Why?" he whispered.

"Why, because you think I'm too dominant to bottom, or why because you're convinced you couldn't bring me pleasure?" As usual, Noah cut to the core of Indy's issues.

"Both." Indy turned down his eyes.

Noah pulled Indy's head back against his chest, maybe understanding that this was scary and vulnerable and that it was way easier to talk when they weren't facing each other.

"Because of the way Josh and I started fucking, I don't have much experience being the bottom guy. Hell, you've seen my experience because you were there."

"You haven't...since?" Indy dared to ask the question that had been plaguing him. He'd heard Noah and Josh but hadn't been able to determine who was doing what.

"No. I've offered, but Josh didn't want to. He said as much as he loved it, he loves being a bottom more. I'll admit I'm way more comfortable being top with him, so I was more than okay with it. But with you it's different. If the only way I can have you is by bottoming, then I'll spread my legs for you anytime. My ass is yours. My whole body is yours."

Yours. Mine. Noah had no idea what these words he used so easily did to Indy. The idea that Noah offered himself like that, Indy couldn't wrap his mind around it. What self-respecting man as big and strong as Noah would volunteer to bottom for a boy like him? Noah had called Indy his, even though they hadn't done anything other than cuddle. How could he ever satisfy a man like that?

You can't. He wants your ass, that's it.

"You don't think I'm too small?" he asked in a timid voice.

Noah's answer was swift and definitive. "Fuck, no. I don't know if it's because I've never bottomed or because I'm unusually tight or something, but taking Josh in wasn't easy for me. Even with the prep we did, it hurt for a long time before we got to the good parts. So frankly, I'm relieved you're not that big. Seems to me you'll be able to hit that sweet spot perfectly and make me feel nice and full. Plus, Josh said my ass felt incredibly tight, so you've got that to look forward to."

Indy snorted as the humor of the situation hit him. He tried to hold it in, but a loud chortle erupted, shaking his body.

"Are you laughing at me?"

Was that mock offense in Noah's voice? Indy let go of Noah's neck, leaned back a little so he could see his face, make sure he wasn't offended for real. The sparkling green eyes assured him Noah wasn't mad in the least.

"Dude, you sounded like a commercial praising your own ass. It was fucking hilarious."

"Well, I had to make sure you knew the unique selling points of my sweet ass."

Indy laughed. "Oh, trust me, I'm convinced."

Noah's eyes sobered. "Don't interpret this as me putting pressure on you, because I'm not."

"I know," Indy said, dropping a quick kiss on Noah's lips. He caught himself right after. "Is that okay?" he asked.

Noah's face softened. "Always. Indy, you can touch me anywhere, anytime. Your touch makes me happy."

"I don't wanna be a cocktease."

Noah cupped Indy's chin in his hand, made him face his kind eyes. "You're not, and I would never think of you that way."

Indy nodded, smiled at Noah's sweet affirmation.

"Now, my first order for today: I'll cut off your cast in a

minute. What's the first thing you want to do now that your wrist is healed?"

An hour later, Noah parked in front of a nondescript building a short drive from his house. 'Adirondack Brazilian Jiujitsu,' the black and red sign read.

"This is it," Indy said. He tightened the brown belt on his combo of white cotton pants and a thick, white cotton jacket —it was called a gi, he had explained to Noah. With a careful gesture he tied his curls back and wrapped an elastic band around them, securing them in a ponytail. It made him look even younger, Noah noted with a soft feeling in his belly.

"You ready?" Noah asked. He'd secured Indy's still-tender wrist in a tight brace to protect it from too much impact. He still wasn't completely on board with the plan, but he understood how much Indy had missed this.

"Can't wait."

When they entered the building, a soft buzzer signaled their presence. They were barely inside when a tall, thirty-something guy appeared. Like Indy, he was dressed in a white gi, though his had a black belt.

Indy bowed. "Professor Kent," he said, then extended his hand. "I'm Indy Baldwin." His drawl was back, Noah noted, even though he hadn't dressed as a woman.

"Blake Kent, good to meet you. You said on the phone you know Matt Fox?"

"He's my professor," Indy said, handing Kent a some-what crumpled and stained letter he'd been holding the whole time. Noah wondered what the letter said. Indy had only explained it gave him the opportunity to walk into any jiujitsu school in the country and schedule a lesson or practice session.

Kent unfolded the letter and read it. His eyes lifted to Indy, studying him for a few seconds. Noah's body tensed. This guy had better be nice.

"You come highly recommended. Fox is a big name, so his praise means a lot. Have you trained recently?"

"I broke my right wrist, the cast came off today—hence the brace. So I've done little grappling, but I've stayed in shape."

Kent nodded. "Okay, then. I have an hour and a half, so let's make it count. Follow me."

He led them into a brightly lit room with wooden benches on opposite sides of a square, thick blue mat. A red padded wall closed off the third side.

"Your friend can wait in my office or watch, whichever you prefer," Kent said.

"I'll watch," Noah said.

Kent focused cool blue eyes on him. "His choice," he said, jerking his chin toward Indy.

"He can watch," Indy declared, his voice confident.

Noah lowered himself on one of the benches as Kent walked onto the mat and took a stance, feet planted slightly apart, his back to the padded wall.

Indy kicked off his flip-flops and bowed before he stepped on the mat. He took position across from Kent.

"Twenty jumping jacks, count them out," Kent ordered and Indy started jumping, his voice announcing the count loud and clear. They continued warming up with lunges, squats, and more. When Kent announced push-ups, Noah winced. He wasn't sure Indy's wrist was ready for that kind of pressure yet, but the boy dropped down immediately and

gave the twenty requested push-ups, his muscles quivering
with the exertion.

"We'll start with you escaping from several positions, so
I can get an idea of your skill level."

During the next fifteen minutes, they went through a
complex series of exercises, all designed to have Indy try to
escape from various positions and holds. Noah watched in
rapt attention as Indy managed to break free again
and again.

"You're good," Kent commented when Indy had once
again broken his hold, a ghost of a smile playing on his lips.
"You've learned to take advantage of your size and speed."

"Thank you, professor," Indy said, beaming.

"Let's see if you can take me down in a grapple. Stay
within the circle." He pointed to the white circle in the
center of the mat.

Indy nodded and positioned himself in the center of the
circle and dropped low on his heels, one foot diagonally
planted behind the other, his hands raised to block his face.
Kent mirrored his position across from him. Noah leaned
forward as the two started an intricate dance of reach and
feign, of grab and duck and trying to tackle legs and feet.
Indy was fast, Noah noted with pride, managing to stay on
his feet despite several attempts to drag him down.

Finally, Kent managed to get a strong hold on Indy's left
arm and he brought him down hard. Indy went with the
downward move, his arms and legs coming up in defense as
he rolled. Kent dove on top of him, but Indy blocked and
rolled and pushed himself off, at one point even managing
to flip himself backward to keep Kent off of him. When he
attempted another swift move to dive under the guy's arms,
Kent's elbow accidentally slammed into his nose, and Indy
went down with a loud yelp.

Noah jumped up. Indy was on the ground, rolled up in a ball, his hands cupping his nose. Blood rapidly soaked the sleeves of his gi. Noah was on the mat before Indy could say a word.

"Let me see," he ordered, cursing his prosthesis that prevented him from kneeling on the floor. Instead, he dropped on his ass as close to Indy as he could, then yanked at Indy's arms until he got the hint and slid closer to Noah.

Indy lowered his hands. Blood was pouring out of his nose. The sight made Noah's stomach clench, which was weird because he'd seen way more gruesome stuff than a bloody nose. He raised his hands to explore Indy's nose as tears dripped out of his eyes.

"It's not broken," Noah said.

Kent dropped a wet towel and an icepack next to Noah on the mat. "Here."

Noah acknowledged him with a nod, never taking his eyes off Indy. He wiped the blood off his face, then held the towel against his nose. "Sit for a bit. The bleeding will stop soon."

He pulled Indy between his legs, letting him rest with his back against Noah's chest. "You dizzy? Nauseous?"

"No. I'm fine," Indy mumbled through the towel, his body relaxing against Noah. Noah brushed a loose curl from Indy's face, then wiped a tear from his eye. Fuck, he hated seeing him like that. He'd ten times rather hurt himself than see Indy in pain.

"You a doctor?" Kent asked.

Noah looked up to find the man studying him with interest. "Physician assistant and before that, army medic."

Kent's gaze dropped to Noah's hands, protectively wrapped around Indy's slender frame. Noah caught the raised eyebrow and ignored it. Indy was his, and he wasn't inclined to explain anything to anybody. If that guy had a problem with it, he could go fuck himself.

"I think the bleeding has stopped," Indy mumbled a while later. He took the towel off. Noah made Indy turn around and face him. He gently cleaned the remnants of blood off Indy's face, who winced as Noah touched his nose.

"It has. Put the ice pack on." Noah wrapped the ice pack in a clean corner of the bloody towel and put it against Indy's nose. He raised his index finger. "Track my finger."

Indy obeyed silently. His eyes tracked well, Noah concluded with relief. He brushed Indy's cheek with a tender gesture, earning a soft smile from under the icepack.

"I take it we're done with the lesson?" Kent asked brusquely.

Indy's eyes sought Noah's. "Noah?" he asked.

"I was asking you, not your boyfriend," Kent said.

Noah's eyes narrowed. What the fuck was this guy's problem? Did he have a problem with gays or something?

Indy raised his chin defiantly. "It's Noah's decision," he said, his voice calm and clear.

Heat rushed through Noah. The sheer joy of Indy submitting to him, it was indescribable. Indy had promised to do whatever Noah told him, but the fact that he kept that promise under these circumstances, in front of this asshole, it meant more to Noah than he could ever put into words. Indy wanted to continue, if only to show his professor what he was made of. And as much as Noah wanted him out of danger, this was something he needed to let Indy do. This was where he needed to trust Indy that he knew what he was doing.

"You're good?" he asked Indy.

Indy nodded. "Yeah."

"Okay. I'll wait."

Indy's face lit up, and Noah couldn't resist a quick kiss on his soft curls. Indy scrambled up. For a second Noah sat worried about how undignified it was going to look to get up, but then Indy extended his left hand, braced his body, and allowed Noah to pull himself up. Noah closed his eyes for a second, fighting against the urge to lift Indy up and kiss him silly for the simple gesture that helped him maintain his dignity.

"Thank you," he said.

Indy's face radiated with the sweetest smile, which did not help Noah's fight against his dark urges at all. With effort, he made his way back to the wooden bench.

"You'd better tell your boyfriend to stay off my mat, or he can wait somewhere else."

Noah whipped around when he caught Kent's words. Indy didn't even flinch with the much taller guy inches away from him.

"You make me bleed again, and I fucking promise you: my boyfriend on your mat will be the least of your worries...Professor."

If Noah thought it was a rush to hear Indy submit to him, it was nothing compared to him claiming Noah as his boyfriend, loud and clear. The way Indy stood there, ramrod straight, his chin lifted to meet Kent head-on, it was an incredible sight.

"You've got balls, kid." There was grudging admiration in Kent's voice.

"So I've been told. We good?"

Kent smiled tightly. "We're good."

They continued grappling after Kent got Indy a new gi jacket, Noah never taking his eyes off them. Kent was good, obviously, but Indy fought hard and never gave up, not even when Kent had him pinned to the mat. Kent gave instructions in between, pointing out moves and tricks to Indy, who was focused and seemed to soak every word up. When they were done, Indy's curls lay plastered against his head and his face was dripping with sweat. He bowed to Kent and stepped off the mat.

They walked to the car silently and didn't talk until they were almost home. Noah wasn't sure what was going through Indy's mind, but his closed-off face told him Indy needed some time to think.

"Thank you for letting me stay," Indy finally said.

"Thank you for making it my call."

Noah turned into the driveway, opened the garage door.

"I need a shower," Indy said, then caught himself. "Is it okay if I take a shower?" he rephrased.

Noah smiled as he shut off the engine. "Care for some company?"

12

---

hy the fuck did I say yes?

Indy's stomach sank as he walked up the stairs and into his room. Noah had blindsided him with that question, and Indy had found himself saying yes without realizing it. Noah's care for him combined with his stubborn indifference toward Professor Kent's attitude, had made Indy melt on the inside. Kent had obviously had some kind of issue with Noah, maybe because he disliked gays or whatever. Noah hadn't given a shit and had claimed Indy. Indy had been so grateful that he'd wanted to say yes to everything Noah asked of him. Including this asinine idea of showering together.

Noah had seen his back, but this was different, way more intimate. In the shower, Noah would see everything up close and personal: every scar, every imperfection, everything that Indy hated about his body, including his small dick. Which, of course, would appear even smaller flaccid.

Plus, showering was inviting more, wasn't it? Kissing, groping, forcing him to do a blow job, bending him over to...

No, Noah wouldn't do that. Would he? Fuck. He was so fucked.

"Change your mind?"

Indy swiveled around. Noah was standing in the door, leaning on his crutches, his prosthetic leg off and buck naked. God, he was magnificent. Breathtaking. So fucking beautiful. The powerful muscles in his chest and arms rippled as he adjusted his stance. Indy had never realized how sexy arms could be, but Noah's biceps made his legs turn into jelly. How could Indy say no? How could he say yes? It was too much.

"I'm scared," he whispered.

"There's nothing to fear, baby. I won't ever hurt you."

Baby. It was the first time Noah had called him that. Indy's heart swelled. Could he trust Noah in this? Maybe he should take a page from his and Josh's book, bring things out in the open.

"What do you expect of me?" he asked, his heart beating fast and his eyes downcast.

Noah stepped close, his finger lifting Indy's chin to face him. "Nothing. No expectations. Anything you want or don't want is fine."

Indy exhaled. Noah meant it. He hadn't been lying: Indy could trust him. He could do this. He wanted to do this.

"Okay."

He followed Noah into his bedroom where Noah disappeared into the master bathroom and turned on the shower. Indy undressed, laying his blood-stained gi, shirt, and boxers on the king-size bed. He shivered with tension, his teeth chattering.

Noah had put his crutches against the wall and was already in the huge shower, holding his head back to let the water fall over his head. The shower had hand rails on all sides, allowing Noah to lean on them for balance. Indy opened the sliding door and stepped in, training his eyes on the floor.

"This is new for me as well, you know. I've never showered with Josh. Seen him shower, of course, and he's helped me a few times when my leg hurt, but never like this," Noah said softly.

Indy bit his lip. Maybe this was as scary and vulnerable for Noah as it was for him. Noah couldn't feel all that comfortable with showing his scars to someone else. His were as bad as Indy's, and he always kept them hidden, except from Josh, but he'd admitted he never even showered with Josh. Was he equally afraid of being rejected? The thought that this big, wicked strong man feared anything was almost incomprehensible.

Indy's eyes traveled up and found those angry scars on Noah's legs. He'd shown him once that his wounds didn't make a lick of difference to him, but maybe he should do it again? Show him how sexy he was? He'd love to gift Noah that, at least. Should he ask permission? No. Noah had said his body was Indy's, that Indy could touch him anywhere, anytime.

He dropped to his knees on the wet tiles and brought his lips to Noah's left ankle, kissing it. Noah let out a gasp and Indy looked up to check it was okay. Noah looked down with so much gratitude and affection that Indy refocused on what he was doing. He followed the trail of the scars with kisses, all the way from Noah's left ankle up to his thigh. The scars were rough under his lips. Fuck, Noah must have been in excruciating pain for weeks, months even. No wonder he'd needed Josh to bring him relief.

He reached out a tentative finger to the stump, brushing the red marks on the bottom. He wanted to make Noah feel better, to ease the pain. His mouth went to the stump, and he dropped kisses there, too. Noah's knuckles turned white in a brutal grip on the handrail as Indy was caressing and showering his stump with love.

Indy leaned back on his knees and looked up, which brought him face-to-face with Noah's thick cock. It was halfway hard, a powerful sight that made Indy's belly quiver. He was uncut, an unfamiliar sight for Indy.

He wanted to touch it. Feel what it felt like in his hand. His mouth. On his tongue. Could he? Should he? Was he ready for this?

Pushing down all logical objections, Indy reached out and stroked the shaft in front of him with one finger. It jumped up, growing harder.

Indy smiled. He caressed it again, dragging his nail all the way from the base down to the crown. It responded with a quiver, stretching and filling even further. The head now peeked out and Indy brought his mouth close, took an experimental lick with the tip of his tongue.

"Holy fuck," Noah exploded, grabbing the other handrail.

Indy looked up with innocent eyes. "You like?" he asked.

Noah's jaw was tight. "Fuck, yeah. Anything you're comfortable with, baby."

Baby. There was that word again. It made Indy feel so wanted, so safe and protected. He licked again, lapping Noah's crown with a wet tongue.

He reached out with his hand and circled the base of Noah's cock. It was so thick and his hands were so small, he couldn't even circle it completely. He took Noah's right ball in his other hand, rolled it, squeezed it softly before doing the same with his left testicle. They were so full and big. Beautiful. Everything on this man was beautiful.

How would it feel to have Noah fuck him, to have that thick cock inside him? He bit his lip. What did it say about him that after all he'd endured, he still thought of himself as a bottom? When he looked at Noah, he imagined himself taking, not giving.

Every now and then when Duncan had been generous and patient enough to bother with prep and lube, Indy had gotten a taste of how good bottoming could be. There was something so fulfilling, literally, in being filled with dick. He could only imagine how much better it would be with someone who respected him, who would treat him as an equal, even when fucking the shit out of him. Someone like Noah.

And Noah was way bigger and thicker than Duncan, so he'd be so completely full with cock. The idea made him hard as fuck, even as his stomach churned at the same time. Fear and arousal battled inside him, and Indy had no idea which would win.

"You okay?" Noah asked between clenched teeth.

Indy got up from his knees, letting his body slide up against Noah's until he could nestle his head against that broad chest, wrapping both his arms around Noah's waist. Noah's hard cock was poking against his stomach, a wonderful feeling.

"I was imagining what it would feel like to have your cock inside of me," he said, opting for honesty.

Noah's right arm came around him, strong and tight. His mouth brushed Indy's ear, as the hot water rained down on their naked bodies.

"And? How did you imagine it would feel?" Noah's voice was raw.

"So full. You'd fuck the living daylights out of me with your thick cock. My mind says you won't hurt me and that it would feel so good, that you would make it good for me. But at the same time I'm so scared, and I'm not sure I'll ever be ready."

A violent tremble racked Noah's body, but otherwise he remained still. The man had promised he wouldn't do anything Indy didn't want, even if Indy was being a cock-tease. He was proving he had a tight rein on his want and temper. Indy's shoulders relaxed.

"Fuck, you turn me on, baby. I can't wait to fill that sweet, round ass of yours with my cock. But I'll wait till you're ready. Even if it takes weeks or months, I'll wait. I get that you're scared, and we won't do anything you don't want, I promise. You can trust me, baby."

The words reached deep inside Indy, turning him on and comforting him at the same time. It was a gift Noah had, knowing what to say. He believed him, but why the fuck would Noah be willing to wait for him? He could have Josh at any time and there would be dozens of others available if he tried. Shit, men and women would line up for him. So why did he want Indy? It didn't make sense. He couldn't deny Noah's reactions, though. The man was aroused by Indy, for whatever reason. Maybe, for now, that had to be enough.

They stood like that for minutes, the warm water cascading down on their entwined bodies. Indy relaxed in Noah's embrace, his heart and mind secure with Noah's honor and control.

"Can I wash you?" Indy asked.

"Please." Noah's voice was still hoarse.

Indy stepped back and grabbed a washcloth and some Axe shower gel, squeezing a healthy amount on the cloth. He reached for Noah's right arm and washed him from his fingers up to his shoulder, turning the arm to get the inside. He had to stretch out to reach all of him.

He did the other arm after Noah had transferred his weight to the other handrail. His chest was next, then his stomach, the tight muscles rippling under Indy's care. He ducked behind Noah to wash his back, daringly dropping his hand to wash Noah's butt.

He hesitated when he came to Noah's crack, but the guy made it easy for him by spreading his legs and giving Indy access. Washing another man's crack and hole should weird him out, but it wasn't. Indy loved sharing this intimacy with Noah, taking care of him.

He dropped to his knees again to wash Noah's legs, first the whole leg and then the stump. All that was left was his dick, which was still rock hard.

"Indy, it's—"

"I'll do it," Indy interrupted him. He washed Noah's balls, taking care to rinse them off well, then continued to soap his member clean. When it was soap-free, he kissed it, because he wanted to.

Indy stood when he was done, proud and happy with what he had done for Noah. He looked up and met Noah's eyes. They shone with such fierce want it made Indy's stomach swirl. Fuck, Noah really wanted him.

"Kiss me," he told Noah.

NOAH WANTED to lift Indy so they'd be on equal heights, but he didn't dare it on the slippery shower tiles without his prosthesis. He shut the water off, the shower cabin still steamy enough to keep them warm. Then he lowered himself to the floor, taking Indy with him, raising him up by his hips once Noah sat down, and placing him on his lap. It brought Noah's cock dangerously close to Indy's ass. Would it be too much for him? Indy wrapped his arms around Noah's neck and pulled him in, fusing their mouths together.

Noah moaned when their tongues met. Finally. It felt like he had waited forever for this. Indy tasted so sweet, like a fresh meal after a lifetime of ready-to-eat shit. He could taste traces of the caramel hard candy Indy seemed addicted to.

Fuck, the man could kiss. He was all in, his mouth exploring and sucking and licking and biting. Noah dug his fingers into Indy's ass to pull him even closer. He wanted nothing between them, not even air.

He kept one hand on Indy's ass, the other in his curls, making sure to never put pressure on him. His cock was throbbing with need, but he ignored it. He'd deal with it later. Right now, he wanted to drown in Indy's mouth, feast on his lips, and nothing else. It was enough.

They kissed for a long time, their bodies growing cold on the outside, though Noah's blood was pumping and cooking on the inside. His cock was unrelenting, bordering on painful after being denied release for so long. He noted with deep satisfaction that Indy was rock hard, his dick prodding against Noah's stomach.

"Fuck, Josh was so right. You kiss like it's the last thing you'll ever get to do," he whispered, tearing his mouth away. Indy's eyes stared at him dreamily, his cheeks rosy and his lips swollen and red. Noah lifted his hand from Indy's hair and brushed his cheeks.

"Can I help you come?" he asked.

Indy stilled. Noah waited patiently, not wanting to put any pressure on him.

"How?" Indy asked.

"I could jerk us off together."

Indy's teeth went in his bottom lip again. "Okay."

Noah smiled. He brought his mouth back to Indy's, diving in for another wet and erotic kiss. Once Indy relaxed into the kiss, he wriggled his hand between their bodies, bringing their cocks together. There was not enough space to maneuver, so he broke off their kiss with some regret. If he could do nothing else but kiss him for the rest of his life, he'd die a happy man, even if his balls turned fucking blue.

"Move back a little," he told Indy, who obediently scooted back a couple of inches, staying on Noah's lap. Indy leaned back, putting his hands on the tile floor. It gave Noah the room he needed to mesh both their cocks together in his hand. There was something sweet about seeing Indy's slender dick next to his thick shaft, so indicative of their differences in build and size.

Noah slipped his thumb over the crown of his own cock, which was dripping with precum. He did the same with Indy's dick, mingling their fluids together in a tantalizing move that made them both shiver.

"You like my hand on your cock?" Noah asked softly.

Indy nodded, his eyes glued to the mesmerizing view of their two members meshed together in Noah's hand. Noah swiped their cocks again, looking for more lubrication. He repeated the move a few times until he was satisfied he had enough lube to slick both their cocks.

Slowly he shafted their dicks downward, rubbing them closely together. It felt unbelievably good, tight and slippery in his hand. He did it again, watching Indy's face for any signs he wasn't okay anymore. But Indy's eyes never left their groins, his cheeks reddening with arousal.

"Your hand is so big and strong," Indy whispered.

Noah swallowed. Fuck, he had to fight to keep himself in check. He wanted nothing more than to flip Indy over and bury his cock deep into that sweet ass. The thought alone made him shiver, and he increased the pressure on their dicks. His insides hummed, his nuts signaling it was time to get a fucking move on.

Sweat beaded on Noah's forehead as he jerked them off in earnest. Indy's mouth went slack, and he let his head hang back, his eyes closed.

"Ooooh," he moaned, shivering. "P-p-perfect, Noah. S-so good."

The sight of Indy losing himself to pleasure was intoxicating, maybe even more than the tight grip Noah had around their dicks. God, Indy was beautiful, his swollen lips mumbling soft encouragements.

Noah couldn't keep this up much longer. He hadn't come yet today, and his body was demanding release. His balls were so fucking full and tight, they were ready to explode by now.

"Indy," he started, then held back a deep moan. He was so close. Too close. "Fuck, I'm...I can't..."

Noah gave another frantic jerk and surrendered to the overwhelming need to come. He held on to their cocks as he spurted thick shots of cum all over Indy's chest and legs. Right after Noah had jacked the last cum out of his own dick, Indy came with a hoarse shout, releasing his jizz in Noah's hand.

"Fuck, that was intense," Noah said as soon as he could form words again. He watched as his cum dripped off Indy onto the floor. "I didn't mean to shoot all over you."

Indy grinned, his eyes still hazy. "You can't tell me you don't like seeing me covered in your cum," he said with a sly smile.

Noah laughed. "Fuck, baby, you're sexier than ever like that."

Indy dragged a finger through Noah's jizz, dropped it on the floor. "I thought the whole idea of a shower was to get clean. Now we have to start all over again."

"You're complaining?" Noah asked in feigned indignation.

Indy let out a carefree laugh that hit Noah hard. "Fuck, no." He slid farther forward and leaned in to kiss Noah. Without meaning to, Noah's cock slipped between Indy's legs and bumped against his hole. They both froze, their mouths an inch away from each other.

"I'm sorry," Noah muttered, "I didn't mean to ..."

"You know what would make me look even more sexy than having your cum all over my chest?" Indy whispered. He gyrated his hips, making Noah's dick slick against his entrance.

"What?"

"Having your cum drip out of my ass."

The visual made Noah's eyes roll back in his head. He was tempted to let Indy know what would happen if he kept teasing him like that until he saw the look of shock on Indy's face. Obviously, Indy's lack of filter had caused him to say something he regretted now. He must have realized the same thing that had flashed through Noah's mind. One thrust, and he'd be inside him.

"Noah, I'm sorry..." Indy stammered.

"You're right, you know," Noah said, kissing him. "That would look even better. Can't wait to see it, to feel my dick inside you. But Indy, until you ask me to fuck you, I won't. Not even if you tease me, tempt me, or shake your delicious butt right in my face. I will not touch you unless I have your permission. Until then, you can say or do anything, tease me as much as you want. I may have to excuse myself to jack off, but I will never break my promise to you."

INDY WAS quiet the rest of the day. Noah could've made full use of the fact he got to boss Indy around, but he didn't. He seemed to feel that their shower encounter had changed something in Indy. It had.

Indy had often gotten into trouble for his lack of filter. His mouth always seemed to speak faster than his brain could process potential problems. More than once he'd gotten the shit beaten out of him for saying what was on his mind. Duncan had smacked him around a few times, for sure. In the last year and a half he'd been with him, it had taken little to provoke Duncan, as coke and troubles with his crew had fueled his temper. Indy had learned to walk on eggshells and above all to be guarded, even if it was completely against his character.

Being with Noah and Josh had freed him from that caution. He heard himself react spontaneously and carefree, like he had when he'd been a kid. The stuff he'd said to Noah about sex and how he felt about him, it could have gotten him into all kinds of trouble with a less honorable and disciplined man. What guy would rein himself in when he was fooling around naked with a guy who talked about cum dripping out of his ass? Shit, he couldn't believe he'd said that.

He'd meant it, wholeheartedly. Fuck, it had been the image that had played in his mind when Noah confirmed how good Indy looked covered in cum. Indy had looked at Noah's cock, that delicious thick shaft, and had once again imagined it in his hole. The idea of Noah shooting his load up his ass had made him hard again, which was why he'd said it.

But fuck, he should have thought first. You couldn't say shit like that without people thinking you meant it as an invitation. Best case scenario, you were considered a damn cocktease and worst case scenario, well, he'd lived through that already, hadn't he?

He couldn't understand how so much had changed in such a short time. Only weeks ago he'd been living as a woman, focused on staying alive, and he had shrunk away from anybody touching him. Now he was living with two guys, and he craved touch, Noah's above all. It was as if his mind and body had been awakened, set free after a long imprisonment. He felt so alive with Noah, so fucking wanted and safe. And horny.

Holy fuck, he'd never been so horny in his life. He was hard half the day, just thinking about Noah or being in his presence. Those powerful muscles, that big, dominant body, the way he saw straight to Indy's soul—it all turned him on.

Yet he'd kept Noah at a distance until today, at least physically. Every time he was tempted to give in, to crawl on Noah's big body and give in to that maddening desire to be fucked by the beautiful man, he held back. Noah wanted him something fierce, Indy didn't doubt that anymore. And the man clearly didn't give a shit about the scars on his back.

But the scars on the inside, that was a different story. Once Noah found out how fucked up Indy was, the things he had done, what he was running from—there was no way he'd still love him.

Wait, love? Want. Noah wants you. He hasn't spoken of love, has he? You're delusional if you think this man could ever love a fuck-up like you.

Indy studied Noah, who was lying on the couch, engrossed in something he was watching on his iPad while Indy was pretending to read in one of the chairs. Did Noah love him?

The thought froze his veins. Nobody had ever loved him. That wasn't a whiny I-feel-so-sorry-for-myself assessment. It was the fucking truth. His mom had been too fucked up to be capable of love, a fact he'd known since he was young and had seen confirmed when she'd handed him over to Duncan.

And Duncan, that fucking piece of shit, had no idea what love was. Had he given Indy a sliver of warmth, of attention, of kindness, Indy would have done anything for him. Even after all the shit Duncan had put him through, he would have stayed had Duncan appreciated him even a tiny bit. But even that had been too much to ask. The guy had sold him out to the devil without a hint of remorse.

Nobody else had even come close to caring, not until he'd met Josh and Noah. He found it difficult to believe their kindness had no ulterior motive, that they weren't after anything else, wanted nothing back in return. But even though he still didn't understand, he realized it was true. Josh had selflessly given him a blow job, and Noah had jacked him off, not even attempting to fuck him. Indy had sat on his fucking lap, naked and talking dirty, and the guy had still not made a move.

Could someone with that much honor and discipline ever love a fucked-up, broken kid like Indy? No fucking way. Noah loved Josh and he might be a basket case, but they knew each other before Josh got messed up. There was no way someone as strong as Noah would ever understand how seriously fucked up Indy was, and how he made the choices he had.

No, if Noah loved him, or was starting to love him, it was because he didn't know any better. Once he discovered what Indy had done, who he truly was, that love would be gone in an instant. Fuck, nobody wanted to be with a son of a whore who'd turned into a whore himself. Because that's what he had been, Duncan's whore. Except he hadn't gotten the money that was paid for him—his mother had. No, Indy was fucked up beyond restoration, and nowhere near good enough for a man like Noah. Noah deserved better, so much better.

Which is why Indy couldn't let him come any closer. And he certainly couldn't let Noah fuck him, because he'd be so screwed after that. How could he ever walk away after sharing what was bound to be such an incredible experience? He couldn't, he wouldn't be able to.

One day, he'd have to. Someday, somehow, Duncan would find him, and Indy would have to disappear all over again. There was no way in hell he was getting Noah involved in this. If Duncan ever found him, he would take down anything and everyone near Indy. Every day he stayed with Noah and Josh, he was putting them in danger.

Soon. He'd have to leave soon. Oh, God. All he wanted was a little more time to feel seen, cared for. Loved.

"Indy?" Noah asked, yanking Indy from his thoughts. "You okay?"

Indy focused. Noah was looking at him with concern. "Yeah. What's next, boss?"

13

Noah's body was draped in a comfy chair in the doctor's lounge. He was bone-tired after a long and busy shift, rubbing his eyes furiously. Thank God he only had half an hour left. Kneading the sore muscles in his neck, he sighed. He was so tired of this. All of it. It wasn't just his stump—though that was still bothering him way more than he'd hoped—but the constant adrenaline that came with working in the ER. It had bugged him in the army, driving him to drink way more than he should have, and it took a toll on him here as well. Plus, the situation with Indy didn't help his mood, either.

Four weeks.

It had been over four fucking weeks.

He'd never been the most patient guy on the planet. He was a diagnose-it-and-fix-it guy who preferred to tackle problems head-on and kept pushing until he'd found a solution. But he was getting a crash course in patience now.

Four weeks, Indy had been staying with them. A full month and Noah still didn't know jack shit about him. To be more precise, he didn't know jack shit about Indy's background or what or whom he was hiding from.

He'd learned tons of other things, like Indy being passionate about football—he'd let loose a string of imaginative curses last Sunday when the ref had made a call against the Pats that had cost them the game. He was eager to learn how to cook, following Josh like a little puppy in the kitchen whenever Josh was fixing something. Noah had found out how disciplined Indy was. Once his cast was off, Indy had resumed a full workout regime including 10k runs and as many jiujitsu training sessions as he could fit in. Josh had driven him to the studio when Noah was at work since Indy had indicated he preferred not to drive himself. Noah had asked Josh how Kent had acted, but after the initial surprise that Indy had shown up with another guy, the man had been okay.

He'd discovered tons of small things, like that Indy was ticklish, hated broccoli, didn't drink coffee, and loved country music. But he had made no progress in getting Indy to trust him. He'd hoped that day of bossing him around had helped, but even after sharing that mind-blowing experience in the shower, Indy had stayed aloof.

Indy hadn't so much as kissed Noah again, though his eyes always followed him, studying him—and more than once Noah had found Indy looking at him with clear desire in his eyes. Something was keeping Indy back, but what was it?

Noah had done everything in his power to show him Indy could trust him, that he had a tight grip on his control. What the fuck did he want before deciding to trust and take the next step? He'd hoped that Indy would feel safe enough by now to share something, anything. Where he was from, for instance. Noah's money was still on Boston—Indy's accent was undeniable, and it was getting stronger by the day.

The door to the lounge burst open and Owens, his attending, dashed in. "Flint, incoming trauma. Shooting with multiple victims, including two cops."

Fuck. Excellent timing, as always.

"On my way."

The adrenaline blazed through him as he made his way through the hallways. In the distance, multiple ambulances wailed, rushing to deliver their loads at the hospital.

"Where do you want me?" he asked.

Owens, a blunt, but highly skilled ER doctor, pointed. "Trauma 2. You run the protocol. Winans will assist you."

"You want me to run the protocol?"

"That's what I said, isn't it? You've seen more trauma and gunshot wounds than all of us combined, Flint. You could do this in your sleep."

Noah nodded, squaring his shoulders. It felt damn good to be trusted like this, even if he had to take that arrogant shit Winans as an assistant. The guy was an intern, but he still thought he was way above Noah because Noah was 'only' a physician assistant. Luckily, Owens didn't care much for Winans either.

The doors to the ambulance bay opened, and EMTs wheeled the first stretcher in.

"GSW to the chest and abdomen," the EMT announced. A young guy thrashed around, restricted by the handcuffs that bound him to the stretcher.

"Trauma 1. I'll take this one, you take the next," Owens ordered Noah. "Have them come get me if you need help."

"They're right behind us. Police officer," the EMT

shouted over his shoulder, hurriedly wheeling the stretcher into Trauma 1.

"Okay guys, get ready," Noah said, stretching his neck and shoulders. Fuck, despite the adrenaline he was still dead tired. This had better go well. Especially with a cop. No room for errors there.

The doors slid open.

"GSW to the left shoulder. He keeps passing out. BP low, but steady," a female EMT called out.

Noah pointed. "Trauma 2. We're ready for him."

She wheeled him in, assisted by her partner. Noah and his team followed.

"On my count," Noah said, grabbing one corner of the sheet. His intern and two nurses grabbed the other corners. "One, two, three."

They transferred the man onto the bed. He was Latino, fit, late twenties.

"How are you doing there, Officer?" Noah asked, his hands immediately exploring the gunshot wound to the guy's shoulder. The man was pale. Sweaty, but awake. For now, at least. Figueras, his name tag said.

"Did someone call my wife?" the cop grunted, his voice barely audible.

Noah looked at Maddie, one of the nurses, for confirmation.

"I don't know. His partner came in with him," she said. "I'll ask him to step in for a minute."

"We'll get right on it," Noah said to Figueras, but the cop had passed out again.

"Linda, cut off his uniform so we can see what we're dealing with and run a trauma panel after that. Winans," he barked at his intern, "Get his vitals hooked up. I'm not liking his color, so get me some info."

The door opened behind Noah, but he didn't look up from his patient, studying him. They'd hooked up a large bore IV in the field, but he might need another one.

"Isn't that a nurse's job?" Winans objected.

Noah was so done with the kid's attitude. "Get out," he ordered without even looking at him.

"What?"

"I'm not gonna repeat myself."

"Listen, you're just a PA. You can't boss me around," Winans said with an arrogance that made Noah's blood boil. An asshole like him wouldn't have lasted a week in the sandpit, let alone in the CSH—the combat surgical hospital Noah had spent a lot of time in.

"I know you're some army veteran or something," Winans continued, "but that doesn't mean you can treat people like this. I'm a doctor, and I don't do nurses' work."

Noah's vision went red, but before he could do anything, Winans was taken by his coat lapels and half lifted off the floor.

"Listen, you arrogant little shit. That's my partner bleeding out on that table, and instead of doing your fucking job, you're complaining. And that army veteran you insulted is a decorated war hero who saved countless lives until he paid the price. Show him the fucking respect he deserves. He gave you an order, now get the fuck out of his trauma room."

Everyone watched in stunned silence as O'Connor— Noah had recognized his voice even before he had seen him —dressed down Winans. When O'Connor let go of his coat, Winans whimpered and ran out of the room.

O'Connor had looked Noah up, huh? How else would he have known all those details? Why would he have been so interested in knowing more about Noah? There could only be one reason. Josh.

Noah had done his own little digging on O'Connor, of course. Sergeant Ignatius Sean O'Connor had quite the career in the Marines until he'd received an honorable discharge after an incident that was kept under wraps. Not even his former CO had been able to get the records on that one—and Noah had damn well tried.

"Thanks, sergeant," Noah said, turning back to his patient. His hands checked the bullet wound, probing the entrance site for shrapnel. "Linda, can you hook up another large bore IV? We may need to get more fluids in."

"Pardon my language," O'Connor said.

"It's nothing we haven't heard before," Linda said with a sideways glance at Noah, while preparing the IV.

Noah shrugged. "The military isn't known for its delicate way with words. Turn him on his side. I need to see the exit wound."

Hands reached out and Figueras was lifted. Noah's fingers probed the exit wound on his back. It felt clean.

"His BP is dropping, but slowly. Pulse is thready," Maddie said.

"How is he?" O'Connor asked, his voice dripping with concern.

"He asked for his wife. Has she been informed?"

"Her escort is under way. She shouldn't drive."

Noah nodded in agreement. He studied his patient again. Something was off. "The wound looks like a through and through, but I don't like his vitals, and he's too pale for the amount of blood he lost. Are you sure he was shot only once?"

"No. We were ambushed and bullets were flying everywhere. It was like being down range."

"Did he lose a lot of blood before the medics got there?"

"No. I put pressure on the wound almost immediately."

Noah eyed O'Connor for a second, noticing a faint trace of blood on the man's bulging neck.

"Bring in the portable. I want a full set of scans: arms, chest, legs, everywhere," he ordered the nurses. "We're missing something."

He stepped back as Linda strode into the connecting trauma room to get the portable and rolled it in. He studied O'Connor. The slow trickle of blood on the neck didn't worry him, but O'Connor looked tense and pale. His uniform jacket was sieved with small holes.

"O'Connor," he said. "You got grazed in the neck. Anywhere else?"

O'Connor's mouth set. "I'm fine."

"I didn't ask if you were fine, I asked where else you got hit. Your uniform looks like a fucking target practice sheet."

Their eyes met, a wordless battle of two strong minds. Noah would win, he had no doubt, as he had never backed down when someone was hurt.

O'Connor finally surrendered, his jaw locked tight. "My chest and back. Probably fragments of concrete from the pavement when the bullets hit."

"Step out," Noah ordered.

"I'm not leaving my partner."

Noah raised his eyebrows. "That was an order, sergeant."

When he saw O'Connor's honest concern for his partner, he softened his tone. "You can't be in the room when they run scans, you know that. Radiation. Step outside with me."

They walked into the hallway, O'Connor moving with

care. Noah rubbed his leg, leaning against the faint yellow wall. Too many hours standing again. The stump was throbbing and burning like a motherfucker right now underneath the liner and prosthetic sock. Didn't matter, he had a job to do.

"What's Officer's Figueras's first name?"

"Manuel."

"You guys been partners long?"

"Little over a year."

O'Connor was not exactly a chatterbox, was he? Well, he was hurt, worried about his partner, and probably half in shock from the shooting. Noah would give him a pass this time.

"We're done," Linda announced, gesturing for Noah to step back in.

Noah moved close to O'Connor, deliberately getting in his face. "You can go back in, but you're parking your ass in a chair. I can appreciate that you're not leaving your partner. You're a tough S.O.B., and I respect that, but you're more hurt than you let on, and there will be no passing out in my trauma room. So hang in there, and I'll check you out when I'm done."

"Yes, sir," O'Connor answered without hesitation.

Noah smiled.

That smile was immediately wiped off his face when he walked back in and saw the scans. Well, fuck. At least his instincts had been spot-on.

"Page vascular, surgery, and call the OR. Tell them we're sending him up right now," he ordered, his face tight.

Shit, this was going to be close. He unhooked the man's monitors himself when Maddie and Linda didn't respond right away.

"You're supposed to wait for the surgery consult. As a PA you can't sign off on surgery," Linda said.

"We don't have time. A bullet fragment traveled down his bloodstream and has nicked an artery in his abdomen. He's bleeding out on the inside. He's going up, now!"

Linda and Maddie looked at each other, then apparently decided obeying would be the wisest course of action. Noah kicked the bed brakes loose and wheeled the guy out of the room. He stumbled when his prosthetic leg hit a chair, cursed as he managed to stay upright. Motherfucking leg.

He spotted an ER resident, Dave, in the hallway. He was a good guy, always willing to lend a hand.

"Dave, can you bring him up?" he called out, pointing to Figueras. "I have another patient." Dave nodded, came running, and Noah let go of the bed. Thank God he didn't have to do the run upstairs, because he wasn't sure his leg would have held him.

He half limped back into the trauma room, where O'Connor was still sitting in the chair, sweating profusely by now.

"Is he going to be okay?" O'Connor asked.

"I hope so. I think we caught it in time."

"You caught it in time," O'Connor said.

Noah held up his hands. "Don't go there. It's my job. Let's find you a bed so we can check you out. You're not looking so peachy, O'Connor."

"Connor. Call me Connor."

Noah nodded. He checked his watch. Damn. His shift had been over half an hour ago, and he wasn't anywhere near done. Josh had been wiped after his therapy session today. Noah had heard it in his voice when they'd spoken on the phone earlier. Josh needed his sleep, but he couldn't sleep until Noah got home.

Another reason why Noah resented this job. He needed something with more regular hours, so it would be easier on Josh.

"I gotta make a quick phone call," Noah said.

"I'm not going anywhere," Connor said, sprawled in the chair.

Noah stepped into the hallway, gestured a nurse to come over. "Can you get a fresh bed in here for Officer O'Connor and start a chart?"

She nodded. "Sure thing, Noah."

Noah sighed as he hobbled back into the trauma room. He debated doing the call in private, but where was the fun in that? Might as well get on O'Connor's case while he had the chance. He dug his phone out of his pocket, speed dialed Josh.

"Hi, Josh," he said, watching with satisfaction how O'Connor's head jerked up. He grinned.

On the other end of the line, Josh groaned. "Tell me this is not what I think it is."

"Sorry, babe." God, the look on O'Connor's face at that word! Fucking priceless. "I'm gonna be a while. I have a VIP patient."

"Who?"

"Your friend, O'Connor."

"Connor came in? Is he okay?"

Noah smiled at the concern in Josh's voice. This was getting better and better. "I don't know, haven't checked him out yet. You wanna come hold his hand when I do?"

"Fuck you," Josh growled. O'Connor seemed to second that exact same sentiment, considering the deadly scowl he aimed at Noah.

"Oh, count on it. Multiple times."

O'Connor's eyes narrowed as he undoubtedly guessed

what Noah was hinting at. Enough with the fun. Josh was exhausted, so Noah knew when to quit.

"It's gonna be a while, so you may want to consider not waiting up," Noah said softly, his voice serious and warm now.

Josh sighed. "I'm too afraid I'll have a nightmare again."

The solution was easy. "Ask Indy."

Silence.

"Josh?"

"Ask Indy to sleep with me?"

"Yes, with the emphasis on sleep. It'll be good for both of you. I gotta go."

He switched off his phone, put it back in his pocket. Two orderlies came with a fresh bed and Noah gestured. "Your ride, man."

O'Connor stared at him, his jaw clenched.

"Oh, I'm sorry, did you want to talk to my boyfriend, too?"

"You're a sick bastard, Flint." With effort, O'Connor raised his broad frame from the chair and made his way to the bed, lowering himself with care. He opened the buttons of his uniform, but Noah swatted his hands away.

"All part of the service here," he said. He removed O'Connor's uniform jacket, revealing his massive torso and back, covered in dozens of small wounds.

Noah whistled. "That does not look pretty, my man." He gently and swiftly probed the wounds. "They're all superficial, though. Looks like you may only need a few stitches, but they'll all need to be cleaned out. You got lots of dirt in there, and we don't want these to get infected."

"Send the intern," O'Connor said between clenched teeth. "Hell, let a nurse do it. Don't waste your time on me and go home."

Noah grabbed a few suture kits and a handful of irrigation kits and pulled up a stool, lowering himself carefully. Damn, his leg hurt. "That arrogant little shit is not going anywhere near you. Lay back, we're gonna be here a while."

He ripped open the first suture kit and spread out the contents while O'Connor leaned back against the bed. "So tell me, on a scale of one to ten, how hot do you think my boyfriend is?"

INDY HAD BARELY FALLEN asleep when he woke up again from Josh's phone ringing in the room next door. Sexy and I know it drifted through the walls, the ringtone for Noah calling. Indy checked the clock. Just after midnight. Poor Josh, having to wait for Noah to come off shift to get some sleep. And poor Noah, because Indy guessed he was calling to say he was going to be late. Again. Working in an ER sucked. Hard to go home when you were still treating patients.

He closed his eyes again, ready to go back to sleep, when Josh knocked on his door.

"Indy, you awake?"

"Yeah, come in," he said. He turned on his bedside lamp and shifted to his side to face Josh. Indy was still using Josh's shirt to sleep in, even though he had his own clothes. He loved the soft cotton and the fact it still smelled like Josh and Noah. Somehow, both their smells were on there, and he felt close to them wearing it.

Josh stepped in, wearing nothing but a pair of his standard-issue tight black boxer shorts that perfectly outlined his cock.

"What's up? Everything okay with Noah?" Indy asked.

"He's working late." Josh sat down on the bed, apparently not realizing or caring how the thin material stretched tight across his shaft. Indy blinked. Josh was hard. As in raging erection hard. What the hell? "Connor came in as a patient."

Josh was using the cop's first name. Interesting. "Is he okay?"

"Noah didn't say, merely asked me if I wanted to come in to hold his hand. Fucking asshole."

Indy suppressed a smile. "I'm sure he wouldn't have been joking if Connor had been badly hurt."

"That's what I figured." Josh sighed, rubbing his cock absentmindedly, sending a jolt through Indy's system.

"So, what I can do for you?" he asked, his voice raspy.

Josh sighed again, then fixed his bright blue eyes on Indy. "It's okay if you say no, but I'd really, really love for you to fuck me."

Indy stilled and swallowed thickly. Holy fuck. Josh had offered before, but Indy had interpreted that as a polite offer to make him feel better. Fuck, Josh had made it right after Indy had confessed his dick was too small. Indy had figured it was a heat of the moment thing, not a genuine offer. Could he accept this? Did he want to?

"Are you sure you want to do this?" he asked.

"Are you?"

All of Josh's usual shyness seemed gone as he stretched himself on the bed next to Indy, his mouth maybe an inch away. Indy shivered.

"Tell me, Indy," Josh whispered, his voice low and seductive, "Do you want me?" He traced the outline of Indy's lips with his tongue, his breath hot and sexual on Indy's mouth. "Don't you wanna know how your cock would feel inside another man's ass? It would feel so good for both of us, I promise."

He kissed him, the softest of kisses, all wet and warm. Liquid heat swirled in Indy's belly.

"I dunno," Indy stammered, licking his lips when Josh broke off the kiss. His eyes fell on Josh's mouth, that soft, sweet mouth that could make him melt with a single kiss. "What about Noah?"

"Fuck Noah."

"Well, yeah, you did," Indy whispered. "I watched, remember?"

"Oh, I remember very well. Fucking him was such a rush with you watching. But I've decided I like bottoming way better than topping, especially with Noah." Josh's eyes lost focus, went all dreamy. "There's this deep satisfaction in taking whatever he gives me, in giving him such pleasure by letting him use me. Fuck, there's probably something wrong with me, but the harder he fucks me, the more control he loses, the better it feels for me. When he orders me, bosses me around, and makes me do what he says, damn, it fulfills me somewhere deep inside."

Indy's eyes went wide. Josh's innate desire to pleasure others. Him coming when Noah ordered him to. The fulfillment he got from being told what to do. It all made perfect sense. "You're a sub," he blurted out.

"I'm a what?"

Indy bit his lip. Was he out of his fucking mind? The guy clearly had a sexual trauma, aside from his PTSD. Who was he to fuck him up even further and complicate things? Fuck, for all he knew, Josh would take offense at the mere mention.

"Indy, you have to tell me. I promise I won't get mad at you," Josh said, probably guessing from Indy's face why he was hesitating.

"Look," Indy said, his voice tight, "I'm no expert in this,

okay? But it sounds like you get off on submitting to someone else, on following orders from a dominant partner in bed. It's a Dom/sub thing."

Josh's eyes narrowed. "You're talking bondage, like being gagged, whipped, and forced to kiss someone else's boots, and drink their piss and weird shit like that?"

"It could be, but only if you're into that. Maybe you're submissive in bed, without wanting more than a dominant partner. Or you could explore this more, discover you crave more domination, or more pain. At the core, it's a relationship based on trust, where the Dom is focused on bringing his sub pleasure, both sexually and mentally. Usually, there's some level of pain involved, but it doesn't have to be extreme. I dunno, spanking, mild whipping, tying someone up, things like that. And the kinky stuff, the gross shit, well, that's only for subs who are into that."

"How the fuck do you know all this? I mean, no offense, but you don't seem like the type to enjoy that."

Indy had expected the question, just like he had expected the familiar pain of thinking about Duncan. Why had Duncan chosen him? He could've had anyone, so why didn't he merely choose Indy to fuck, but to keep as well? It would have been so different if he'd fucked him and discarded him. It still would've hurt, but he wouldn't have been betrayed, forced to do what he did, and be on the run for the rest of his life.

He startled when Josh put a soft hand on his cheek. "I'm sorry, I didn't mean to dredge up bad memories. It's okay if you don't want to talk about it."

Indy kissed Josh's hand. "You're right, I'm not a sub. Very much not, even though I'm a natural bottom. I've seen guys who get off on inflicting pain for the sake of it, but that's not what I'm talking about."

Indy swallowed as fresh anger rolled through him. After all he'd done for Duncan, he'd still handed him to that sadistic son of a bitch. Fuck, the pain had been so horrific he'd hardly been able to breathe. He shook his head and tried to focus on something else. Josh's blue eyes filled with compassion, and Indy held on to his hand as a lifeline.

"I had a friend, TJ, who was in a Dom/sub relationship with his boyfriend. He asked me to watch him and his boyfriend once because they both got a kick out of that. Jack, his boyfriend, he didn't just bring pain, he brought pleasure with it. And TJ clearly loved being told what to do, being submissive. Man, Jack fucked the living daylights out of him after spanking him and ordering him to do all kinds of stuff, and TJ loved every second of it. That's how I knew that first, I wasn't made to be a sub, because I could never surrender to someone else, and second, that bringing only pain has nothing to do with being a Dom, but only with being a major asshole."

Josh's face was serious, but he didn't look offended at all. Indy breathed a sigh of relief.

"So being a natural bottom is not the same as being submissive?" Josh asked.

Indy grimaced. How had he ended up in the role of expert here? "No. I know I'm a bottom, but I'm not submissive. My fight reflex is way too strong for that, and my big mouth isn't capable of saying only 'yes, master' and shit like that. But like I said, you can be submissive without being any more extreme than having a dominant partner. It's a whole subculture, a lifestyle, but that's only for those who need that, or crave it."

"Again, you don't need to answer, but if your experiences with sex haven't been all that good, as you said, and you've

never topped, how do you know you're a bottom?"
Josh asked.

"Because I do love cock in my ass, and the idea of
topping scares the fuck out of me. I don't think I'm built for
it physically, but I'm also not wired for it psychologically.
When I think about Noah..."

He stopped. Fuck, it was completely inappropriate to
talk about Noah with Josh. He was Josh's boyfriend, for
fuck's sake, regardless of what they called their relationship
themselves.

Josh smiled. "Continue," he said. "I'd love to compare
notes on Noah. I promise I won't be offended or mad, Indy."

Indy bit his lip. Before he shared anything more, he
needed to ask the question that had been hounding him.
"Why aren't you two together-together?"

Josh let out a shaky breath. "You don't pull your
punches, huh?" He rolled on his back and folded his hands
behind his head.

"It's okay if you don't wanna talk about it," Indy said
softly. He rolled on his back, too, wanting to give Josh space
if that was what he needed.

"I've loved Noah since the day I met him, when he stood
up for me in that fight. He was everything I wasn't: strong,
courageous, never giving a fuck about what everyone else
thought. I looked up to him, couldn't believe he wanted to
be my friend. Then his mom got sick and she died. It all
went so fast, and something broke in Noah. Him and his
dad, they never got along, and with his mom gone, Noah
lost his compass for a while."

Josh stayed silent for a spell. Indy turned his head.
"You okay?"

Josh jolted, as if shaken from deep thoughts. "Noah told
you about our first time, right?"

"With him in the hospital, yeah. And the first time you guys fucked."

Josh turned his head so their faces were a breath apart. A delicious blush stained his cheeks. "That wasn't our first time," Josh whispered.

14

Cleaning out O'Connor's wounds took forever. Noah could have asked Winans to help. Hell, even a nurse could have assisted, but he didn't want that. He needed to get a sense of the kind of man the cop was. O'Connor hadn't said much, merely ground his teeth as Noah cleaned out some deeper wounds on his back and stitched up two bigger ones. He'd been right, it looked like shards of concrete had hit him, sent flying by bullets.

"Okay, time to flip and do the other side. Way less damage on your front, so we're getting there," Noah announced, stretching his arms above his head. Two AM. Sweet heavens, he'd been at this for an hour and a half.

O'Connor pushed himself up on his arms, but sagged down again with a muffled curse.

Noah took pity on the guy, knowing he'd been through a lot. "Come on, big guy, I'll help." He raised O'Connor up with ease and turned him face upward.

"Painkillers working?"

"Yeah. Can't feel a damn thing. Just dead tired."

"Feel free to doze off. I'll need another thirty, forty-five minutes tops."

"Nah, thanks, I'd rather watch you," O'Connor said.

Noah raised his eyebrows. "Really? You're hitting on me now?"

"Fuck off," O'Connor said, but there wasn't much force behind it. He closed his eyes for a second, then seemed to resign himself to something. "He's a ten."

"You're ready to talk about this now?" Noah asked, amusement lacing his voice.

"Just making conversation. We have another half hour to kill, after all."

"And you figured that pissing off the guy who's treating you was the smartest way to go."

"It wouldn't be, if you were actually pissed off, but you're not. You seem to find it all strangely amusing, and that makes me wonder why."

Noah smiled. How long would it take the guy to figure it out? "He is a ten, isn't he?" he mused. "That lean, tight body, those bedroom eyes, that soft, kissable mouth... He's got that whole innocent boy look that shoots straight to your balls, doesn't he?"

O'Connor clenched his teeth. "What do you want from me?"

Noah's hands stilled, and he met the guy's eyes straight on. "Honesty. Complete, brutal honesty. And believe me, I'll know when you're lying."

O'Connor didn't blink. "I can see why they call you The General," he said. "You take after your old man."

Noah put his instruments down. He had to be careful now. "That is not a button you want to push, O'Connor, trust me."

The cop blinked now. "Sorry, that was below the belt."

Noah took a deep breath and got back to stitching up a nasty gash near the guy's collarbone. "Apology accepted."

"What do you want me to say?" O'Connor asked, a trace of embarrassment in his voice. "Yes, I like your boyfriend, okay? Yes, he is cute. I didn't know he was involved, didn't even know for certain he was gay."

Noah snorted. "Dude, if you can't tell Josh is gay, your gaydar is worse than his."

"In my defense, he'd been making out with Indy. Granted, not initiated by him, but he sure as hell wasn't objecting."

And of course, Connor thought Indy was a woman. That would make things confusing. "True, but you could've asked him."

"I'm not out."

The confession was quiet, but honest, and Noah's hands stilled again. What reason could O'Connor have to keep his sexuality a secret? Sure, being a gay cop wasn't easy, but in this day and age he wouldn't be the only one. Plus, he wasn't the bottom type, like Josh—*no offense, lover,* he apologized in his mind. O'Connor was built like a fucking truck and possessed enough testosterone to make people back the fuck off for harassing him, so what was the deal? Did it have to do with him being a Marine? They weren't known for being the most rainbow-friendly, that was for certain.

"Not out at work, or not out at all?"

Noah felt bad for asking because clearly the guy assumed Noah was gay as well and took him into confidence for that reason. He froze. He *was* gay. Shit, that label really took some getting used to.

"Not out at all. I enlisted before I had accepted it myself, and I sure as hell wasn't gonna come out while serving. Then I became a cop, and I never quite got there."

Noah avoided eye contact now, wanting the other guy to feel safe enough to share. Meanwhile, his hands continued irrigating the wounds, putting bandages on where necessary.

"And your family?"

Connor tensed under his hands. "I broke with my family when I became a cop. They're not big on law enforcement."

"That sucks," he said.

"Now that I've apologized for encroaching on your territory, can we stop embarrassing me and drop this topic?"

Hell, now he'd actually started to like the guy. What was the world coming to?

"You're not. Encroaching on my territory, that is. Look, I'm not gonna explain it all, because that's between you and Josh, but Josh and me, we're not what you think. If you really like him, talk to him. He's worth coming out of the closet for."

"WHAT DO YOU MEAN?" Indy asked Josh.

Josh kept his eyes down. "We had sex before, but Noah doesn't remember…"

Indy frowned. "How the fuck can he forget something like that?"

"Because we were both drunk, but he a little more than me. It was after his mom had died. God, Noah was lost in those months. He kept drinking himself into a stupor, and most of the time I stayed sober to take care of him, made sure he made it home safe. But it was my birthday, and we'd gone out to celebrate, so I'd been drinking, too. We made it back to his house, and…"

Josh sighed. "Noah gets horny when he drinks. Like

really horny. It's one of the reasons he doesn't drink anymore. Well, that, and he was turning into an alcoholic. So we get back to his house, where his dad refused to put the AC on, even though it was ninety degrees out. Noah's room was in the basement, but still a fucking furnace. We strip to our boxers because of the heat, and then he asks me about this hookup I'd had. I'd gone to a gay bar, met this older guy, and let him fuck me. It was nice, you know. Wanted to get that whole virginity thing over with. I tell Noah I discovered I love sucking cock, and he's horny as all get-out, so he drags his underwear down and tells me I could suck him."

Indy couldn't help it. He grinned. "That sounds like him."

Josh smiled, a flash of relief on his face. "He was fucking gorgeous and of course, I'd been lusting after him for years by then. So after some obligatory protest on my part I suck him off. He comes like a fucking volcano, and damn, my cock is aching and leaking. And he's sweet and clingy and desperate to be held, you know, as he was in those months. So we cuddle, and he gets all hard again, and of course I'm still sporting a boner... He gets all bossy Noah, tells me he wants to fuck me. I refuse at first, but he simply tells me to stop pretending I don't want it. Sends me to the bathroom for Vaseline, orders me to lube up... How could I say no when he didn't ask, but commanded me? He was irresistible."

Josh's eyes glazed over, and Indy smiled. "I rode him until we both came so fucking hard. After that, he fell asleep instantly. I cleaned him up, tucked him in."

Indy rolled on his stomach, stared at Josh with big eyes. "Noah doesn't remember any of this?"

Josh dragged his knuckles over his chin with a raspy

sound. "No. I was afraid to tell him. At first, because I thought he'd feel ashamed or disgusted. Then I'd kept it silent so long, I feared he'd get mad at me for not saying anything."

"Josh, you have to tell him. He needs to know." Indy couldn't believe Josh had kept a secret that big from Noah when they were supposed to share everything with each other. It was what their whole relationship was built on, the very foundation. How could Josh have kept that from him?

Josh's eyes clouded over. "I know." He sighed deeply. "I'm afraid of how he'll react."

Noah wasn't going to be pissed about having drunk sex with Josh, that much seemed obvious to Indy. But the fact that Josh had never told him, had led him to believe that time in the hospital had been their first time, holy crap. That was a biggie, and he didn't see how Noah would let that one go.

"But that's not why the two of you aren't together," he gently steered the conversation back to his question.

"No, it's not. What Noah and I have, it may work for us right now, but it's not healthy or viable in the long term. The official term would be codependent. I'm dependent on Noah to take care of me financially and keep the nightmares at bay, and he depends on me for sex and release to keep his pain at a tolerable level and deal with his anger issues."

Indy frowned. Anger issues? What was Josh talking about? Noah had mentioned it before, too. A cripple with anger issues, he'd called himself. Indy had never seen the man angry, not beyond normal irritation. "But that's all based on the deep love you have for each other."

"Love, yes. But friendship-love, not a romantic love. Fuck, I wasn't even sure Noah was into guys until we met you. At the risk of sounding too touchy-feely, the fact that we're best friends with benefits doesn't mean we're meant to be together as a couple."

Josh rolled on his side again, scooted close to Indy and put his hand on Indy's hip. "I know it's hard to understand, but trust me when I say that Noah and I aren't good together. He will always keep seeing me as damaged, someone whose pain he needs to take away."

A deep hurt flashed over Josh's face, so painful to watch that Indy's breath stopped for a second. He took Josh's hand, not able to find words to express his compassion.

"I can't talk about it too much, because I'm not ready yet, but something happened to me, something bad, and Noah can't stand to see me hurt."

"And if he could stop seeing you that way, would that change things?" Indy wanted to know.

Josh's answer was fast and resolute. "No. Because I'd still see him as the guy who saved me. I love him, Indy, but not like that. I could have, if things had been different, if he and I weren't so fucking damaged, maybe. Listen, letting Noah fuck me, it's not a hardship for me. I'm gay, I'm a bottom, he's my best friend, and he makes me feel good. But sometimes he's in so much pain or so angry, that it's not fucking anymore. It's a release for him that's much deeper than a mere orgasm or a fuck. I love Noah, but there's still so much anger in him, and he doesn't know how to deal with it. He releases it on me, and I can take it, crave it even, because for some sick reason I love rough sex. I shouldn't, not after what happened to me, but I do." The insecurity was clearly audible in Josh's voice.

"I'm the last person to judge, Josh, trust me," Indy said. "It's not what you get off on that makes you a sick person. It's what you do with it, how you act on it. It's the choices you make. Consensual sex between you and Noah, even if it gets rough, that's nothing to be ashamed of."

Josh brought his mouth closer and kissed him, a gentle and warm kiss. "You are so sweet, Indy, you truly are. You're perfect for Noah, you know that?"

Indy blushed fiercely. "I don't know about that," he stammered.

"What are you afraid of?"

Fuck, where to start? "I don't know if I'll ever be able to bottom again, let alone have the kind of rough sex Noah wants."

Josh shook his head. "He doesn't want that. He needs it because he hasn't learned to deal with his anger in an appropriate way. As long as he has me, he doesn't have to, but with you he can't. That's a good thing, as it will force him to process his emotions in a more healthy way."

It made sense, what Josh said, but would it be that easy? What if Noah couldn't learn? What if he forgot, if only for a second, it was Indy and not Josh, what would happen then? Indy could not, would not endure sex like that. He'd fight Noah off, hurt him even.

"Indy, a simple 'no' is enough. No matter how angry Noah is, he would never, ever hurt you."

"How do you know?"

"Because even when he's half out of his mind with pain, he still makes sure I come first. He may fuck me as hard as he can, but he will not allow himself to come before me. That's how tight his control is. If I said no, he'd pull out in a second."

Hadn't Noah said something similar, weeks ago when they'd talked about sex for the first time? He'd stated the exact same thing, that even if they ended up in bed together, he'd stop as soon as Indy said the word.

But the rough sex, that wasn't the real issue, now was it? Nope, his biggest fear was something else entirely. Despite Josh's analysis of Noah being fucked up as well, Indy was certain whatever issues Noah had paled in comparison to his own. If Noah ever found out what Indy had done, he'd stop wanting him. Stop loving him. Anyone would.

It wasn't just where he was from, who his parents were, or what Duncan had done to him. It was what he himself had done. He'd stayed with him for over four years, had never so much as protested against anything Duncan had inflicted on others. He'd stood by, watched, silently. He'd known who Duncan was, the horrible acts he'd committed, and he'd never breathed a word to anyone.

And worse, the first two years, when the sex still had been somewhat decent, he'd reacted. He'd been hard, had come, had enjoyed some of it. Duncan had fucked him— and he had liked it. Or at least, his body had. How the fuck could he explain that to anyone? How could anyone forgive him for that? How could he forgive himself?

"What happened to you, Indy? Do you want to tell me? I won't tell Noah if you don't want me to."

Could he tell Josh? Trust him with this horrible, horrible secret that was eating him from the inside out, like the acid had eaten the flesh on his back? Josh knew about trauma, knew about making choices that others would deem sick and twisted. And he could be a test case, to see how he would react before Indy told Noah. If Josh could accept him with his past, maybe, just maybe Noah could, too?

Indy didn't think anymore, he put his arms around Josh, sought the comfort he needed to tell his story. God, where did he start?

"My real name is Stephan Moreau, and I grew up in South Boston. My mom got pregnant with me by accident, and she doesn't know who my dad is. Most likely he's one of the men she fucked for money. She wasn't an all-out prostitute, I guess, more of an occasional one when money was tight. When she couldn't find enough odd jobs, she started dealing drugs for the Fitzpatricks, one of the most notorious crime families in Boston. She was good, because she looked young, innocent. I look like her. Her contact was Duncan Fitzpatrick, the heir apparent to the empire. He's..."

Indy's voice broke. He couldn't do this. How the fuck could he ever find words for what had happened, for what he'd done? If he told Josh, he'd never look at him the same. He'd never hold him again, and he definitely wouldn't want to have sex with him anymore.

But what was the alternative? Never telling anyone? Never trusting anyone, not ever again? That wasn't living. It was surviving.

No, he wanted to live. He wanted to trust, to connect, to love. He clenched his fists, forced air into his lungs.

Josh kissed his head. "Take your time, Indy. I'm here."

"Duncan is seven years older than me, but he started working for his uncle, the Fitzpatricks' boss, when he was a teen. By the time he was nineteen, he ran the Fitzpatricks' drug operations. He knew me, had seen me a few times when he'd met with my mom. Everyone knew who he was. He was handsome, you know, a charmer. Black hair, bright blue eyes, a sexy smile. When he smiled at me, I felt it in my stomach. Then my mom fucked up. She'd just gotten a shipment to sell, fifty thousand worth of coke. She had a customer at home and forgot to hide the drugs. He knocked her out cold, then took everything she had. She owed Duncan fifty grand, and he's not a man you wanna owe that much money to. Duncan came to collect, and she made a deal with him."

He swallowed, hid his face against Josh's shoulder. "Me, in exchange for the money. I had no choice. He threatened to kill her if I didn't cooperate. For four years he had me. Four years of a hell that was gradually getting worse. He started using, became unpredictable, more and more violent. I wasn't innocent before him, had given a few guys blow jobs for money. I know I was way too young, but it was the only life I knew. But Duncan robbed me of every shred of innocence. He used me, and then he threw me away."

15

When he was done, Indy stayed where he was, his face hidden against Josh's shoulder. What would Josh think of him now that he knew? His heart was racing, his hands clammy, and his stomach was revolting viciously. But Josh lifted his chin with a gentle move and made him slide backward so they could see each other.

Josh's eyes were filled with tears.

Tears of pain, compassion, not disgust.

"My God, Indy..." Josh raised his hand, brushed Indy's cheek. "Honey, were you scared of how I would look at you?"

Indy nodded, his throat too constricted to speak.

"Indy, you were a child. You did not choose this; this happened to you. Whatever you did in those years with that monster, you did it to survive. Whatever you felt, even if you had feelings for him, defended him, it's okay. You were a child, an innocent victim. You survived this, and I would never judge you for that."

Something broke free in Indy's heart, something that had been bound and imprisoned for a long time.

"I feel so guilty for how I felt, how I responded, even when we had sex."

He forced the words out, knowing he'd never find the courage to say them again if he kept silent now. "It wasn't always bad, you know. He could be loving and gentle, if he wanted to, and sometimes when he took the time to make it good I liked it. I liked him fucking me. That's sick, right?"

"Look," Josh started, then stopped. "Can I touch you?" he asked.

Indy nodded.

"Everywhere?"

Indy hummed his consent.

"Can I take your clothes off?"

More nodding.

Josh pushed Indy aside with a gentle shove and sat up. Seconds later, Indy's boxers and shirt had disappeared, and then Josh whipped off his own underwear.

"Better. Come here," Josh said and pulled Indy on top of him, their bare cocks brushing up against each other. "Our bodies react to stimuli, even if we don't want to."

Josh worked his hand between their bodies, gripped Indy's cock which had become hard from the naked friction with Josh. "You love Noah, but you respond to me as well. That's because we're both gay, and we're naked, and we're talking about sex. Even bad sex, illegal sex, horrible sex, is still sex—and that means we may react physically, even if we don't want to."

Indy understood. Josh was saying that however his body had reacted to Duncan, it was okay. He shouldn't judge himself for the physical reaction.

"Did you...react?" He kept the question vague, didn't want to push too hard.

Josh met his careful gaze, his blue eyes full of pain. "I was hard as a rock until they tore my insides to shreds."

Josh understood. He truly, deeply understood. It was like the sun had reached a part of Indy's soul that had been dark and shaded for so long. Josh had given him something precious with this trust, this vulnerable admission. Indy felt lighter and warmer than he had in ages. Free. Like heavy shackles had been taken off of him.

"I want to fuck you," he whispered. "If you'll let me."

"Fuck, yes. Please." Josh's answer was swift and emotional. "But Indy, and I will only ask this once, are you sure you want to do this? You know, because of Noah and everything else?"

"If Noah can fuck you while he wants to be with me, so can I. I want this more than anything else, and if it turns out Noah has an issue with it, that's his problem. He doesn't fucking own me."

Josh's face broke open in an unexpected laugh. "Fuck, you two are made for each other. You'll be so good for him, honey."

Indy leaned on his forearms, brought his mouth a breath away from Josh's. "Lesson number one: when you want me to fuck you, stop talking about how good your other lover and I would be for each other."

He kissed Josh deeply. Every emotion he had, every bit of gratitude for the freedom Josh's words had brought, he poured in there. For a few precious minutes, they were one soul, he and Josh, connected on a level he couldn't even describe.

"Point taken," Josh panted when Indy let go. "Fuck, I love kissing you."

"Josh, I don't know how to do this. I want to make it good for you, but I don't know how."

Never had Indy felt so vulnerable, yet safe at the same time. He wanted to bring Josh pleasure, but also wanted to experience for himself that sex could be good. He trusted Josh to do right by him, by both of them.

Josh kissed him again. "I'm gonna talk you through it, okay?"

Indy nodded, determined to get this right.

"I'd like to see your face, so I can see how you're doing. So maybe we could start with you literally topping me and me on my back if that's okay with you?"

Indy bobbed his head.

"If you're topping, it's your responsibility to prep your bottom. My ass is flexible, and I know how to relax, so I don't need much stretching, but if you fuck an inexperienced guy, you need to take your time. Noah was tight and had trouble relaxing, so if you fuck him make sure to stretch him properly. Sit back on your knees."

Indy listened intently. He should know this, but he wasn't taking any chances. Not with Josh. If he ended up hurting him, he'd never forgive himself. Plus, Noah's offer was still on the table. If Indy ever took him up on it, he wanted to make it an unforgettable experience for both of them.

Indy climbed off Josh and took a spot between the guy's legs, which were spread wide now. Josh opened the drawer of the night table and reached blindly for something and came up with lube and a condom. He pulled up his legs, spreading them even wider.

Josh squirted lube on his fingers. "I'll start, and you can take over whenever you want to, okay?"

Josh brought his fingers down to his hole and slipped a finger in. "There's lots of ways to prep a guy. But the baseline is that you can't fuck a guy until you've managed to get two or three fingers in with ease."

Josh swirled his finger around, added a second one. "Can I...?" Indy asked hesitantly.

Josh nodded and pulled his fingers out. Indy carefully dripped lube on his fingers. He stared at Josh's pucker for a few seconds before he stretched his arm ever so slowly and brought his fingers forward. He bit his lip.

"It's okay," Josh said softly.

Indy put his middle finger against Josh's hole and pushed in. He let out a surprised little yelp when his finger slid in all the way. Fuck, it was so different from this perspective. He'd never touched a guy's hole before, not like this. Not even his own. Duncan had fucked him so often he'd never even had the urge to experiment with himself.

"More." Josh's voice was gruff.

Indy pulled out, added his index finger and slid back in. Josh's breath caught, then released audibly. Josh's ass hugged his fingers tight. Fuck, that silken heat would fit his cock like a glove. It sent a powerful wave of excitement straight to his balls.

"Slide back and forth a few times and widen your fingers."

Josh let out a groan, his body twitching. "This already feels good." His cock was visibly growing harder. Josh really loved having something in his hole. Indy added a third finger. Josh's hole relaxed around him, the muscles giving up their iron grip on his fingers.

A tiny tremor made Josh's muscles jolt. "Fuck, you feel good inside of me."

A slow smile spread across Indy's mouth and without being told, he pulled out and slid back in a few times, moving his hand. It was a completely new sensation, bringing someone else pleasure like this. Not passively, not by being used, but actively. It rushed through his veins, the satisfaction of getting it right, of doing this to Josh.

"Ungh!" Josh's hips bucked off the bed. "Do that again."

Indy's hand moved again and Josh shivered. "Oh, so good." Another deep tremble tore through his body. "I'm ready when you are."

Indy retracted his fingers. Oh, fuck. Showtime.

"Indy, do we need a condom?"

"I'm clean," Indy whispered. "But I don't have proof or anything."

"Your word is good enough for me. We can use one if you want, but I believe you."

"I'd love to go without..." Indy said, his eyes cast down.

"Perfect. Put some lube on your cock," Josh told him, and Indy obeyed with slow, almost mechanical moves. His heart was hammering in his chest. Fuck, he was going to do this. He was fucking another man for the first time in his life.

Josh reached up, pushing Indy's chin up with his index finger to make eye contact. "I need you inside me, Indy," he said softly. "I want to share this with you. It'll be good, I promise."

Indy took a deep breath and let himself fall forward on his arms till his cock was right at Josh's entrance. His body was shaking as he angled his hips and ever so slowly tilted them forward. His cock found the slick hole and wanted to push in. Indy gave the tiniest of thrusts and Josh pushed back to let him in.

He let out a high yelp when his cock breached the first ring, Josh's body welcoming him into a snug, slick heat.

"Deeper," Josh commanded.

Indy slid forward without hesitation now, his face flushing with want. Oh, fuck, it was exactly as he had imagined. Warm, moist, soft as silk. He thrust in deeper and deeper until his entire cock was buried inside of Josh. The pressure on his dick was incredible.

"So wicked hot...so good," he stammered, his eyes fluttering and his heart hammering in his chest.

He pulled out, surged back in. Josh let out a loud moan, and Indy's face burst into a delighted smile. He repeated the move, earning another vocal reward from Josh.

"Fuck, you feel so good...just like I imagined." Josh bucked his hips as Indy slid in again. "Angle slightly to the right." Indy shifted, retreated, and dove back in.

"Holy... Ungh!" Josh yelped. "Right there."

Jackpot. Indy repeated the move. That had to be that elusive male pleasure spot he only knew from stories.

"Harder." Josh's hands reached for his ass and grabbed his cheeks to push him in with every move.

Indy found a rhythm, as hard and deep as he could go, making sure to hit that angle Josh had pointed out. Josh panted, his eyes rolling back in his head. His cock was rock hard, Indy saw with deep satisfaction.

Indy wanted to savor this moment, wanted to revel in the fact that he was topping another man for the first time. And dammit, he was bringing him obvious pleasure, judging by the excited groans and moans Josh was letting out. The experience of having his cock in this tight, warm cavern was unreal. It was so snug and slick, he wanted to stay there forever.

His body was about to show him the improbability of that option as every muscle was tensing for the impending release. Hot white pleasure thundered through his veins, setting course straight for his balls. His head was spinning with delicious ecstasy. Holy motherfucking shit, he was gonna come so hard, so long. This was gonna be the best orgasm of his life.

Josh hasn't come yet.

The thought pierced through his orgasm-focused ramblings. As a top, he was responsible for Josh's pleasure, otherwise he would be as big an asshole as Duncan had been.

Why hadn't Josh come yet? He'd been fucking him as hard and deep as he could, and Josh trembled every time he hit that magic spot inside. Maybe Duncan was right all along. Maybe his dick was too small to make the guy come. Maybe it only felt nice—but nice guys finished last. Or in this case, not at all.

He bit his lip, fighting hard to hold back his own release. Fuck, he had to do something. What could he do? He did not want to let Josh down, didn't want to fail. He reached out with one hand, grabbed Josh's dick and jerked him off, while keeping up his deep thrusts. The guy's long shaft was rock hard and trembling in his small hand. Clearly, the problem wasn't that he wasn't turned on.

Suddenly, he remembered. It was so obvious. Josh was a sub. He needed to obey.

Lowering his voice as much as he could, he shouted with uncharacteristic authority: "Dammit, Joshua, let go!"

Josh howled as he exploded in Indy's hand, painting them both with thick ropes of cum. Indy surrendered to the violent climax tearing through his own body, tears forming in his eyes as he clenched them hard. His hips jerked, his dick spewing deep inside Josh. He couldn't hold his own weight anymore, dropped like dead weight on top of Josh, muscles spasming with the effort and release. Josh's arms came around him, and Indy found a safe place for his head against Josh's chest.

It took forever for his heart rate to slow down, for his breathing to return to normal. When it did, he couldn't hold back the embarrassing tears that were coming. He shattered into a million pieces, crying hot tears for no apparent reason at all.

All that time, Josh held him, a strong hand on the top of his head, never pushing or holding too tight, the other hand on his lower back. He mumbled soft, sweet words that twined around Indy's heart like beautiful gift wraps, each word a present for his starving soul.

Finally, he started making sense of his surroundings again.

"You did so good, Indy, I'm so proud of you," Josh was saying, his hand making small comforting circular rubbing motions on Indy's lower back.

"I'm sorry," he managed after three hoarse, failed attempts.

"Sorry for what, making me come?"

"For crying. Again."

"Don't be ridiculous. I'm honored that you trust me enough to share your tears with me."

Indy bit his lip. Josh's words rang true. He hadn't cried in such a long time, not until he'd met Noah and Josh. And as much as it frustrated him to be so emotional all the damn time, it was because of their trust.

"I did make you come, didn't I?" he said, allowing pride to brighten his voice.

"Damn right you did. You totally ripped off Noah's trick, by the way."

Indy chuckled. "I can't quite pull his tone off, but it came close enough."

"Yes, you little bossy top, it certainly...came."

They cuddled for a long time, not saying much and not

caring about the mess they had made of themselves and the sheets. Finally, they dragged themselves out of bed to clean up.

"Indy, would you be offended if I asked if we could sleep now? I'm exhausted, and I have an early therapy session tomorrow. If it's okay with you, we could sleep in our bed? I don't want Noah to come home to an empty bed."

Indy sighed deeply. "I'd love that."

WHEN NOAH PULLED into the driveway, he was so tired he could barely function anymore. Shit, it hadn't been exactly safe to drive. He rolled the car into the garage and closed it behind him. At least the lights upstairs were out. It looked like Josh had taken his advice and had bunked with Indy. It would help Josh in his journey to not depend on Noah alone. And it would be good for Indy to get comfortable being touched again, with intimacy. As much as he respected Indy's issues, Noah hoped he'd find a way through them, because he longed for more intimacy between them.

Yawning, he made his way inside. It was different, coming home to an empty house. Well, not empty but Josh was always waiting for him when he got back. Funny how much he'd gotten used to that.

He switched off the few lights Josh had left on downstairs as he made his way upstairs. Where would they be, Indy's bed or theirs? His body tightened at the idea of them sleeping in his bed. Their bed. Much to his surprise, both bedroom doors were open. His breath about stopped when he stepped inside his room.

They were sleeping, all right, Josh on his back and Indy on his stomach, almost on top of Josh. Indy's head was resting on Josh's shoulder, his arms around Josh's waist, his legs on either side of Josh's right leg...and Indy's perfect, round butt was sticking high in the air, a sheet precariously draped over his waist. It was the single most beautiful sight Noah had ever seen: his two men together, sleeping. Naked.

Wait, naked? He'd rarely seen Indy's naked back, the man always self-conscious of the scars. Was he wearing underwear under those sheets? Sure didn't look like it. Josh slept in the buff but Indy didn't, and there was no way Josh would've done it if Indy had been uncomfortable. But why would he have stripped?

Unless... They had sex. There was no other explanation for them being naked and so at ease with each other's bodies. Had Josh...? No, Indy wouldn't let Josh fuck him, no way. Not when he knew how much Noah wanted him.

Something had happened. He swallowed. Fuck knew he had no right to be jealous, no matter who had done what with whom. Josh wasn't his, and Noah had no right to Indy. It would be hypocritical of him to object to Josh and Indy doing anything when he himself was still fucking Josh.

And yet.

If Josh had taken... No, he couldn't go there, couldn't do this. You have no right. Not after how he had treated Josh. Fuck, ever since he'd met Indy he'd realized how little he had given Josh. He'd tried, maybe, but all the affection Josh had wanted to show him in the tiniest gestures, Noah had always held him back. And he hadn't fucking understood until Indy. Until he wanted nothing else than to touch that sweet man, kiss him, hold him, all fucking day long. He ached for him, longed for him deep within his body and soul. If what Josh felt for Noah was even a fraction of that, he'd been a fucking cruel bastard to deny him the opportunity to express it.

Even if, and his stomach soured at the thought, even if Josh had been able to express that now with Indy, even if Indy had given him what he hadn't wanted Noah to have yet, Noah would have to suck it up. Karma was a bitch, wasn't it?

He switched the hallway light off, waited till his eyes had adjusted to the dark and closed the door. He'd have to be grateful to be invited here tonight. And he was. They hadn't excluded him, had invited him in. It had to be enough.

He lowered himself on the reading chair in the corner of the room and removed his shoes, his socks. With effort, he took off his scrubs, his stump burning and throbbing as he unhooked his prosthetic leg. Fuck, he was getting tired of this pain. The massage oil he rubbed all over his legs soothed his stump, but it still stung.

Wearing only his boxers, Noah leaned back in the chair and watched them sleep. He had to swallow at the images popping up in his head. He clenched his teeth, his jaw aching from the force. Why had Indy chosen Josh when he'd known how much Noah wanted him? Watching Indy lie on top of Josh made Noah want to drag his best friend's ass out of that bed and take his place.

Indy was his.

He gasped when the realization hit him. It was Josh he envied, not Indy. He did not want to kick Indy out and take his place in Josh's arms; he wanted to be the one to hold Indy and love him.

Wait. Love him?

Where had that come from? Fuck, he was too tired to deal with all of this.

He hesitated for a second, debating sleeping by himself in Indy's room—then rejected it. Fuck it. They chose to sleep here, meaning they'd known he'd come back at some point and see them. That calmed his jealousy somewhat.

They hadn't even tried to keep it a secret from him; it was all in the open. They could deal with this. He could handle this. After he'd gotten some sleep. Which was not happening with this burning, aching leg...and a throbbing cock. It was hard as steel, responding to the images of Josh and Indy fucking that he'd conjured up in his mind.

Well, too bad. He wasn't going to wake up either of them for a pity fuck right now. Indy wasn't ready, and he couldn't wake Josh for a booty call, especially not since he'd already been busy with Indy.

Not helping, Noah chastised himself as his cock jumped up. Not helping at all.

Josh and Indy were parked on Josh's side of the king-size bed, which meant there was more than enough room for him. He dragged down his boxers, told his cock to forget it, and lowered himself on the bed as quietly as possible. He lifted his stump to place it in a comfortable position and grunted despite his efforts to be quiet. Fuck, it hurt so damn much.

He hated this stupid stump, hated his missing leg, hated his job that made him so worn out, hated his gut that was all tied up in knots over Indy and Josh and sex and whether he was gay. Dammit, he hated it all.

"Noah?" Josh stirred and opened his eyes. He turned his head to look at Noah and smiled softly.

"Go back to sleep. It's okay," Noah said, keeping his voice low.

"You're not okay." He should have known Josh would pick up on his pain. He always did, tuned in as they were to each other. "You're in pain."

He ground his teeth as he nodded. "Stayed longer to treat O'Connor. He was hit by concrete fragments, had dozens of small wounds."

"Is Connor okay?"

The concern in Josh's voice put Noah over the edge, and he dragged himself to sit up. "Really? You wanna talk about your precious Connor right now? While you're lying in bed, naked, having fucked the man I want? Fuck you, Josh!"

"He's not my Connor. I've met the guy twice, for fuck's sake. You're being ridiculous. And keep it down or you'll wake Indy," Josh said.

"Noah." Indy's soft voice sounded happy.

"Yeah." He didn't know what to say. What was there to say? Had Indy heard his crude accusal?

The bed moved as Indy rolled off Josh and crawled close to Noah. He let out a sigh of contentment as he lowered his head on Noah's shoulder and wrapped his small arm around Noah's chest. "I'm glad you're home." His voice was sleepy and fucking adorable.

Noah stayed still, not trusting himself to touch Indy right now. Not when he was feeling this powerful urge to show him whom he belonged to. "So am I."

His voice was so much colder and rougher than Indy deserved. Fuck, he was going to ruin it all.

"Do you want me to move?"

Insecurity laced Indy's voice, and Noah cursed himself.

"He's angry because he thinks you let me fuck you," Josh said matter-of-factly.

"Well, did you?" Noah couldn't help himself. He had to know. "Because I come home to find you two naked and way too comfortable with each other, so tell me the truth. What the fuck happened?"

Indy gasped and untangled himself from Noah, leaving him cold and feeling alone. God, he was such a bastard. What the hell was he doing?

Josh put a calming hand on Indy's arm. "Remember that

anger issue I mentioned? This is it. He lashes out when he's in pain. It's not personal."

Indy swallowed as he sent Noah a pained look. "It sure as hell feels personal."

"He's worked a sixteen-hour shift, something his body and his mind can't handle. He's dead tired, he's in pain, and I don't think finding us in bed helped."

"I can hear you!" Noah shouted, slamming a fist on the covers. "Stop fucking talking about me as if I'm not in the room!"

"Indy," Josh's voice was ice cold, "You need to consider if you can handle this. Noah, back the fuck off. You're scaring him."

Noah buried his face in his hands. He was being a total asshole, but he'd lost the grip on his self-control. He was too tired, too angry, too jealous, and too fucking horny.

"What are you going to do?" Indy asked Josh. The concern in Indy's voice stabbed Noah through the heart. Fuck, he didn't deserve him. Neither of them. No wonder Indy chose Josh over you. Josh can give him the sweetness he needs instead of all this pain and anger.

"If it's okay with you, I'm going to let him fuck me till he's too worn out to do anything else but sleep."

Noah's body froze, the anger still buzzing through his veins. What did Josh say? Surely he'd misunderstood.

"He could hurt you."

Indy voiced his own fears, and Noah didn't even blame him for saying it. He had the physical power to break Josh in half. Why would Josh even offer this?

"Remember what I told you? Noah would never hurt me...or you. You have no idea how tight a grip he has on himself. It's why he's in so much pain, because he doesn't know how to let it out. So I'll let him fuck me. It's how I take care of him."

"Josh..." Noah said, his voice faltering.

"Shut up," Josh said. "He needs to understand this."

Noah let himself fall back on the bed, turning on his side to watch them both.

"I told you, I like it rough. Noah is about to fuck me senseless, and where that may scare others, the idea makes me so fucking hard that I'm trembling."

Josh reached out to grab Indy's hand and put it on his shaft. Noah inhaled sharply at the sight, his cock quivering.

"You're hard as steel," Indy said with amazement.

"I crave his power and the raw anger he's bringing. I love being the bottom, the caretaker, the soft and weaker one. It completely turns me on."

"I understand," Indy whispered. He let go of Josh's cock, then leaned toward him and kissed him tenderly. "Go to Noah, take care of him. He needs you."

"He needs to leave," Noah snapped. "I don't want him to see this."

"It's Indy's choice," Josh said with the fuck-off tone Noah recognized from using it himself way too often.

"Josh, I'm on the edge. I'm so tired, and the pain is so fucking bad. I'm afraid I'll go too far, hurt you, scare him."

"I know, but if you want him to trust you, you must allow him to see this part of you. Let out the pain, Noah. I can take it, and Indy's a hell of a lot stronger than he looks."

"I want to stay," Indy said. He rolled over to the other side of Josh, wrapped the sheet around his body, and leaned back against the headboard on the far edge of the bed.

Noah clenched his fists. "I don't have it in me to be gentle," he gave a last warning.

Josh shot Indy a look over his shoulder, then smiled that slow, sexy smile at Noah. "Who says I want you to?"

Noah held on to the last shreds of his control. "Lube me," he told Josh.

Josh grabbed the lube from the night table. Noah groaned as Josh spread a generous amount of lube on his cock. Somehow, Josh seemed to grasp that this was not the time for foreplay, or games, or even a blow job. He needed it to get out of his system, this sizzling anger burning so hot and close to the surface.

Josh piled two pillows on top of each other, lowered himself on his stomach on top of them and pushed his ass back, opening his hole wide for the taking. It was still stretched, probably from Indy taking him. Good. Noah didn't wait a second, but dropped his weight on top of Josh, grabbed his hips and entered him in one desperate thrust.

"Oh!" Josh groaned, pushing his ass back even farther to accommodate Noah.

Noah shoved his arms under Josh's chest, gripping his shoulders in a tight hold, then moved him downward on his cock, while slamming upward at the same time. Josh's tight ass engulfed him, and the sweet friction was too much.

His vision went red, and he plunged in, again and again and again. He felt nothing but his cock, wanted nothing but to thrust it in deeper and deeper, so hard and so deep he would stop feeling at all. He kept drilling, didn't stop when Josh came with a loud moan, not even when he came so hard himself it made him dizzy.

With the waves of his release crashing through him, he kept up the feral rhythm, his cock still hard as hell, burying it deeper in Josh's warm cavern than it had ever been before. When his muscles gave out, he grunted in frustration. Letting go of Josh for a second, he lifted his stump in the right position, then sat up, dragging Josh with him. He leaned back against the headboard and jammed a pillow behind his back for support. He didn't wait for Josh to adjust, merely lifted him up, his biceps and chest bulging, and sat his lover down on his cock, facing away from him.

"Ride me," he commanded with a low and broken voice, lifting Josh's hips and shoving them down again.

Josh rose, slammed down, taking him hard and fast and deep. They were completely in sync. No dirty talk or sweet whispers, the only sounds slapping and grunting and moaning and ragged breaths. Noah's heart was racing, his body hot and sweaty, his need blinding him. His vision blurred, his balls throbbed and wrenched flush against his body. His muscles clenched and strained as he lifted his hips and thrust with desperation.

Noah's fingers dug into Josh's hips, lifting him and jamming him down on his deep thrusts. When Noah came again, his orgasm was so hard it almost knocked him out. He cried out in a fierce wail. He held on to Josh, putting his head on Josh's shoulder, their bodies pressed together as he shuddered and shook with the force.

And then he broke. He hadn't cried when his mother died, leaving him with his asshole of a father. He hadn't cried when he had lost friends to roadside bombs and attacks. He hadn't cried when he'd discovered what had happened to Josh. He hadn't even cried when he lost his leg or when he'd been in the hospital, desperate with pain. But he cried now, big sobs that tore through his body.

Josh lifted his hips to let him slide out, then turned on his lap to face him. He opened his arms wide. Noah leaned in and, rocking Josh on his lap, held on for dear life. He didn't know how long they sat there, Josh hugging him and Noah's body shaking with violent sobs and shivers. He wasn't even crying tears but seemed to let something out that was way deeper.

Finally, his body and mind found peace, and he stopped shaking. Josh let go and cupped both of Noah's cheeks, kissing him softly on his mouth.

"Josh..." Noah said, his head full of apologies. Where could he start? How could he apologize for what he had done?

"I love you," Josh said, kissing him again. "God, I love you so much."

It brought him to his knees, this declaration of love. Josh still loved him, despite it all. He had let his anger out, taken it all out on Josh, and the guy came back with "I love you." He didn't deserve him. Either of them.

"I love you, too." Suddenly he was desperate for Josh to know that, to understand that he did love him, even when he'd used him to release his anger.

"I know you do. Lie down, Noah, you need to sleep."

Too tired to protest when Josh pushed him back, Noah let himself slide down on the mattress. He opened his arms to hold Josh, but instead, his lover straddled him.

"What are you doing?" His eyes sank closed. He was so tired.

Josh's hands fisted his still half-hard cock, guided it back into his ass that was still dripping with cum.

"Go to sleep, Noah. I'll ride you till you fall asleep."

He wanted to protest, needed to, but was too exhausted to even lift a finger. When Josh set the most tender, sweetest rhythm ever, he smiled. Barely awake, his cock responded to the love it was getting from Josh's ass. He drifted in and out of sleep until he released so gently, it rippled through his body. He fell asleep with his love's name on his lips.

"Indy."

16

He was a fucking mess. There was no other word to describe the emotional chaos in Indy's head. Despite everything he'd been through over the years, he'd never had so much to process as right now. Leaving Duncan—and the whole Fitzpatrick clan for that matter—had been an easy decision, despite the dangers. It had been a life-or-death choice, and he'd wanted to live too much to stay.

But Noah and Josh and all the feelings they evoked in him, that was an entirely different matter. Topping Josh had been exactly what he needed. It had been healing, he'd realized afterward. The deep satisfaction he got from bringing Josh pleasure, from making him come—it had been an amazing experience. Plus, Josh had touched his scars, both literally and figuratively, and had not bolted in the slightest. Of course, he was used to Noah, who was as damaged as Indy was. In more than the physical sense.

Indy hadn't grasped how broken Noah was on the inside, not till last night. Noah had always been the strong one, the one keeping it together, but yesterday he had broken. Grief, that's what it had felt and looked like to Indy. Grief over the loss of his leg, maybe, over the life he'd had to give up. And it hadn't come out until Josh had given him an outlet for the anger that had contained it.

It had given Indy hope. If Noah had so much pain inside of him, pain that caused him to do things he regretted, maybe he'd understand Indy's pain. Maybe Noah's damage wasn't all that different from Indy's. Maybe they could be damaged together—at least for a little while, until Indy had to go.

The sex, it had scared Indy, until he'd seen how willingly Josh had taken it, how much pleasure it had brought him. He hadn't lied when he'd told Indy he got off on bottoming, being dominated, and rough sex. Noah had been too deep in —Indy smiled at his own choice of words—to notice, but Josh had come so hard. But even when he'd been hammering Josh so hard the bed had shaken, Noah had still held Josh, touched him. He hadn't hurt him, had kept his physical strength in check even when he'd been blind with need.

And oh, when Josh had ridden him, Noah half asleep, it had been such a beautiful sight. Noah hadn't realized it, but Josh had been saying goodbye. Indy had felt it, had seen it in the way Josh hadn't held back his love for once, in the tears that had streamed down his face as he'd softly fucked Noah into oblivion. Afterward, Indy had held Josh, kissed him, wiped the tears from his face while Noah had slept peacefully. And Josh had held him too, had whispered in his ear, "He's yours now, too. Take good care of him."

Josh had rolled off Indy to the other side of the bed and had pushed Indy to the middle. Indy had fallen asleep between them, snuggled up to Noah, with Josh spooning him from the back.

Loved. He was loved, for the first time in his life.

When he had woken up, Josh had been up already, but Noah had still been asleep. He'd been spooning Indy, his strong arms holding him close and his chest warm and safe against Indy's back.

Safe.

No panic at being held, no fear at the thought that Noah had the strength to crush Indy. He wouldn't. Sweet fuck, Indy wanted him so much. But Noah needed to sleep, so he'd crawled out of Noah's arms without waking him.

It was past noon when Noah came downstairs on his crutches in just boxers, his eyes still soft and cloudy from waking up. Indy watched him as he stretched, the powerful muscles in his chest and arms rippling.

"Hey," Noah said when he spotted Indy at the breakfast counter.

"Hey yourself."

Noah lowered himself on the bar stool next to Indy and dropped his crutches.

"How are you feeling?" Indy asked, pushing the fresh mug of tea he had made for himself in front of Noah.

He took a careful sip. "Still tired. Better than last night."

Indy turned his stool toward him. "That was some serious fucking you did."

He winced. "We're skipping the pleasantries, I see?"

"We are."

Indy studied Noah, the emotions that played on his face. Resignation, but fear as well. Indy understood where that was coming from. He'd seen Noah at his most raw and vulnerable. Noah had to be afraid it had been too much. Having your damage, your issues so out in the open, it was scary as fuck. It was time to restore some balance. Before they had sex, Noah deserved to know at least a little of his story.

He took a deep breath. "My real name is Stephan Moreau, and I grew up in South Boston."

For the second time within twenty-four hours, he told his story. But he didn't stop there. Noah deserved to know it all. The whole ugly truth.

∼

Two and a half years before

"Fucking hell, where are you?"

Stephan woke up at the sound of Duncan's snarl and a door that was slammed shut. Fuck. He was angry. Possibly high. He was out of bed in a second, not even bothering to put on more clothes than the boxers he'd been sleeping in. Duncan would only rip them off anyways.

"I'm here," he said, walking into the small parlor, hoping against hope he was wrong.

Duncan threw down his Red Sox cap and unbuckled his belt. He turned and faced Stephan, his dilated pupils and flushed face confirming Stephan's suspicions. Damn, he was high as a fucking kite.

"I'm horny," Duncan grumbled, unbuttoning his pants and dropping them. "Suck my dick."

He was already hard, his cock jutting forward. Stephan hesitated for only a second. Once, only once had he refused Duncan in the four years since he'd been bought—and it had not ended well for him. He'd broken Stephan's arm, blackened his eye, and had fucked him so viciously his ass had hurt for a week. Not an experience he was keen to repeat. Not that he couldn't defend himself by now—he'd gotten his brown belt—but fighting back would only cost him more in the end. You could not escape the Fitzpatricks, and if he ever lifted a hand against Duncan, retribution would be swift and fucking deadly.

Stephan dropped to his knees—Duncan preferred him in that position—and reached for the guy's member. He could do this with his eyes closed, literally. When Duncan was jacked up on coke, he would come in a minute, two at the most. It was one of the very few advantages Stephan could spot in Duncan's increased drug use. For the most part, it was a fucking nightmare.

He took Duncan's dick in his mouth, grabbed the base with his other hand, and started. The one thing he was grateful for was that Duncan wasn't all that big. It's how the guy had gotten the nickname Tiny Tim, though no one ever used it to his face, not without consequences at least. It was one reason Duncan wasn't keen on fucking Stephan—or any of his other whores—in public, as many of his lieutenants did with their whores. He didn't want everyone to know what a small dick he had,. The women he fucked were too impressed by his status to say anything and the few who had ridiculed him had paid a steep price. You did not fuck with Duncan Fitzpatrick, no matter how tiny his dick. Not that Stephan had any right to say anything because his dick was even smaller. A crayon, Duncan had called it.

Duncan thrust in Stephan's throat, as he always did. Not that big a deal with a dick his size once Stephan had gotten used to it. The first ten times he'd gagged violently. That sensation of choking while your mouth was full of dick and the tears were streaming down your face, damn, he'd gotten nightmares from it. It hadn't deterred Duncan in the slightest. He'd told Stephan to get used to it and learn to relax. He had, but he'd also learned to hold one hand around

Duncan's base. That way, he could at least control some of his moves, prevent him from choking him with his dick.

Blowing Duncan was mechanical by now, nothing Stephan was invested in emotionally. It had been a hard transition from the still somewhat naïve fourteen-year-old who had a boyish crush on the high and mighty Duncan Fitzpatrick, to the jaded eighteen-year-old he was now who knew what a first-class motherfucker the man was. And with his mother in prison for drug trafficking, he didn't exactly have other options.

Duncan moaned, thrusting harder. Stephan groaned with him, as if it brought him pleasure to suck the asshole off. It was expected of him, and he had become quite the actor. One did not survive otherwise. He'd always pretended everything was fine. In school, being Duncan's bitch— Duncan's term—had brought him a weird status amongst his peers. No one had ever dared mess with him and his teachers had been repulsed. Not one of them had been concerned or even asked if he had chosen that role himself. Fucking idiots.

He'd loved school, though. One reason was because he was away from Duncan. In school he could at least pretend his life wasn't fucked up. The bigger reason was that he liked learning new stuff. Maybe he got that from his father—the man whose name he didn't even know. He did well in school, graduated with decent grades. In another life, he would have gone for college. Instead, he was stuck here, with his crime lord boyfriend who showed no inclination of getting enough of him. Stephan's only hope was that Duncan would accidentally OD—though fuck knew where he'd end up then. Or with whom. There were worse fates in life than being Duncan's bitch—that much Stephan did know.

Duncan was close now. Stephan recognized the signs and increased his own moaning and motions. He hated to swallow and if he couldn't avoid it, often made himself throw up afterward. He pulled the dick out of his mouth, pointed it at his face, pumping him furiously.

"Come all over me, baby," he breathed seductively.

Fucking Oscar-winning performance. Having cum on his face beat the hell out of having to swallow it, and Duncan seemed to find it highly rewarding to spray him all over. How the guy could be so dimwitted he'd believe Stephan was enjoying this was beyond him, but whatever. It worked.

"Mark me with your cum, Duncan. Fuck, you're so wicked hot!"

Yup, Mr. Predictable erupted and blew his wad on Stephan's cheeks and neck. By the translucent quality and the little amount, he'd been doing more fucking before with fuck-knew-who. Fine with Stephan. It meant he wouldn't be able to get it up again to fuck him, so yay.

"Fuck, Steph, nobody sucks cock like you," Duncan grunted. "That was the balls."

"You know I take good care of you," Stephan panted.

Duncan dropped back on the couch, not bothering to pull his pants up.

"I'm gonna go clean up," Stephan said, retreating into the tiny bathroom. For someone who made a fortune dealing drugs, Duncan sure had bought a shitty house for Stephan. The house wasn't his, of course. It was Duncan's. Stephan only lived there like a kept man. A whore, really. Duncan bought houses left and right, a solid investment, he'd assured Stephan, and incidentally also a good way to launder drug money.

The Fitzpatricks weren't stupid. They didn't draw attention to themselves with tons of expensive houses and over-the-top cars. So, a shitty house it was for Stephan, while Duncan stayed at expensive hotels often, wasting money on liquor and ridiculously pricey food, entertaining his friends and business partners. And of course, Duncan stopped by Stephan's house for a fuck at least daily—often more than once.

Stephan was smarter. If he ever, ever wanted to get away, he needed money. So he'd been siphoning off cash. He'd ask for money to buy groceries, clothes, to go to the movies, buy gadgets. He'd give Duncan fake receipts, inflated prices. Nothing so much over he'd get suspicious, 'cause Duncan wasn't stupid. That was the whole problem. If he'd been stupid, he'd be way easier to fleece. Stephan had to take five, ten, maybe twenty dollars at a time. A few times, he'd been able to take bigger amounts, but mostly it had been slow gathering.

And he'd taken notes. Detailed notes, about everything he heard, every transaction he witnessed, every act of violence he saw. He had pictures and videos, too. Duncan wasn't dumb, but he was a digital amateur—as opposed to Stephan. His smart phone had been all he'd needed, besides a cloud backup and wipe he had installed. Once his phone had sent off the info, it deleted everything, and you had to have serious hacking skills to get it back. Or the password to his cloud backup, which was all but unbreakable. If Duncan ever tried to fuck him over, Stephan needed insurance. No one else would have Stephan's back, that much had become clear over the years.

He cleaned the cum off with a washcloth. Thank fuck he hadn't gotten it in his hair; that was a bitch to wash out.

Duncan was talking on the phone to someone when Stephan walked into the bedroom to get dressed.

"Will that settle our score? ... Your word is good enough for me. You know I'm a man of my word. All right, then."

He hung up.

"Put something nice on, baby, we're going out," Duncan yelled at him from the living room.

Fuck. Stephan hated the parties Duncan took him to. Duncan treating him like his bitch was something he had learned to live with, especially since the guy had been territorial and hadn't even allowed his friends or associates to look at him. Stephan had been grateful because it had kept him from being passed around, like some of the other girls and boys. Duncan had allowed no one else to fuck him in the four years he'd had Stephan—another tiny little thing to be grateful for.

But lately, that had changed. Duncan had made some crude remarks about Stephan earning his money, had joked with his friends about how good he was at sucking cock and how tight his ass still was, even after all these years. He'd bragged about Stephan in a way that had made his skin tingle, and not in a good way. Fuck, two weeks ago at a party he'd joked with his lieutenants about how much they'd pay for the experience of having Stephan suck them off, or to fuck him. Ever since, Stephan had been on edge, suspicious.

Maybe it was time to make a run for it, find his freedom. He had almost fifty grand hidden, enough to last him for a bit. He'd hoped for more, but wasn't sure how much more time he had before things went south. Not much, that was becoming clear.

He picked dark dungies, a tight light-blue shirt. Duncan liked him to look even younger than he was, and he didn't want to piss him off. That was a bad idea in general, but especially when he was high.

Duncan walked in as Stephan was putting gel in his blond spikes.

"Put on your tight dungies," he ordered. "They make your ass pop. And wear that red string. I want you to look hot and sexy."

Stephan's stomach sunk. Fuck, where was Duncan taking him? Red string? Nobody would see that, unless... Oh, this was not good. His insides churned as he got changed, going over every possible scenario. None of them were positive, but he knew better than to ask Duncan. He'd have to be careful, on his guard.

A limo brought them to an expensive hotel near Prudential they'd been to before, close to the city center.

"Where are we going?" he asked in the elevator.

"It's a surprise," Duncan said, winking at him. Stephan swallowed, turned his gaze away. Duncan pretended to be relaxed, but he was on edge. Stephan recognized the signs, the shifty eyes, biting his fingernails, not being able to stand still. Some of it was the coke but there was more. Something was going on. Fuck, Stephan hated surprises, since they were rarely good.

"I can't wait, honey," he purred. He had to keep up the front, stay alert on the inside.

Duncan put his hand on Stephan's ass as they walked through the hallway to a suite, at least that's what it said on the little plaque next to the door. Duncan knocked and the door was opened almost immediately by a handsome guy, dressed in expensive clothes, judging by the name brands.

"Stephan," he said, reaching for his hand and pulling him inside. "It's such a pleasure to meet you after hearing so much about you from Duncan. Come in."

Stephan wanted to say likewise but had no earthly idea who the guy was. "Thank you," he said, stepping into the room. He had expected a party, or at least a small gathering, but there was no one else there.

"Steph, wait here for us, all right? We'll be right back."

Stephan nodded as he couldn't do much else, and Duncan and the well-dressed guy left the suite. Damn, he'd never given Stephan his name. Everything about this felt bad, but what could he do?

He walked around the gigantic suite, checking out the shower with the double shower heads and the bathtub with jet streams. It didn't mean shit to him, all that expensive stuff. All the riches in the world meant crap without your freedom—a lesson he had learned the hard way the last four years.

He checked the slim golden watch he was wearing—a rare, expensive present from Duncan. It would fetch at least a grand in a pawn shop, which was the only reason Stephan liked it. It had been five minutes since the guys left. What the fuck was going on?

The door lock released and it opened. Stephan retreated back into the suite, his whole body tight with tension.

"Hello, Stephan."

He recognized the man's voice immediately, even before he walked into Indy's line of sight, and his body froze. Eric Fitzpatrick, Duncan's cousin. Equally handsome, but an unimaginably sick fuck. He was way, way worse than Duncan. Got off on rape. Stephan had seen him brutally violate a guy who had stolen from him, right in front of everyone. Fuck, what the hell was happening?

Eric was dressed in an expensive suit, as always. Out of habit, Stephan checked the guy's pupils. Would he be fucked up on something as well? Didn't look like it.

"Duncan didn't tell you, did he?"

Eric made a tut-tut-tut sound, while taking his jacket off, carefully hanging it on a chair.

"Tell me what?"

"He gave you to me. Well, for tonight at least. He owes me, you see, and this is his way of paying off that debt."

Stephan froze. Duncan had handed him over to Eric? Holy motherfucking hell, he was in so much more shit than he'd ever imagined.

"No response?"

Stephan shrugged with feigned indifference. "Does it matter what I say?"

Eric's laugh was chilling. "No, but I do hope you'll resist, at least a little. Struggling turns me on, as you know... You remember Tony, do you?"

Images flooded Stephan's mind. The guy who had stolen from Eric. Oh, he had struggled, all right. Eric could've had him hogtied and gagged, but he didn't. Even then, Stephan had realized the sick fuck had wanted to hear the guy scream, had gotten off on it. And damn, he had screamed. The rape had been ruthless, ferocious. Eric had fucked his straight, virgin hole until Tony had passed out from the pain, his ass a bloody mess. Stephan had had nightmares about it for days.

"I do," Stephan said, keeping his voice level. What were his options? Playing it cool and cooperating? Hope that Eric would get bored? Somehow, he doubted the bastard would allow that to happen. He'd make it interesting, somehow.

"Then you know what happens when you struggle." Eric unbuttoned his shirt sleeves, rolled them up meticulously.

"But if I don't struggle, how will you get off?" The words flew out of his mouth and he wanted to take them back immediately. Duncan would have backhanded him, but Eric laughed.

"You're a feisty one! Duncan hasn't fucked that out of you, huh? No wonder, with a dick that size." Eric pulled a knife out of his pocket, whipped it open with a lazy gesture. "We're going to have a wonderful time together, you and me."

INDY DIDN'T LOOK at Noah. He'd never be able to finish if he did. "He raped me," he said, fighting to keep his voice level. "I couldn't do a damn thing until he had to let go of the knife to tie the condom he'd used. I don't think he even expected me to fight back at that point. Nobody ever won against the Fitzpatricks, you know. I grabbed the knife, jammed it straight into his thigh. I stood in that hotel suite, Noah, and I watched him bleed out. Waited till I knew for sure he was dead until I called the cops."

"My God, Indy..."

Indy knew Noah wanted to comfort him, hold him, but he needed to finish the story before he lost the courage.

"I didn't wanna get charged with murder, so I needed the cops to collect evidence, to prove that he'd raped me and wanted to do it again. Otherwise they'd have never believed me had they ever arrested me. They would've thought I was loyal to the Fitzpatricks, had done it to help Duncan. Even then, they weren't fully convinced. But because I had solid inside intel about the Fitzpatricks' organization, they agreed to safeguard me and drop the charges for murder in exchange for my testimony. One of the cops turned out to be on the Fitzpatricks' payroll, however, and ratted my location out to Duncan. He brought three of his strong men and they held me down, tied me up, beat the living crap out of me."

"Your back." The words were forced out between Noah's clenched teeth. His eyes spewed fury.

Even thinking about it made Indy nauseous. The pain had been so blinding, he had passed out. "They poured some sort of acid on me. It burned straight through my skin. The pain knocked me out cold."

"Oh, baby..." Noah said, his voice thick with emotion.

"I was found hours later by a passerby. They had broken both my arms, my jaw, a couple of ribs, and I had a skull fracture. And my back was nothing but seared flesh. The rape kit came back negative, though. My guess is they planned to but backed out after they'd poured the acid on me. It would've hurt them as well, so they left me there, assuming I'd die. I spent months in the hospital recovering, having skin graft after skin graft."

"How did you know where to stab this guy?"

Indy flashed a wry smile. "I needed to hit a main artery so he'd bleed out fast. I went for the femoral artery. Something I picked up from Grey's Anatomy. I watched every episode at least twice."

Noah nodded with a hint of pride, but his face still showed the barely veiled fury. "Were they ever charged for their attack on you?"

"I was still willing to testify after that. They put me in protective custody, kept me under heavy guard all the time I was recovering. The DA was building his case with me as the star witness. After the attack on me everyone was finally convinced I was the real deal, that I wasn't playing them. My mom died in prison while I was recovering. She was stabbed by another inmate, bled out before the guards could get to her. I'm pretty sure Duncan was behind it. He did warn me he'd go after her, after all. I felt kinda upset, but not all that much, since she'd sold me to him. It felt like she brought it on herself, you know? I didn't have any other family, so no one Duncan could threaten me with. But two months before the trial was supposed to start, when I was finally recovered enough that I could start living again, I received an envelope. I was staying at a hotel on the other side of the country under surveillance, but still they managed to send me a message."

"What did it say?"

He swallowed. "'If you talk, we'll finish the job.' They had included a picture of me after they'd beaten me up, passed out on the floor, bloody and broken. I threw up when I saw it. The next day, I escaped my surveillance and took off."

He grabbed his tea back from Noah and took a gulp to soothe his achy throat.

"I've been on the run ever since. He hasn't stopped looking for me, and he never will. I had someone help me with a fake identity as a woman, and for the most part, I've lived as a woman for the past eighteen months. Until I met you and Josh…"

"Indy, what do I do? How do I help you through this?"

Noah's voice was warm and calm, but the suppressed anger showed in his tense jaw, his clenched fists, his eyes that had not quite pushed back the violence brought by Indy's story. He was angry on Indy's behalf and fuck, that felt good.

"Be patient with me. Before yesterday, I thought anything between us was impossible. Maybe I would've let you fuck me at some point, because I wanted you too much to keep saying no, but I was determined not to let you in. You were so wicked strong, and what you had with Josh was so special. I felt too damaged for you, was certain you'd never want to be with me if you knew my past and how fucked up I am. But then yesterday evening..." His voice trailed off, searching for the right words.

"You saw I'm as fucked up as you are, only in a different way," Noah finished the sentence.

Indy nodded, biting his lip.

Noah said, "Did it scare you? Did I scare you? As you put it, that was some serious fucking."

"No. It helped me see that we're all messed up, you, me, and Josh, but we cope in different ways. You reached your limits yesterday, and Josh helped you through that. It was beautiful."

Noah's brows raised, his head reeling back. "Beautiful? That's not what I expected you to say."

Indy smiled. "You should've seen Josh's face when he came. Pure bliss."

"How was it, you and him?"

There was curiosity in Noah's voice but also traces of hurt. He had to tell him everything. This was a conversation he needed to have up close and personal, however. Indy slid off his stool and stepped between Noah's legs. "Put me on your lap."

Noah's eyes grew big, but he lifted him and set Indy on his legs, turning his stool so Indy's back was supported by the counter. Indy was only wearing a shirt and boxer shorts, and the two layers of thin fabric did little to prevent him from feeling Noah's crotch. He put his hands on Noah's bare chest and let his fingers explore the skin, stroking his pecs, his nipples. The skin was deliciously rough under his fingers. He breathed in Noah's smell, more sweaty than usual. God, even the tangy odor of the man's sweat was intoxicating.

"It was healing," he said. Noah's muscles tightened where Indy touched him, and he reveled in Noah's sheer power. "It was what I needed to help me get ready for you. Josh may look like an angel, but his kisses alone are wicked and enough to make me hard as steel." Indy put a finger on Noah's lips. "He does this thing with his tongue, where— well, you've kissed him, so you know."

Noah cleared his throat, his breaths quickening. "We haven't kissed all that much, so feel free to tell me more, and don't be skimpy on the details."

"He let me top him," Indy said, grinding his crotch against Noah's hardening shaft.

"Did he now?" Noah managed, putting his hands on Indy's hips and pressing him down, increasing the contact between them.

Indy smiled.

"He sure did. He helped me prepare him and everything."

Indy rocked his hips back and forth, causing a delightful friction between their bodies. "And then he let me fuck him. It was so much better than I had imagined. My cock all snug and slick in his ass. He's so tight, so fucking hot. It was wicked fucking pissa."

"You know you're killing me here, right?" Noah grunted, pushing his groin upward.

The outline of Noah's thick erection pressed against Indy's ass. Indy threw his head back, laughed as delightful tingles teased his body. It was good to see Noah relax again, let go of the anger Indy's story had caused. "He had trouble...letting go. So I stole your trick."

Noah met his eyes, laughed. "You called him Joshua."

"Yup. I barked 'Dammit Joshua, let go,' and he blew his wad."

The deep laugh rumbled through Noah's chest.

Indy sobered. "I needed that experience with him. To

see sex differently, to feel what it can be like. He was so sweet to me, so perfect."

"I'm glad," Noah said.

Indy cocked his head and studied him. "Do you mean it? Aren't you jealous of Josh...or me?"

Noah kissed him, a feather-light touch on his lips. "Yeah, I mean it. And no, I'm not jealous, not anymore. I was yesterday, when I discovered the two of you naked, but that was because I was fucking exhausted and in too much pain. It does things to me, when I'm like that."

"I didn't mean to make you jealous."

Noah smiled. "I know. And just so you know: I was jealous of Josh, not you. I don't mind sharing him, but the thought that he'd had you first, that was a tough one."

"He didn't fuck me," Indy whispered, strangely warmed by Noah's admission. "And you know that I don't want to fuck things up between you two. But I'm ready."

Noah's face softened, and he blinked. "For me." He breathed in deeply, a look of reverence on his face. "I'm yours now, too," he said. He understood. "I'll take good care of you, Indy," he whispered.

"I know you will. I trust you."

"You're mine now."

Indy felt the words in his soul. "I am. And I know I'm sharing you with Josh, and I'm fine with that. He still needs you, and you may need him, because I can't take your anger. Not yet anyways, and maybe never. But sleeping between the two of you last night, it was special. It felt like home."

Footsteps sounded on the stairs and Josh walked up into the kitchen from the cellar, wearing running shorts. He gulped down half a bottle of water, then noticed them sitting together. A broad smile lit up his face.

"I see you two have found each other," he said with a happy smile.

"He's mine now," Noah said in an over-the-top stern tone, "So hands off."

"Oh," Indy said, pouting his lips, knowing Noah was joking. "Can I at least still kiss him? He's such a great kisser, and he can make me all hard and ready for you…"

"I can do that my damn self," Noah grumbled, before yanking Indy's mouth close and fusing their lips together. Indy's eyes crossed, and he vaguely heard Josh laughing. Noah's hot mouth attacked his with so much fervor, Indy wanted to crawl into him. His arms came around Noah's neck, and he wrapped his legs around Noah's waist. The deeper contact with his cock sent a shiver through his body. He was gasping for air when Noah let him go.

"You still wanna kiss Josh?" Noah teased, putting his hand between their bodies and squeezing Indy's shaft. "Seems to me you're plenty hard."

Indy moaned. "Who's Josh?" he said, grinding into Noah's hand.

"Exactly." Noah pulled back his hand, much to Indy's disappointment. He was even more surprised when Noah lifted him off his lap. "As much as I like this, we're not going to have sex right now."

"We're not?" Indy made no effort to hide his disappointment. What the fuck? He was finally ready to let the man claim him and now Noah didn't want him?

"No. I'm off today, and you and I are going on a date." He got up from the stool and kissed Indy on his mouth. "As much as I want you, we're gonna do this right. Get dressed warmly and we'll find a nice, secluded spot for a picnic, since the weather is brisk, but beautiful."

Indy stared at him, his mouth slightly open. "You want to take me on a picnic," he repeated.

Noah lifted his eyebrows. "Problem?"

Indy closed his mouth, considering it. "I guess not. I'll go get dressed."

Josh grinned. "I'll pack you guys some sandwiches."

17

Noah took Indy to a spot he'd heard about from Owens, who was an avid outdoors fan: a secluded lake in the Adirondacks. The lake was a short hike from a dirt road, a distance he could just about manage considering the pain in his leg. He'd taken the prosthesis off as soon as they'd gotten to the lake, content to let Indy see the real him. He loved that they could share their scars.

It was a bright and clear day, the stark blue sky contrasting with the autumn-colored trees. The crystal clear water of the lake reflected the surrounding mountains, creating a picture many painters would be drooling over. The air hummed with birds, and the water rippled every now and then. Could be beavers, Noah thought, his eyes spotting a beaver dam on the other side of the lake. It was October at its finest; the temperature hovering in the fifties.

"It's beautiful here," Indy said, stretching out on the thick fleece blanket they had brought. The tight jeans stretched around his perfect legs and round ass, and it hit Noah how much better he looked compared to four weeks ago. His cheeks had filled in, a rosy color enhancing his soft, pure skin, and his body showed four weeks of healthy eating.

"This time of year it is. Between June and the end of August, the bugs will eat you alive."

"Did you grow up in this area?"

"No, I've lived everywhere. Army brat, remember? I even spent two years in Germany as a kid. Hated it. Met Josh when my dad got transferred to DC and we moved to a suburb in Maryland. Josh and I only moved here 'cause I got that job at Albany General."

"Germany? Wow. I can't even imagine what that must have been like."

"It was okay. It's an American base there, so I had little contact with German kids. I learned some German, but it's all gone. If you learn a language as a kid but stop speaking it before you're ten or so, you forget it again."

Indy's eyes widened. "Really? I never knew."

Noah nodded. "The brain is weird that way. I became a Patriots fan in Germany, by the way."

Indy's brows shot up. "I never even wondered about that. Growing up in Boston, I never had a choice. It's Pats Nation, you know. Never even realized what an odd choice it is for you and Josh. How come?"

Noah smiled at the fun memories bubbling up in his brain. "My dad wasn't into football. On the base in Germany, I became friends with this kid from Western Massachusetts, Robby. His dad was the biggest football fan ever, and of course he supported the Patriots. Hanging out with Robby, I sorta got into it and cheered for their team. The Pats have had my loyalty ever since. And since they were from Boston, I became a Red Sox fan, too. When Josh and I started hanging out, he got into it as well. More to please me at first, but now he's as much of a fan as I am."

"Well, I'm glad Robby was a Pats fan. Had he been from Texas, you and I would have had a wicked serious problem."

Indy rolled on his stomach, his face morphing to serious, and studied Noah for a few seconds. "Why did you enlist?" he asked. "You said it was never your dream."

Noah sighed. Even thinking about his mom made him sad all over again. "My mom died two months before my graduation. She had breast cancer. When she died, I kind of lost my way. Got blind drunk for a while, woke up not remembering where I was or how I'd gotten there. My mom, she had tried to support me best as she could in what I wanted, but my dad didn't give a shit. He wanted me to become a career soldier, like himself. I didn't know how to stand up to him, so I signed up to become an army medic. Did my basic training, then did medical training in Texas. In the field, I took more courses and gained a ton of experience. Graves, my CO, liked me, liked my work, so he recommended me for the physician assistant program, which I had just completed when I got blown up. He helped me transfer to a civilian hospital as a PA."

"So what did you want to do?"

Noah hesitated. He had never told anyone else but Josh. "I wanted to be a psychologist. Maybe even a psychiatrist. Too late now."

Indy nodded. "It suits you. You read people like a book."

Noah shrugged, happy with his praise. "Like I said, too late now."

"Why? You don't love what you're doing now," Indy said. "No, don't deny it, it's true. You like it, because you like helping people, but you don't love it. It wears you out, and it's more than the physical aspect. You're drained after a shift."

Indy was so right. Noah had realized it more and more the last few weeks. Something had to change, because he wasn't sure how long he could do this anymore.

"I'm not the only one who can read people," he said, touched that Indy had seen it, seen him. He sighed, a long heavy sigh. "It's the adrenaline. I've had years and years of it, and it breaks me. Plus, the standing and walking is hard on my wounds."

"So quit."

"Just like that, huh? And what would we live on?"

"What, you and Josh?"

"Josh, me...you. Somebody has to pay the mortgage, you know."

"That's a patronizing remark. I don't need you to pay anything for me. I can take care of myself."

The anger was palpable in Indy's voice, and his eyes were blazing. He was right, of course. "I know. I don't mean to insult you, Indy, I swear, but it's how I'm wired. I take care of people."

"I don't need you to take care of me," Indy said.

Noah sighed. "I know. But maybe you could let me, just a little?"

Indy bit his lip, apparently thinking about it. "Why isn't Josh working, is it because of his PTSD?"

"Josh was in a bad place after I got hurt, and he was in no shape to work. Plus, in all fairness, I needed someone to help me, so it worked out well for both of us. He likes being home, so I'm not sure if he'll ever want to get a job. I won't pressure him."

"What did he do in the army?"

"He was a sharpshooter...a sniper. And a damn good

one. He seldom missed and had the patience of Job to get his target. But killing people like that, even when they're enemies, it's personal. It's taken a toll. He hasn't found a good way yet to live with it."

"Why did he even enlist? He seems like the least likely candidate."

A wave of guilt hit Noah. "For me. He did it for me. I had made up my mind to enlist, and he went with me. Fuck, I leaned so hard on him after my mom died. He was my best friend, was always there for me. He was my wingman when I'd go out to get drunk, always made sure I got home safe, even cleaned up after I puked my guts out. He took care of me even then."

Something flashed over Indy's face, as if what Noah was saying wasn't news to him. What had Josh shared with him already?

"Don't you think he maybe did it for himself, to stay as close to you as possible?" Indy asked.

"No. Maybe. I don't know. It was messed up, and I was furious with him for enlisting, yet relieved at the same time."

Indy frowned. "If you don't have good memories of your time in the Army, why are you both still wearing dog tags?"

Indy was so perceptive. It was one of the character traits Noah admired about him. He truly listened. "Josh was advised to wear them, because of his PTSD. If something were to happen to him, they'd know who he was. Plus, like you experienced, if he acts strange and people see the tags, they're more likely to be understanding. Since he had to wear them, I wanted to as well. Solidarity, and all that."

"Was it hard for Josh, serving?"

Noah's face hardened. "No. Surprisingly enough, he did really well. He liked the routine. And as I said, he was damn good at what he did. But he should've never signed up, with him being gay. The army wasn't a safe place for him, and he got hurt because of me."

Bile rose in his throat. It was his fault. Without his stupid decision to join the army, Josh would have never signed up, would have never been in that fuck-awful place, would have never gotten—he couldn't even wrap his mind around it, couldn't fathom soldiers doing that to a brother-in-arms.

"What happened?"

Indy's voice was soft, warm. Noah hid his face in his hands. He didn't want to look at Indy. Hell, he wasn't even sure if he should tell him this. Would it trigger bad memories? Was it even his place to share Josh's story, when Josh himself could barely talk about it? Shit, what good would it even do? Once he told him, Indy would never look at him the same. He'd recognize it was his fault Josh got hurt.

"Noah." Indy's arms came around him, cradling his head. "It's okay. You don't have to tell me now. Wait till you're ready."

He hugged him back, seeking his mouth, then kissing him with a desperate urgency to forget. He wanted to feel anything else but guilt and shame over what he had done, what he had caused. Indy accepted him in, pulling him tight and kissing him back with sweetness. Noah lifted Indy on his lap and he circled his legs around Noah, his arms around Noah's neck.

Indy was his.

Noah's desperation eased, taken away by Indy's sweet lips. Oh man, that tongue—he wasn't sure if he'd learned that from Josh or not, but the slick dance Indy did with his tongue in Noah's mouth made him weak and dizzy inside, quivering with desire. He laced his fingers through Indy's beautiful curls and pressed him close.

"This is my favorite spot for you, you know that? You belong on my lap," Noah said after what seemed like hours of kissing. He leaned his forehead against Indy's, his eyes closed.

"I love being here, too. It makes me feel wicked safe."

"I will do anything to keep you safe, baby. Anything."

Indy sighed. "The Fitzpatricks, they're not people you want to mess with. Look at what they did to me. I wasn't meant to survive that, you know."

Noah's stomach rolled at the thought of what those bastards had done to his Indy. The pain Indy must have been in, both physically and emotionally. He couldn't even imagine. And he understood what Indy was saying. The threat was real. How could he not take it seriously after hearing Indy's story? These guys were real-life criminals who would not hesitate to kill anyone who was a threat to them. But how could Noah not vow to protect what was his? Somehow, he'd find a way.

He kissed Indy's nose, holding him tight. "I know, baby. I'm not being flippant about this. But I love you too much to ever let you go, so we'll find a way for you to be safe, okay?"

Indy froze in his arms, and Noah realized what he had said.

Love.

He'd used the big L-word, had blurted out what was in his heart. And nope, he didn't regret it one bit, since it was true. He loved Indy, loved him with every fiber of his being.

He opened his eyes and leaned back slightly so he could see Indy's face. He stared at Noah with big eyes, his mouth slightly open.

"You love me?" he managed.

"I love you. Not as a friend, but as in I want to spend the rest of my life with you, protect you with everything I've got, take care of you till the day I die. That kind of I love you."

Indy bit his lip in that adorable way he often did when he was pondering something. Noah waited. He couldn't rush him now.

"What about Josh?" Indy asked, his eyes downcast. He was still on Noah's lap, but he felt a thousand miles away right now.

"Don't make me choose between you." The thought of having to make that choice made it hard to breathe. Choosing between his best friend to whom he owed everything and this man who had managed to make him fall in love so hard and so deep—he couldn't.

"I would never do that. I'm asking because I don't want you to stop loving him. I don't want to take his place."

How had this tender heart stayed so pure despite everything that had happened to him? How did a boy who survived so much come out with his kind heart intact? He and Josh were so much alike, in that aspect.

"You could never take his place, baby. Josh is my best friend, my sanity. I don't want to go through life without him, and he still needs me as much as I need him. But I love you, baby, as much as I love him, though in a different way. My heart is big enough for you both if you are willing to share me. I know it's not how it's supposed to be, but it's all I can give."

Noah was all too aware of his heart's fragile state. Indy had the power to break it into pieces that could never be whole again.

Indy looked up, his eyes solemn. "Nobody has ever loved me before, so I don't know the first thing about love, or what it's supposed to be like. But I have little to offer you in return."

"Do you love me?" Noah dared to ask.

"I don't know what love feels like. What do I have to compare it with? I don't want to hurt you—I just want to be honest. You and Josh, you make me feel safe and wanted and special. I want to be with you enough to ignore my urge to run. Is that enough?"

"How do I feel to you?" Noah asked.

"Fuck, Noah, you know what you do to me." A delightful blush crept up Indy's rosy cheeks.

"Tell me anyway. I want details," Noah ordered.

Indy's eyes narrowed, his breathing quickening. "You want details? You sure?"

A smile spread across Noah's lips. Fuck, he was about to regret this, but he wanted it anyway. "Bring it."

The next second he was flat on his back, Indy stretched out on top of him. Indy's warm hands slid under Noah's jacket and found his skin under his shirt. He brought his mouth close to Noah's ear. "Promise me you'll stay still."

"I promise."

"I love how strong you are." Indy's hand slid up under Noah's shirt and found his right biceps. "Fuck, even looking at your arms makes me feel weak inside."

Noah hummed, closing his eyes to revel in the sensation of Indy touching him. Fuck, he'd missed that touch so much. Craved it.

Indy's hand traveled to his pecs, gently squeezing each nipple. Noah shuddered. "Your chest, damn, it's perfect. When you hold me, I feel like there's a strong wall around me, like a protected castle."

His other hand came up to Noah's cheek, rubbing his stubble, and Noah's eyes opened. "I love how rough you are everywhere. I'm such a boy compared to you, and I love it. Makes me feel small, but in a good way."

He kissed Noah. "You should smile more. It makes my heart stutter when you do. Your smile can light up an entire room." Noah couldn't help but smile at those words, and Indy let out a sigh. "Fuck, yeah, like that. Brings me to my knees, every single time."

Noah balled his fists. He'd made a promise to stay still, and he was fighting hard to keep it, because, damn, he wanted his hands on his man. On his ass, on his cock, everywhere.

Indy dropped soft little kisses all over Noah's face. "Those freckles of yours are totally cute. They shouldn't fit a face like yours, but they do. They soften your face, make you look a tad less arrogant. Because you are arrogant as shit, you know that, right? And what's even worse is that that fuck-you tone of yours totally turns me on."

Noah was developing a love-hate relationship with the way Indy was worshiping his body. He loved his tender touch, his frank words, but was regretting his promise not to touch. Deep need pulsed through his veins, rushing to his cock. His balls hung heavy, thrumming with arousal. He was getting to a point where he'd have to beg Indy to back off, because he wouldn't be able to control himself.

Right then, Indy leaned up on his elbows and pressed his crotch hard against Noah's. "What's doing, loverboy?" Indy teased. He wriggled his hand between them and cupped Noah's cock. Noah raised up to push against Indy's hand. Fuck, the man was killing him.

"You about done with the dirty talk?" he ground out through his teeth.

Indy laughed and the sound shot straight to Noah's balls. "Just getting started."

Noah groaned. "Fuck, kill me now, would you? Not sure how much more of this I can take."

"I've got something better than killing you."

With one swift move, Indy pushed his hand under Noah's track pants and whipped out his cock. Before Noah could react to that unexpected move, Indy dropped off him sideways, kneeled and engulfed Noah's cock in his mouth.

"Oh, fuck!" Noah let out, bucking his hips at the sudden sensation of his dick in a hot, wet mouth.

He pushed himself up on his elbows, wanting to make sure Indy was okay, that he was doing this for the right reasons. His gaze fell on Indy's head, bowed over him, his curls hiding part of his face. The only part that was visible was that hot mouth around his shaft. Damn, he'd never seen anything more sexy than that.

"Indy, you don't—Fuuuuck!"

Indy deep throated his entire cock with ease and Noah saw stars. Actual, literal fucking stars. He let out some unintelligible sounds, then moaned harder than he'd thought possible. Indy let his cock slide out a little, sucking him like a lollipop, then took him right back in. His throat engulfed Noah's cock, and he clamped the base of Noah's cock tight with his hand. If Indy kept this up... Damn, his balls tingled already.

No, he couldn't come like this. This one-sided pleasure, it was not okay. But damn, that mouth. Noah bucked again, unable to restrain himself. His eyes clenched shut, his senses overloading.

"Damn, I can't...I don't want to...baby, I'm too far..."

He moaned again, embarrassingly loud. Indy's mouth never let up, kept sucking him in in that wet, tight space. His hands gripped, pressed, nipped his balls in exquisite torture until Noah was a liquid mess of heat and want.

Noah lost all coherence as his body took over. Thrashing, tensing, tightening...and then releasing with a roar that seemed to come from his toes. He blasted deep into Indy's mouth, who sucked it all up, licked him clean till the last drop, letting out happy hums.

His vision dizzy and his ears still buzzing from the force of his release, Noah sought with his hand till he found Indy, then pulled him back on top of him.

"Please, tell me I didn't hurt you, didn't force myself too hard in your mouth."

Indy kissed him, his mouth still salty and creamy with the remnants of Noah's cum.

"You didn't," Indy said between kisses. "Didn't you feel my hand around your base?" More kisses, each deeper than the one before. Damn, Noah loved tasting himself on Indy's tongue. "Little trick I learned to prevent guys from pushing in too far."

They both stilled.

A trick.

Indy had learned to do this to prevent guys from going too far.

White-hot rage barreled through Noah's veins at the thought of anyone raping his Indy's mouth.

Indy pushed away from him with both hands. Noah wanted to stop him, but he couldn't hold Indy against his will. Not now. Not ever. Indy rolled off him, sat up with his back toward Noah.

Noah put his cock back in his pants. Fuck. That innocent remark must have triggered a shitload of bad memories for Indy. What could he say to take away Indy's pain?

"I'm sorry, Noah..."

Wait, what? What the fuck did he have to be sorry for? He rolled on his side, facing Indy's back. "What's going through your head, baby?"

It took forever for Indy to answer. "I'm not a whore."

What the fuck? Noah's fingers itched to grab Indy and make him face the other way, but he held back. "Where's that coming from? You're not, and I would never think that."

He voiced it much sharper than he had meant it, and he winced.

Indy's head sunk low on his chest. "I didn't mean to make you feel cheap, like a client or something."

Noah shook his head. "You didn't. You gave me an amazing gift, why would I feel cheap?"

"Because I compared you to Duncan and other guys I've...had."

Was that what Indy was upset about? Not the bad memories, but the fear of hurting Noah's feelings? "Damn, baby, I never even went there. I thought you pulled away because your own words triggered bad memories. It made me so angry to think that you had to learn to defend yourself from guys going too far with you."

Indy turned around, his shoulders still hunched and his eyes peering upward to Noah's. "You're not angry with me?" he asked in a timid voice.

Noah did what his heart told him. He opened his arms wide. "No, my sweet baby. I was angry for you, not with you."

Indy made his way into Noah's arms, leaning against him sideways and exhaling. Yeah, not close enough, Noah decided and plucked his man under the arms to pull him on his lap, right where he belonged. He nuzzled his neck and let out a grunt of contentment.

"Your mouth is heaven, baby. Thank you for giving me so much pleasure."

"Noah, will you do something for me?" Indy whispered against Noah's chest. It hit Noah how little Indy asked. He couldn't remember a single time that Indy had asked for a favor.

"Anything."

"Will you please fuck me when we get home?"

INDY WAS out of the car before the garage door closed. He laughed hard, racing inside with Noah on his heels. They'd barely spoken a word in the car, both too eager for the next step.

"How was the picnic?" Josh asked as they entered the kitchen. He was at the breakfast counter, reading a book and sipping a cup of tea.

"Who cares," Noah growled, smacking Indy's ass. "Get your butt upstairs, right now."

Indy shot a teasing look over his shoulder, pouted his lips. "But Noah, I thought we could watch some TV first."

He let out a loud squeal when Noah picked him up and slung him over his shoulder. Damn, his man was strong. Fuck if that brute strength didn't make his heart skip a few beats. In a good way. He wasn't scared, not even a little bit.

"We're done talking. Let's go." Noah started walking, hauling Indy with ease. "Josh, my man, we'll be busy upstairs for a while. We'll let you know when it's safe."

Indy slapped Noah's ass with both his hands since it was so easily within reach. "Put me down, you big brute."

"Erm, no. Not a chance. Not letting you go now. Not ever."

Indy's heart warmed at the playful words that rang so true. Forever with this wonderful man, now there was a dream he could get behind. It was a pipe dream, but oh, damn, it was a good one. He stopped struggling, allowed

Noah to carry him if only because it made him feel all gooey inside to be hauled off.

"Have fun!" Josh yelled after them, laughter in his voice.

Noah didn't stumble once carrying him upstairs into the big bedroom, kicking the door shut behind him. He lifted Indy off his shoulder, laid him down on the bed on his back.

When Noah towered over Indy, panic rose for a second. He pushed it down hard. This was Noah. This was the man who had held him naked in the shower and had not lifted a finger. This was the man whose first concern had been that he'd hurt Indy when he'd given him a blow job. This was the man who had respected his boundaries every step of the way. He had nothing to fear, nothing.

Noah stilled, as if sensing Indy needed a second to calm himself. "Remember what I promised you. A simple 'no' is enough, at any time."

Indy nodded at Noah's soft words, felt them in the deepest depths of his heart to be true. "I trust you."

"What do you want, Indy? You have to tell me. Do you want to go slow? Do you need some time to adapt?"

Indy shook his head. "No, I'm done waiting. I want you now."

Indy sat up and whipped off his own shirt, gripped by the powerful need to feel Noah's skin on his, nothing between them. His pants came off next, then he yanked off his socks and stripped down his boxers. The fear and shame he'd half-expected to pop up at being naked in front of Noah never came. Fuck, he wanted this more than anything.

"Hurry the fuck up, would you?" he said, climbing over the bed toward Noah. Noah's eyes radiated such want and desire it made Indy shiver.

He kneeled on the bed and pulled at Noah's shirt until

the man moved with something resembling urgency and undressed.

"Yes!" Indy let out a token sound of appreciation when Noah stood naked in front of him. Damn, that body of his. He was so fucking hot. Every single muscle perfect, every inch of skin strong and masculine. And oh, that thick cock ready for action, pointing straight at him. Every sliver of fear Indy had ever entertained about never being able to enjoy sex ever again disappeared as his mouth watered at the thought of taking this man in.

Without taking his eyes off Indy, Noah unhooked his prosthesis and let it drop on the floor.

"How do you want us?" Noah asked.

The strangest feeling flooded Indy. It was a warm buzz that pulsed through his entire body, made him tingle from his toes to the top of his head. It dizzied him, made it hard to think over the overwhelming sensation of...love. This had to be what love felt like.

Damn, he loved Noah. Completely. He loved this man who always put him and his needs first, never his own.

"I want to see you," he whispered.

Noah nodded. "Get on your back, put some pillows under your butt."

Indy complied without hesitation, scooting backward on the bed and propping two soft pillows under his ass. He spread his legs wide, pulling his feet up. Now that he'd made the decision to give in to what he'd wanted all along, he couldn't wait.

Noah threw a bottle of lube from the nightstand drawer on the bed, then sat down between Indy's legs. He trailed his index finger from Indy's ankle all the way up to his thigh. Indy shivered in response.

"You're so beautiful," Noah said reverently. "You have no idea how badly I want you."

Indy took a deep breath. Noah had said it himself, he had to say what he wanted. "Noah, as much as I appreciate your words and everything, can we do the slow stuff another time? I want you. I need you, and the longer you wait the more time I have to get scared, so could you maybe hurry the fuck up, please?"

Much to Indy's delight, Noah let out a relieved sigh and smiled. "Fuck, baby, that's music to my ears. I wasn't sure if I had the patience to go slow."

He grabbed the lube, squirted out a glob, and settled himself between Indy's legs. "Open wide for me, baby."

Indy let his legs fall open even wider and scooted down lower on the pillows so Noah had free access. He was wide open, vulnerable, about to surrender to this powerful man who could hurt him if he wanted to. But the panic never came. Instead, there was trust, anticipation, a wave of sheer desire that licked at his insides like a starting fire, ravenous to burn brighter.

Noah's index finger found his hole and probed. Indy breathed in, out, and let him in.

The heat roared higher as Noah circled his finger, pushed it in and out. Fuck, the mere sensation of Noah's finger gave Indy goose bumps, and a low moan stirred in his throat. He wanted more, needed so much more.

"More," he whispered.

Noah smiled, pulled out and added a second finger. Indy bore down, let them in with ease. It stung when Noah pushed in deep, but it also intensified the liquid heat in his belly. Pleasure was already assailing him, making his cock grow even harder. He closed his eyes and focused on relaxing his muscles, giving Noah the access they both so desperately wanted.

Noah would take care of him. The thought kept circling in his head, pushing all other thoughts out. There was no room for bad memories, fear, or even the mention of Duncan. His body, mind, and soul were tuned in to the man between his legs.

"How are you doing, baby?" Noah asked huskily. He widened his fingers, and Indy let out a soft moan as the man grazed a sensitive spot inside him. The flames inside him licked at his cock, his balls, setting them on fire.

"Good, I'm good."

Noah hummed. He pulled out again, then added a third finger. Indy froze for a second as the intrusion breached his outer ring. Noah stopped immediately. Indy let out a shuddering breath, relaxed again.

Noah resumed his movements, but slowly. The man was focused on every minute signal Indy's body emitted to make sure he was all right.

Love. It really was a fucking miracle, wasn't it?

Noah twisted his hand, rotating it so his fingers pointed upward. He pushed in deep, stretching Indy farther open. It was that strange mix of pain and pleasure where the sting of the burn and the stab of pleasure intertwined, both sending electric shocks through his ass, radiating to his cock and nuts. He shivered, impatient for more.

"You're so damn tight." Noah's voice rang with concern.

Indy understood. Noah was scared of hurting him. "Imagine how good that's going to feel around your cock," he teased.

"Oh, I can imagine just fine. I've had my eye on that perfect ass of yours since the day I met you."

This was it. His body was ready. And fuck, his mind was

ready too. He wanted this, wanted Noah. "What are you waiting for, then? I'm ready."

Noah's hand stopped. "You sure?"

"More than anything."

Noah pulled back his hand.

"I'm tested and negative," Indy whispered.

Noah nodded. "Good. I want nothing between us when I make you mine."

He sat up straight, poured more lube in his hand and coated his cock. He hesitated, so Indy grabbed his arm, pulled him. Noah lowered himself on top of Indy, letting his weight rest on his arms.

Indy looked up. Noah's eyes shone with love and want. Indy's heart stumbled, then went into free fall.

Damn, the sensation of a big, strong man on top of him intoxicated him. He was born for this, to be with this man. He didn't say anything, wasn't capable of forming words, but nodded.

Noah's cock lined up against Indy's hole, Noah guiding it into position with one hand. As soon as Noah pushed, Indy breathed out and bore down, welcoming him in. Noah slid in as if they'd done it a thousand times before, as if his dick knew the way home.

"Oh, fuck," Noah breathed when he inched in deeper, past the snug entrance. "Oh...fuck."

Indy smiled. It wasn't the most eloquent of expressions, but it sure as hell was sexy to see his man throwing his head back in ecstasy.

Noah pushed in a little deeper, Indy's ass adjusting quickly. Oh, it burned all right, but nothing he couldn't handle. Nothing that didn't bring pleasure as much as discomfort. He closed his eyes, squirmed a little. God, his muscles were squeezing Noah's cock like a vise. Even halfway in, Indy felt deliciously full.

"Keep going," he encouraged Noah, who had stopped moving.

"Give me a second," was the quick reply.

"I'm fine!"

"I'm not," Noah bit out. "You're so fucking snug around my cock that I'm gonna blow my wad if I don't stop."

Indy opened his eyes. Noah's jaw was tight, his teeth clamped down and his brows furrowed. Every muscle in his body was on full alert. It was clear he was fighting as hard as he could.

It was an unbelievably arousing sight. To know he had this effect on this strong man, that he could bring him to his knees—Indy had never felt sexier in his life.

"So let go. You have another round in you."

Noah's eyes opened. Narrowed with a solid dose of stubbornness and pride. "No. You have to go first."

Indy remembered what Josh had told him, how Noah always made sure Josh came first and how Noah's sense of guilt played into that. Was Noah somehow feeling guilt toward Indy as well? He didn't want this beautiful experience with Noah sullied by a false sense of guilt.

"I'm not Josh, Noah."

His words were steel wrapped in velvet. He was willing to go to war over this. What he and Noah had, it had to be right from the start. He couldn't allow it to get burdened with destructive patterns they'd never get rid of again.

"Damn it, Indy, I know."

Noah kept holding still, their eyes locked in a battle of wills.

"Then why do I have to come first?"

"Because I want to make it good for you."

"Yeah, so? Who says you can't do both, allow yourself to come first and make me come afterward?"

Noah stubbornly shook his head.

Fuck, this was a deeper issue than Indy had anticipated. And here he'd thought he was the one who was all fucked up about sex. "Pull out."

Noah didn't hesitate even a second, but drew back—letting out a groan as the sensation undoubtedly brought him even closer to the edge.

Indy felt empty inside when that wonderful thick cock left him, leaving him cold and yearning for that fullness and friction. As soon as Noah was out, Indy hooked his leg around him, put Noah's arm in an arm bar and flipped him on his back with ease. He unhooked himself and stretched out on top of Noah, their faces a breath apart.

"I need you to listen. I know that my notion of sex is pretty fucked up, considering my past. But so is yours. You've created this pattern where you associate sex with guilt. Somehow, you feel guilty for taking pleasure, so you compensate by making Josh or me come first. You fucking refuse to let go until then. Even today when I was blowing you, you were fighting it. You have to stop this. If you want to be with me, it can't only be about me, what I want, and my pleasure. You have to be able to take as much as you give, or this won't ever work."

"I need to take care of you," Noah said, a hint of desperation in his voice. "I can't help it, it's how I'm wired."

"First, that's bullshit. You always have a choice, no matter how you're wired. But more importantly, that's a narrow view you have of what taking care of someone means. Don't you realize how much joy it brings me to know I can pleasure you, make you lose control, make you come minutes after being inside of me? You're robbing me of that experience if you always want to delay your pleasure for mine. How's that taking care of me?"

Noah was quiet for a long time, studying Indy with eyes that seemed to peer deep into his soul.

"You're right," he said. "I never looked at it that way."

"Okay, then," Indy said, relieved. "Now, where were we?"

Noah's eyes widened. "You still want to...?" His voice betrayed his insecurity.

Indy didn't say anything, just moved his body downward until he'd lined up with that thick, gorgeous cock. He raised himself on his knees, took Noah's shaft in his hand and lowered himself.

Noah's eyes closed, his hands white-knuckling the sheets as Indy took him in, inch by inch.

Indy breathed calmly, easing downward on the exhale, never once tensing or panicking until he had every inch of that glorious dick inside of him. He let out a deeply content, "Fuck, yes!"

Noah's hands gripped his hips as the man angled his hips to slide in even deeper. Noah's balls bumped against his ass and wasn't that the most erotic sensation ever? Hot damn, he'd never thought it could feel this good.

He raised his hips, came down again in an experimental move. This was a new position for him as he'd always been fucked either doggy style or on his back—never on top. He loved the control it gave him—though there was something to be said for having a strong, big body towering over you— but also how deep he could take Noah in this way.

Indy rose up again, surged down in a controlled move. He moaned as Noah's cock hit a sensitive spot inside that made him tingle all over. Oh, he'd discovered the perfect angle! Indy lifted his hips, rose and lowered, rose and lowered, setting a steady pace, his face drawn in fierce concentration. Hot damn, his ass was loving the shit out of Noah's cock, the tip tagging that spot inside that made him fucking dance with pleasure.

Beneath him, Noah groaned and tensed, his fingers digging hard into Indy's hips. He never pulled or pushed. It felt like his hands were there to steady them both.

Indy leaned backward, changing the angle just so and moved up and down faster.

"Ungh!" Noah let out. He spasmed, that big chest heaving as he panted.

Indy smiled. The man had to be close. He could feel the powerful muscles trembling beneath him.

"You ready, big guy?" he teased, before lifting his ass and slamming down hard.

"Oh, fuck!" Noah shouted.

Another slam. Indy let out a curse, his pulse racing. Damn, he hit that spot again and a full-body tremor tore through his body, his legs nearly giving out. He had to angle to the right to get there. But first, he wanted to get Noah off so they could both take their time for the next round. A few fast and hard moves should do the trick.

Indy pulled up, moved down hard and deep. Noah's legs pulled tight under him, the muscles of his stomach taut. Noah sucked in air, gasped. Indy's chest squeezed tight, watching his man in the throes of pleasure. He did this to him.

Another deep thrust.

Noah bucked, came halfway off the mattress, spasmed again, then released with a shout. He held Indy's hips as he shot his load deep into Indy's ass, his eyes pinched closed, his head in his neck.

Indy lowered himself on top of his man, wanting to be held while Noah recuperated. The strong arms came around him, pulling him close. Noah's chest rose and dipped under Indy's cheek, the muscles still contracting every now and then with the aftereffects of his powerful release. Their torsos were slick with perspiration.

"Damn, baby, your ass is heaven. It's like a constant compression sleeve that fits my cock perfectly, and when you move—I'm seeing stars."

Noah's words made Indy's heart sing. What a rush it was to bring this man to his knees.

Noah's cock slipped out of his ass, and Indy let out a soft protest.

"Do you want to switch?" Noah asked, his breathing returning to normal.

Indy frowned. "What do you mean? You want me to lie on my back again?"

"No, I mean do you want to switch...fuck me, I mean."

The question was so unexpected, Indy was floored. Noah had said he'd be fine with Indy topping him, but somehow the reality of that option hadn't sunk in yet until now. He'd meant it. He was serious about letting Indy be top.

Indy considered it. It had been an amazing experience fucking Josh. The sensation of his cock in that tight, velvet heat had been beyond anything he'd ever experienced. But it had also been nerve-racking and had fueled his insecurities about the size of his dick and the responsibility of making it a good experience for the bottom. Was that what he wanted right now?

He'd felt so full with Noah inside of him. So complete. Like he was whole for the first time, part of something bigger and better than only himself. Nothing had ever made him feel like that, not even close. Even now, despite being so close to Noah, his body felt strangely empty. Maybe it was because he hadn't come yet, but he was craving Noah. Craving his cock, more precisely.

"No," he said, his voice strong. "But thank you for offering."

He inched up higher on Noah's chest, lifted his head and found the man's soft lips, that delightful stubble sanding his skin. He licked Noah's lower lip, sucking on it before entering his mouth with his tongue. Noah growled against his mouth, his hands dropping to Indy's ass to knead both cheeks.

Cum dripped out of his hole, and the sensation reminded Indy of that conversation he and Noah had in the shower. He pulled back his mouth.

"I have something you need to see," he said, his voice husky.

"What could possibly be so important that I need to see it right now?" Noah all but whined.

Indy chuckled. "Trust me. You don't want to miss this."

He rolled off Noah onto the bed.

"Sit up," he told him.

Noah's curiosity was piqued, judging by his quick response to Indy's order. He obeyed, looked at Indy with brows raised.

Indy climbed on all fours, then turned so his ass faced Noah, pushing it back and widening his legs to give his man an unobstructed view.

"See that?" he whispered.

He looked back over his shoulder, caught Noah shamelessly ogling the sight before him, his breath catching. His mouth hung open, like he was gasping for air.

Indy shot him a sultry smile, then reached backward between his legs and drew more cum out with his index finger. Damn, his hole was sopping wet with Noah's juices.

"That is the single most delicious sight I have ever seen," Noah offered in a raspy whisper. "Hot damn, baby, you were so right. Your gorgeous ass looks even more perfect with my cum dripping out of it."

The low rumble of Noah's voice shot straight to Indy's balls, and everything in him purred. His hole twitched hard under Noah's erotic gaze. It knew exactly what it wanted and so did Indy.

"Fuck me, Noah. I need you."

18

Noah's ears buzzed. Sure, his man had said he was up for a second round, but somehow Noah had thought that would change as soon as he pulled out after coming so fucking hard. Maybe it would hurt, or Indy would realize he had gotten no pleasure out of it, or something.

But instead, he had offered Noah this unbelievably erotic sight of his twitching hole, cum leaking out of it, ready for the taking. He wanted it, wanted Noah to fuck him. The mere thought of burying his cock in that snug hole again made him shiver. His cock twitched, craved. The slick heat, the hot pressure of that tight place—he'd never felt anything like it.

Noah didn't even think. He reached out and yanked Indy forward until his ass was in the perfect position. Indy canted his ass at the perfect angle, inviting Noah in. With one thrust, Noah plunged to the hilt, never encountering even the slightest resistance. Indy's ass was squeezing him so fucking hard, putting pressure on every single inch of his throbbing cock. He pumped his hips, the angle changing until Indy let out a deep groan.

Jackpot.

He vowed to make Indy see fucking stars before he himself came again.

Rocking his hips backward, he withdrew to his crown, then surged right back into that silky haven. Feeling his entire cock sink in till his balls slapped that perfect round ass sent stabs of rapture through his dick, to the deep core of his balls.

The pace he set was steady and deep, fluid thrusts hitting that sensitive place inside Indy spot-on. Indy pushed back his ass, met him thrust for thrust, panting and moaning in erotic sounds that spurred Noah on even further. Pleasure surged through his body, gathering in his balls, making them heavy and full all over again.

Indy was enjoying this, no doubt about it, maybe the first time in his life he was getting pleasure from being fucked. Noah felt a swell of pride that he was causing this, that he was part of a healing process that would help Indy enjoy sex again.

His hand came around Indy's slender waist, finding his rock-hard dick dripping with precum. Noah's thumb brushed over the slit, spreading the liquid so he could jack him off nice and smooth. He loved that his hand could easily hold Indy's cock—like he was protecting him, taking care of him.

His hips pumped faster, his hand settling in the same rhythm. Indy was thrashing under him, so close to his release he was jerking. Noah was fucking the shit out of him, wrenching a constant stream of moans and groans from Indy's lips. His own heart pounded, his chest rising and falling fast, his breaths ragged.

"Oh, Noah... Please!"

The pressure on Noah's dick increased, signaling to him that Indy was tensing up before his release. He slammed home, making sure to hit that sweet spot, jerking Indy's shaft at the same time. Indy's breaths became erratic, hard. Noah squeezed Indy's dick again, shoving in deep at the same time.

Indy cried out hard, a shudder tearing through his body as he erupted in Noah's hand.

"Noah! Fuuuck!"

Thick streams of cum sprayed over Noah's hand and the bed, eliciting a deep satisfaction in him. His body purred with approval. Damn, it felt good to make Indy come so hard.

Noah braced himself, expecting Indy to go slack any second, and he caught him when he did. Noah lowered him on the bed with his stomach on some pillows, spread his weak legs and found a perfect spot between them, sliding right back inside. He wasn't ready to leave that ass yet, but he had the patience to wait till Indy had returned to earth.

Noah kept sliding in and out in the sweetest of rhythms. Beneath him, Indy sighed, a soft shiver rippling through his body.

"You okay, baby?" Noah asked.

"Fuck, yeah."

He leaned up on his elbows for a better grip, picked up the pace. His cock was recovering from his second orgasm that way, well on the way to come a third time, though he'd still need time.

Hmm, maybe it would be too much for Indy. He hadn't bottomed in a long time, and it hadn't been easy for him. "Do you need me to stop?"

Indy kept quiet so long that Noah stilled. He cursed as a

sob tore through Indy. Clenching his teeth, he pulled out, then rolled off Indy. "What's wrong, baby? Did I hurt you?"

Indy was still on his stomach, his hands hiding his face. His body shuddered with sobs, every single one stabbing Noah in his heart. What had he done? He reached out, put his big hand on his man's soft curls, stroking his head.

"Please talk to me, baby."

After what seemed like an eternity, Indy spoke. "Can you take me on your lap?"

Noah scooted farther up the bed, sat down with his back against the headboard. "Come here."

Indy scrambled half up, deep sobs rendering him weak, so Noah carefully lifted him up under his arms and dragged him on his lap, his legs pointing sideways. Indy circled his arms around Noah, hid his face against his chest. Noah held him tight, whispering sweet nothings in his ear, stroking his back tenderly.

Whatever he had done, at least Indy still wanted to be comforted by him. Maybe he could still salvage it. If only Indy would tell him what had happened. One second he'd been recovering from what had looked like a deep orgasm, and the next second he'd been crying. All Noah had done in the meantime was continue to fuck him and...

Realization hit. He'd asked if Indy wanted to stop.

These were good tears, healing tears. The tears of someone coming to realize not everyone was an asshole who took what he wanted without giving a shit about everyone else.

"I love you, Indy. I would never do anything deliberately to hurt you."

He kept holding him tight until Indy's body quieted. Indy let out a shaky breath.

"I think I love you."

Indy's voice was barely audible, and for a second, Noah thought he'd misheard. But no, he'd heard right. His heart started a happy dance inside of him, the likes of which he'd never felt before. Like a salsa or something, all wild and hot and fucking awesome.

"You do?" he couldn't help asking. How he wanted to see Indy's face, but he kept hiding against Noah's chest.

"Yeah," was the soft reply.

"And how do you feel about that?"

Indy moved, leaned back to meet his eyes. The sweetest brown eyes stared deep into Noah's, love radiating out of them in such overwhelming measure it made Noah's head spin.

"I'm fucking terrified."

～

THAT NIGHT, he once again slept between them. Well, they slept and Indy lay awake. Noah held him close, spooning him from behind, while Josh had fallen asleep holding his hand. They were naked, all three, and what should have been awkward and scary comforted him instead.

Fuck, he loved being touched by them. No one had touched Indy—Stephan—since that night, aside from medical professionals in the hospital. No one had so much as held his hand, let alone kissed him. And before that, there had only been Duncan.

He tried to think back to his childhood. Had his mom ever hugged him? Told him she loved him? If so, he couldn't remember. She hadn't been a bad mom, not compared to some others. He'd been well-fed, had clean clothes to wear. She didn't usually do drugs, kept the house reasonably tidy. There were her customers, but she'd been low-key about it.

He'd heard them with her, but she'd kept them separate from him, had simply told him to stay in his room.

The last year had been slowly worse before she'd sold him out. She'd gotten sloppy with her drug use, had used more than what she was allowed of the drugs she had to sell. And then she'd fucked up with that customer. Indy still couldn't believe she'd been that stupid.

That was it. She'd had no other way to repay her debt to Duncan. So she'd sold Indy to him. Simply sold him. She'd known what Duncan would do to him. Hell, of course she knew. Everyone knew.

He'd been between two houses for four years, sleeping in his own room one night, in Duncan's bed the next. He never knew where he'd be, would simply follow Duncan's orders. His whole life had been Duncan, for four and a half years. Even when he'd prepared to escape, siphoning off money, he'd never aimed to betray Duncan to the cops. What he'd written down, the pics and videos he had taken, it had been insurance, nothing more. If Duncan hadn't handed him over to Eric, if Indy hadn't killed him, he would have kept his mouth shut. Instead, he was a man on the run.

Noah's breath warmed his skin. Indy loved him so much, more than he'd ever thought possible. It was this big, powerful thing in his heart that demanded attention. It also fueled this equally big, powerful fear in his brain that told him to fucking run.

It wouldn't last.

It couldn't last.

Someday, Duncan's men would find him. No matter what the world thought, the Fitzpatricks knew he was still alive. They would not stop looking, not after he'd not only killed Eric, but had gone after the whole organization by agreeing to testify. No, they'd find him. And when they did, they'd nail him to a cross and watch him die. He would not get lucky a second time.

It wasn't that concept that scared him to death, though. It was what Duncan would do to Noah and Josh. If he found out how much they meant to Indy, he'd not just kill them. No, he'd torture them to get back at Indy, to force Indy to do what he wanted. They'd be perfect leverage, because there was nothing Indy wouldn't do to protect them, to keep them from harm.

He should run, should leave them. He was endangering them all by staying. But dear God, how? How could he leave? They had his heart. He'd never be whole again.

Behind him, Noah stirred. "What's wrong, baby?" he whispered in his ear. "You're all tense."

Indy swallowed. "Nothing. Bad dream. Go back to sleep."

Noah nuzzled his neck. "Mmm, okay. I love you."

Tears formed in Indy's eyes. How could he turn his back on this? "I love you, Noah. So much."

Noah kissed his neck again, then went slack as he fell asleep.

He couldn't walk away from the first person who had ever loved him exactly the way he was. Not when he loved him beyond words. He'd stay, for now. But at the first sign of trouble, he'd have no choice but to run.

Fuck, it would break him more than Duncan ever had.

(To be continued in No Limits...)

MEET NORA PHOENIX

Would you like the long or the short version of my bio?

The short? You got it.

I write steamy gay romance books and I love it. I also love reading books. Books are everything.

How was that?

A little more detail? Gotcha.

I started writing my first stories when I was a teen...on a freaking typewriter. I still have these, and they're adorably romantic. And bad, haha. Fear of failing kept me from following my dream to become a romance author, so you can imagine how proud and ecstatic I am that I finally over-came my fears and self doubt and did it. I adore my genre because I love writing and reading about flawed, strong men who are just a tad broken..but find their happy ever after anyway.

My favorite books to read are pretty much all MM/gay romances as long as it has a happy end. Kink is a plus... Aside from that, I also read a lot of nonfiction and not just books on writing. Popular psychology is a favorite topic of mine and so are self help and sociology.

Hobbies? Ain't nobody got time for that. Just kidding. I love traveling, spending time near the ocean, and hiking. But I love books more.

Come hang out with me in my Facebook Group Nora's Nook where I share previews, sneak peeks, freebies, fun stuff, and much more:

https://www.facebook.com/groups/norasnook/

Wanna get first dibs on freebies, updates, sales, and more? Sign up for my newsletter (no spamming your inbox full... promise!) here:

http://www.noraphoenix.com/newsletter/

You can also stalk me on Twitter: @NoraFromBHR
On Instagram:
https://www.instagram.com/nora.phoenix/
On Bookbub:
https://www.bookbub.com/profile/nora-phoenix

And please, leave reviews of the books you read and loved (including this one, hopefully). It's the most helpful thing you can do for an author!

ACKNOWLEDGMENTS

Writing a book is anything but a solitary effort. I am indebted to a whole bunch of people, so let's hope I don't forget anyone.

A massive thank you to my beta readers: Kyleen, Michele, Karma, Susi, and Amanda. Your feedback made the book so much better. I want to thank Kyleen and Michele especially for answering tons of questions for me, and constantly cheering me on. You rock.

Sloan, thanks for the awesome cover and the hilarious FB banter. Please stop making all these gorgeous pre-mades, because my credit card can't take it anymore.

Dianne, thanks a bunch for your editorial input. I learned a lot.

Courtney, your proofreading was invaluable. You caught a whole bunch of stuff I missed. Any remaining mistakes are wholly my fault!

I owe a mountain of gratitude to the members of my FB group Nora's Nook. You guys believed in me before you read one word of this book, and I cannot tell you how much that meant to me.

A huge thank you to you as reader, for taking a chance on a new author. I hope you loved this book...and the many more that are to follow.

My last acknowledgement is to my two real life besties. AM, your love, friendship, and support has been a constant in my life for the last years. You are and always will be my person. KJ, the universe got it right when we two met, because you're my sister from another mother. You allow me to be myself, and damn, it feels good.

NO LIMITS

Don't miss the next installment in the No Shame Series! In No Limits, we'll follow Josh on his journey to a happy ever after:

Josh is convinced he'll never find someone who'll love him the way he is. He's not exactly a catch with his PTSD, which has transformed him into a homebody most of the times. Sweet, maybe, but also boring as hell. Plus, there's that submissive tendency he recently discovered and is dying to explore. His complicated relationship with Noah and Indy don't make it easy, either. When Connor shows interest in him, he can't believe the sexy cop would look at him twice, let alone make an effort to get to know him. When he does, Josh discovers they have more in common than he'd ever thought possible.

Connor had survived the ordeal that left his best friend and fellow Marine dead, but that survival came at a price. He's a robot, going through the motions, but barely alive. Until fate intervenes when he meets Josh. The vulnerable man triggers all kinds of protective and dominant urges in

Connor, but what would a cute guy like Josh want with an inexperienced, closed-off, bossy steamroller like him?

When Connor discovers his past endangers Indy, all hope for a future between him and Josh seems lost. After all, there's no way Josh will ever choose Connor over Indy's safety and Noah's lifelong friendship. When a crisis hits, can Connor prove he's strong enough to deal with everything that's thrown his way?

ALSO BY NORA PHOENIX

No Shame Series:

No Filter

No Limits

No Fear

No Shame

Irresistible Omegas Series (mpreg):

Alpha's Sacrifice

Ballsy Boys Series (with K.M. Neuhold):

Rebel

Tank

Stand Alones:

The Time of My Life

Printed in Poland
by Amazon Fulfillment
Poland Sp. z o.o., Wrocław